Poole-Carter, R. (Rosemary)
Women of Magdalene:

JAN 23 2009

# Women
## Of
# Magdalene

# Women Of Magdalene

A NOVEL

## Rosemary Poole-Carter

KÜNATI

LARGO, USA

# WOMEN OF MAGDALENE

For information, contact Kunati Inc., Book Publishers in both USA and Canada.
In USA: 6901 Bryan Dairy Road, Suite 150, Largo, FL 33777 USA
In Canada: 75 First Street, Suite 128, Orangeville, ON L9W 5B6 CANADA,
or e-mail to info@kunati.com.

FIRST EDITION

Designed by Kam Wai Yu
Persona Corp. | www.personaprinciple.com

ISBN-13: 978-1-60164-014-7     ISBN-10: 1-60164-014-5
EAN 9781601640147              FIC000000 FICTION

Published by Kunati Inc. (USA) and Kunati Inc. (Canada). Provocative. Bold. Controversial.™

http://www.kunati.com

TM—Kunati and Kunati Trailer are trademarks
owned by Kunati Inc. Persona is a trademark owned by Persona Corp.
All other trademarks are the property of their respective owners.

Library of Congress Cataloging-in-Publication Data

Poole-Carter, R. (Rosemary)
   Women of Magdalene : a novel / Rosemary Poole-Carter. -- 1st ed.
     p. cm.
   Summary: "A fictional account of a doctor in post-Civil War Louisiana who
exposes the head of a women's asylum as a fraud and a murderer, built around
themes of mysogyny and racism"--Provided by publisher.
   ISBN-13: 978-1-60164-014-7
   ISBN-10: 1-60164-014-5
   1. Physicians--Fiction. 2. Asylums--Fiction. 3. Women--Institutional
care--Fiction. 4. Louisiana--Fiction. I. Title.
   PS3616.O64W66 2007
   813'.6--dc22
                         2007028103

# D e d i c a t i o n

---

With love to Nicholas and Katharine

## Acknowledgements

My abiding thanks to Jay Evans and Dr. Doug Lyle, who took the devil out of some details; Sherman Judice, who read the very first draft; Dr. Richard Walker, who recovered from malaria; Dorothy Poole, Dorothy Carter, Aaron Berenson, Robin Carter, Peggy Nance Lyle, B. K. Johnson, Jack Edmondson, Dr. Debra Osterman, S.M. Moore, James McKinnon, Derek Armstrong, Kam Wai Yu, Luisa Amaral-Smith, Dolores Rieger, CoraLynn McCabe, Sarah Harris, Jeri Fahrenbach, Carolyn L. Harrell, and Charlene Hudgins, who have encouraged, inspired and advised; and to the Museum of Southern History for the boots.

# Chapter 1

The Magdalene Ladies' Lunatic Asylum was my destination. On the day word had reached me that I had been granted a position there as general practitioner, I set off walking south and southwest from Baton Rouge to meet my new obligation. I remember that day more clearly than many that came after it: leaving my parents' house—my mother closed up in her room, my father standing in the front doorway as if to bar my return.

My father, a physician himself, had already assured me that my services were not needed in our home community; the poverty that followed the War between the States left little paying business to go round, and I would not be going into practice with him. But Father's old friend, Dr. Kingston, had offered to keep me occupied at his private facility. I suspected Mother's hand in that arrangement. Though I could not share in her belief that Dr. Kingston was my benefactor, he might make use of me.

Attending to the ills of madwomen would make a change from my duties during what my genteel mother referred to as the "late unpleasantness." Indeed, it had been unpleasant, amputating limbs of the wounded, dismantling whole cartloads of men. I wore a special pair of boots with rows of horseshoe nails embedded in the soles for cleats to keep me from slipping and falling as I hurried through my work in the surgery tent, the floor awash with blood.

Lugging my satchel and black bag, trudging down farm roads in fitful spring rains and across fields mired in mud, I was often grateful for my sure-footed surgeon's boots, more grateful still when scuttling down a slick incline of riverbank.

In the steaming heat of a midday, I had found sanctuary, a river road lined on either side with live oaks, their branches arching and meeting overhead like cathedral beams, enclosing a cooler, rarefied air. I smelled the river long before I glimpsed it between the broad tree trunks, a subtlety of clay and mud and fetid reeds filtering upward from the invisible water.

Then came sounds, voices, at first low and muffled like the moist air rising. I left the road for a break in the foliage to look down at a gathering by the river's edge. A preacher who would have been a slave a few years before, sloshed his way into the river and exhorted his congregation to let their sins be washed away.

"I saw the Spirit descending from heaven like a dove, and it abode upon him. And I knew him not."

His words rolled out, unfurled like a banner, over the crowd that responded in pulsing chants, with clapping and moaning. Though I stood apart, unnoticed, unwelcome if I had been seen, I was drawn in by the magic of it.

Such mysterious cadences had always disturbed my mother, whose careful religion left no room for possession of the soul. As for me, it seemed that the washing away of sin was a far easier thing than atoning for it, paying for it, even with one's life.

One after another the sinners came forward to be saved. They waded waist deep into the river, into the arms of their minister, whose powerful hands thrust them below the water's surface and brought them up clean. Though the river churned dark with mud and silt, the water glittered clear running from the bodies of the newly baptized.

"He that sent me to baptize with water, the same said unto me, 'Upon whom thou shalt see the Spirit descending, and remaining on him, the same is he which baptizeth with the Holy Ghost.'"

A girl, her head wrapped in a red madras *tignon*, began to sing "There Is a Fountain Filled with Blood." Drawn by her song, I stepped from between the trees, meaning no harm. But a startled look entered her black eyes as she caught sight of me, and a momentary tremor ran through her strong voice. Gripping my luggage, I hurried on along the upper bank, this time in the sunlight outside the nave of live oaks.

Distance and a bend in the river soon put me out of the girl's sight. Before long, I was out of earshot of her singing and heard only the occasional chirp of a mockingbird.

I left the trail by the slow, wide stretch of the Atchafalaya River flowing southward and followed a swifter, narrower tributary upstream. In choosing locations for field hospitals, I had always preferred a swift stream to any other source of water, the quicker to carry away refuse.

Recalling the directions sent to me, I reckoned the Magdalene Asylum lay less than half a mile northeast. The journey so far had been as convoluted as the labyrinthine paths that followed the sinuous courses of bayous and streams. I was ready for a respite.

Spanish moss drooped from the low branches of cypress, overhanging the tributary, whose shadowy course was rarely lit by a patch of sunlight. There was a dark, damp closeness in the air. No birds sang here, no squirrels chattered in the trees along this particular stretch of water. Pausing to wipe the sweat from my brow, I felt a soft breeze and took a deep breath of it. And then I understood the quiet. My head and lungs filled with the biting odor that silences Nature.

Slowly, I set down my bags and approached the bank. On the far side of the stream, a long, pale shape was caught and bobbed among the rough gray cypress knees that broke the surface. Sound returned: the buzz of flies, the plop of a turtle entering the water.

I had committed myself to being a healer, yet from the war and on, all the days of my life were bound up with the destruction of human flesh. There were times when even my own substance seemed to dissolve around my mind in intermittent bouts of malarial fever—my wartime legacy.

The turbid downflow jostled the form, twisting its loose white garment, shifting it into the path of a sunbeam. Yellow hair fanned out, surrounding a featureless face. Suddenly, a swirl of water lifted the body, freed it of restraints, and whipped it out into the stream, leaving behind a sheaf of hair clinging to the rocks.

The horseshoe nails in my boots dug into the viscous mud as I scrambled down the bank. Wading in knee-deep, I snatched for the gown whirling past me. It slipped through my fingers like the water that carried it. The body, borne away on the tributary's current, rushed to feed itself into the river. I plunged after, waist-deep, shoulder-deep—first weighted down by my suit and boots, then buoyed by the deepening water that drew me forward, always at arm's length behind the object I pursued.

The current slowed. I heard the singing girl's voice rise again, then fall abruptly silent. My eyes had been intent upon the floating body, but now I looked up. Sunlight, caught in ripples, shone on the surface of the deep water with the opaque luster of milky glass. Down river, the minister raised and released a dripping boy, who clambered up the bank and disappeared into the crowd. But the minister continued to stand in the water, chest-deep. He stood and waited as the body slowly turned until it was crossways on the stream and floated to his outstretched arms.

I thrashed ahead through the water, gaining a foothold in the loose silt, to reach the thing already caught and held. Gasps and exclamations issued from the congregation. Most of the members recoiled up the bank, though some edged closer, gaining a better view.

This aberration once had been a woman, but now the figure was bloated to grotesque proportions beneath a thin covering of ragged gown. The few strands of yellow hair, not yet slipped from the scalp, attested that this had been a white woman, a fact indiscernible if looking only at the dark gray-green decomposing flesh that makes us all one race in the end. A hand, devoid of nails and wrinkled as a washer woman's, floated outward as if at any moment it might leave the body for a journey of its own.

I pulled off my suit coat and with it made an effort to swathe the corpse, to contain the fragile remnants of bone and tissue. As I took hold of the body, the minister, with silent understanding, shed his flowing robe and wrapped the dead woman in its folds.

Together, we brought the body from the river and laid it on the rust-colored mud. Kneeling beside it, I opened the robe already soaked with murky liquid and arranged the arms over the chest. It was then I noticed the darker marks that encircled the wrists like blackish purple bracelets.

I looked up at the minister, who stood back, his congregation now all behind him. "Do you know who she was?" I asked.

No one replied.

"She's been in the water for days. Has anyone round here gone missing?"

Silence again.

Then a boy's voice rasped from the crowd. "She be one of them mad women."

I surveyed the host of dark faces, the unfathomable eyes that stared down at me.

"From the asylum?" I asked. "That's where I'm bound—Magdalene

Asylum. I'm the new general practitioner, Dr. Mallory."

"Well, sir, you better take her with you." The minister pointed at the body.

Carry this cold, long-dead thing—I shuddered in spite of myself. I was more accustomed to carrying the newly dead, whose bodies were still hot with fevers.

"Could one of you help me? Please. I have luggage."

"Asa," the minister called over his shoulder.

The newly-baptized boy, who looked about fifteen, lurched forward with a push from someone in the crowd and suddenly stood apart, river water dripping from his overalls and pooling around his bare feet.

"Asa Wilkins got a sister work up there. He give you a hand, sir."

The boy stared at his minister. "Not me, Reverend Jonas. I ain't touching her."

"The Lord carried this man and his burden into our midst, Asa. We got to help him."

The boy winced, and I could well sympathize with his revulsion. "Not me, Reverend. They see me carrying that body, they string me up for sure."

"Carry the doctor's bags, son. No harm in that." The Reverend Mr. Jonas settled the matter.

"Much obliged," I said, and lifted the shrouded body, my pride making every effort to mask the strain of the maneuver.

Asa Wilkins scampered off ahead of me, glancing back now and then, as I slogged after him.

As we neared the river bend, turning to follow the tributary stream and collect my luggage, the girl in the red *tignon* caught up with us at a run. Seems she had pulled my hat from the water and now offered it to me. I could only tilt my head and ask her to place the soggy thing there. She stood on tiptoe to accomplish the task, then lit off before I ever had a chance to tell her God had given her a voice to lift up a man's cares.

# Chapter 2

In another quarter of an hour I made my inauspicious appearance at the wrought iron gates of the Magdalene Ladies' Lunatic Asylum. A grizzled, stoop-shouldered porter let me in, taking my bags from Asa, who would go no farther. I guessed the porter's sense of smell was as weak as his clouded eyesight, for he seemed unperturbed by the thing I carried.

"You done got Miz Poncet there, sir?"

I said I didn't know, then added, "Is it likely?"

"We was sent looking for her. Little bare footprints stopped at the riverside. 'Bout time she washed up," he said, with disquieting calm.

We walked on, each with our own burdens and impediments—he toting my luggage, hobbling ahead on rickety legs, I carrying a corpse, plodding after in mud-caked boots.

The asylum was housed in what had once been a plantation mansion of the Greek revivalist style, with broad veranda and towering Doric columns. The only obvious clue to what now lay beyond the gracious facade was the presence of bars on the upper windows—painted white and curved in fancy scroll designs, but bars nonetheless.

My father told me Dr. Kingston had bought the property for a song, the previous owners having been bankrupted by the war, and then turned it into this private refuge for disturbed women. The weight in my arms reminded me just how disturbed a woman might be. Had she thrown herself in the river? Had she despaired, as had my own sister? And had no one comforted her?

The porter led me up the drive of packed red earth, shaded by live oaks with resurrection ferns growing thick in their branches. When we were a yard from the steps, the double front doors swung open and a finely-featured, silver-haired man advanced to meet us.

Stinking of wet wool, river mud and decay, I presented myself to my employer, Dr. Douglas Christopher Kingston.

And then the shrieking began. A gaunt, pallid woman at a downstairs window screamed and slapped the pane until a pair of heavy dark arms pulled her from sight. One patient, taking a turn on the veranda, laughed and babbled gleefully, pointing a trembling finger at the corpse. Another wailed, and still another rocked herself violently to and fro, murmuring in an incomprehensible language. All were soon whisked into the house by hard-faced caretakers.

Only a solitary young woman remained, hardly more than a girl, in a plain brown dress and white apron, chestnut hair plaited and draped over one shoulder. She had been sitting alone on the top step, back straight, hands folded in her lap. Without a word, she rose, descended the steps, her blue eyes glancing at me in passing—at me, not at the thing I held. I followed her with my own gaze as she proceeded around the house and out of sight. Then I spoke to Kingston.

"The body was in the creek," I began, looking up at my employer, who remained at the top of the steps. "A preacher named Jonas helped me pull it out. Someone said she may have been a patient here." I cast a questioning look toward the oblivious porter. "A Mrs. Poncet, perhaps?"

Dr. Kingston frowned and stared over my head, down the empty drive and into the distance. "Best take it to the back of the house—to the carpenter's shed." He covered his nose and mouth with a white linen handkerchief and disappeared behind the double doors.

Kingston had changed little since I had known him in my student days. Perhaps his hair was a trifle thinner, and lighter now than the gun-metal gray of his closely trimmed goatee. But at this first encounter at the asylum, he struck me once again as he had years ago as a frequent guest in my father's house: the man was overfastidious.

When I had said as much to my mother, she had defended him to me; although, in her ceaseless yearning toward gentility, she sometimes mistook form for substance. When I commented that he cared more for his own opinions than for the facts of medical science, she allowed she would excuse that remark, springing as it must from my own lack of experience.

Should I criticize him? Had I not been guilty of emulating Kingston's preciseness when I began my studies, when I, indeed, lacked so much of experience? He had been good enough to give me a reference when I went east to medical college—a favor to my father, not to me. Seeing him again, I still wondered at his own choosing of the profession—for even the most careful physician must occasionally bloody his hands.

The porter led the way, opening the shed for me, waiting while I laid the body on the floor inside, and shutting it up again. Then he shuffled away, leaving me and my bags in the yard at the back of the big house. I took a deep breath and waited for feeling to return to my arms.

The quiet girl, who had rounded the house ahead of me, stoked an already smoldering fire in the yard. Above the flames a black cauldron of a washtub hung from an iron support. I watched the girl carry two buckets back and forth from the cistern, where she filled them, to the washtub, where she poured them out, adding the water to that which already steamed in the tub. Her slender arms hoisted each bucket in turn high above the tub and poured its contents in a graceful, shining arc. Then she repeated the pattern as if it were a dance she'd learned and only she could hear the music.

Setting down the buckets, she motioned for me to approach. I wondered if she were mute or simply shy, but I followed her wordless instructions. She led me toward a sort of stall—small, roofless, four-sided, its wooden walls reaching just above my shoulders. Opening one side that was hinged like a gate, she ushered me inside. The floor of the stall was an arrangement of flat stones without mortar between them.

The girl brought me two buckets full of water, a cake of lye soap, and a towel.

"Am I to wash up in here, miss?" I asked.

She nodded, casting a glance at my filthy shirt, then looking toward the washtub. I closed myself in the stall, peeled away my clothes, and dropped them over the side. Garments someone else might have thought fit only for the fire she collected and stirred in her cauldron. She brought a third bucket of water to the stall and set my satchel within easy reach.

Dr. Kingston and a large-boned woman in a starched cap—Matron, I assumed—crossed from the rear of the house to the carpenter's shed, hardly glancing in my direction. Dr. Kingston carried a black bag and the woman a length of oil cloth and a lamp. They were in the shed some minutes, and when they left it, the woman carried at arm's length not the oil cloth but my jacket and the minister's robe. She dropped them near the washtub and followed Dr. Kingston back into the house.

While I lathered myself with greasy brown soap and rinsed with tepid rainwater, the girl went on with her washing and rinsing and hanging clothes to dry. The porter returned, seated himself on the back steps, and with a wire brush slowly began scraping the mud from my cleated boots.

It was a rare thing for me to find my needs anticipated and attended to by others.

Bathed and dressed in my better suit of clothes and dry boots, I came to thank the girl for her help. She nodded but said nothing.

The porter was more forthcoming, accepting my gratitude and, when asked, introducing himself as Gaston. Taking up my bags, he offered to show me my quarters.

"You ain't sleeping in the big house. No, sir. You got overseer's old cottage all to yourself. How 'bout that?"

He chuckled as we passed the stall where I had bathed, his lips curling back from ragged teeth, and I asked him what amused him.

"Never seen no gentleman in there before," he replied. "They calls that the water treatment place—puts them crazy women in there what's having fits and pours cold water on 'em. Wet hens, yes, sir!"

I had heard medical men refer to such procedures and other devices for exorcising the demons of insanity, but knew little of them first hand. My years as an army field surgeon's assistant had shown me more of the creation of madness than of its treatment. And I understood my primary duty at the Magdalene Asylum was to attend to the typical ailments of the institutionalized: bed sores, lice, dysentery and so forth. Ministering to the mind was Dr. Kingston's province.

The cottage stood at some distance from the asylum, across the side yard. Though still within the confines of the broad fenced and gated lawn, the white clapboard walls and porch were half hidden by honeysuckle and wisteria vines and the shade of willows.

Gaston tucked my black bag under the arm that held my satchel and pushed open the door with his free hand, stepping sideways to let me pass in before him. The small square-shaped house had four connecting rooms:

a parlor converted to consulting room and a sitting room on one side, a kitchen with its own pump and cook stove and a bedroom on the other. What the builder had lacked in imagination he at least made up for with neatness. The separateness and self-sufficiency of the cottage pleased me, especially after years of bunking in tents and crowded boarding houses.

After setting my black bag in the consulting room and my satchel at the foot of the bed, Gaston continued to shuffle about the dim rooms, raising shades and opening shutters, all the while explaining how he had cleaned and swept the place himself. Never mind that I could write my name in the dust on the kitchen table.

He was, however, quick to offer an excuse for the cobwebs above the shelves in the consulting room, reminding me of their use as a Cajun home remedy. "I left them webs specially for you, doctor. Nothing better for putting on sore spots and pulling wounds together."

I had never owned a slave. Living in town, my parents had no need of field hands, but sometimes had hired slaves, paying their masters for the use of them as cooks or house servants or for attending to my father's horse and carriage. But Father and Mother made the careful distinction that they were not slave owners—a position based, I suspected, less on piety than on their mutual distrust of one another—and of no consequence to the slaves themselves. My father believed a wife should devote herself to domestic duties; too many servants allowed a lady too much idleness. My mother's objections ran deeper.

Mother had been more than glad to leave her family's cotton plantation and move to the city with her physician husband. She impressed on my sister and myself how much she hated and feared the system of masters and slaves—the vile liberties taken by white men with black concubines, the ever-present danger of black men to white ladies. I sometimes wondered, for all her strict Protestant upbringing, where my mother came by this vivid picture she had of plantation life as an endless orgy of sweating bodies worked to a breeding frenzy. As a married woman, she would abide only plain or aging servants in her house. Even then she was ill at ease, although, her anxiety and watchfulness may have been misdirected.

Gaston went on in a singsong, assuring me of his attention to my comfort, as if trying to impress a new master. Perhaps this mask of devotion had spared him a whipping in the past often enough to become habit, but it embarrassed me.

I changed the subject to the body in the river.

"How do you think she came to be there?" I asked. "Assuming the body is that of Mrs. Poncet, had she run away?"

Gaston twisted his mouth side to side before he answered. "Seems to me she was 'posed to be locked up that night she went missing, in one of them little rooms with the mattress ticks on the walls."

"A padded cell?"

"I heard Oralia was on watch, but she done dozed off. Doctor weren't pleased, no, sir."

"Has this sort of thing happened before?" I asked, recalling that only a few women, all of them patients, had displayed any shock at the sight of the body.

"Not my place to say," the porter drawled. "Don't rightly recall another drowning. But myself, I never seen one of them leave here, 'cepting for the graveyard."

Then he bobbed his head and backed toward the door, as if this were enough talk about dead folk. I walked with him to the porch steps and looked across the lawn. It was near dusk, the big house blotting out the lowering sun.

"By the way, Gaston," I said, keeping my tone indifferent, "how did that girl come to be a laundress in the asylum?"

"Effie? Oh, Miss Effie ain't no hired help, sir. She be a patient."

A patient. And yet performing a servant's task. I remember the odd jolt his words gave me. But any change in my demeanor was lost on him, and he trudged back toward the big house.

Even if she had been hired help, I would have been out of bounds to take notice of her, a lone girl without father or brothers to look after her welfare. Still, I had noticed her—despite the circumstances of my arrival and while holding the ruin of a woman's body in my arms—involuntarily and irrevocably noticed her. Learning that she was a patient, I realized she was more than unapproachable. She was as impossible as undoing the past.

Now that I no longer practice medicine, I look back on my days at Magdalene Asylum, at last resigned to the events that brought me there. And more than that—in some measure grateful for them, for from my window I can see Effie once again, as she was that first day, pouring a silver arc of water.

# Chapter 3

I lit an oil lamp and unpacked my bags. Until leaving for university and medical school, I had lived only in my parents' carefully kept house, among my own carefully kept possessions: rows of books in glass-fronted shelves, neatly displayed rock and insect collections assembled when I was ten and eleven, a framed map of the North American continent, equally weighty volumes of *Pardue's Illustrated Classical Mythology* and the King James Bible lying parallel on the bedside table. But I had little enough in my satchel now and nothing to mark a room as particularly my own— comb and brushes, soap and razor—anyone's things set out on a dresser scarf. My old suit presently hung on a clothesline, the better one on my back. My few other garments hardly filled one bureau drawer.

At medical school I had earned a reputation for meticulousness, affecting that trait as if I could thus order my life, and was sometimes ridiculed by more spontaneous classmates. The rush to war, to service and duty, without adequate planning, preparations, and supplies had disconcerted me. Until then, I had viewed life and death—and procedures in the operating theatre—from a safe distance, often from too great a distance to discern fully what I was supposed to see, what I needed to learn. Suddenly, the distance vanished. I stood beside a regimental surgeon, assisting him to extract Minié balls and to amputate shattered limbs. For the first time I was close enough to be drenched with other men's blood.

I learned. I witnessed the powerful significance with which some men endowed objects: a dying soldier clinging to a token—a locket, a ribbon, a ring of braided hair given him by mother, wife, or sweetheart—a talisman against despair and death. But men died anyway.

I tried to relinquish attachment to personal possessions as far as I was able. We were so often on the move. Things wore out, were lost, stolen, needed desperately by someone else. The war taught me to live within myself; my possessions were only what I could carry with me in satchel and black bag. Some felt naked without their accustomed finery, furnished homes, rich food and wine, elegant entertainments. Some felt bereft of ordinary comforts—I was one of those. But I was also free, invisible, as if the only evidence of my existence were in the tasks I performed, the services I rendered to others. When I stopped work, I disappeared.

Carrying the lamp into my new consulting room, I opened my black bag and lifted from it a rectangular wooden box: the amputation kit with its scalpels, tweezers, tourniquet, long-bladed slender knives, and small hand saw. May I have no need of it at the Magdalene Asylum, I murmured. Pills in clear vials, rolled bandages, jars of ointments and salves, tonics in brown glass bottles, and my essential quinine I arranged on a shelf. I left in the bag my army revolver, carried for self-defense, though I had used it more than once to end the misery of a cavalry horse. A badly wounded rider once begged me to give him the same treatment rather than amputate his legs; later, I heard he died of a fever while being transported out of Chattanooga. Why had I been able to keep my oath in the face of his suffering—to give no deadly medicine—and yet broke it in the face of my sister's?

That first evening I again presented myself at the front door of the big house, this time receiving a slightly more cordial welcome.

Dr. Kingston introduced me to Lila Fentroy, the woman who had accompanied him to the carpentry shed; she was indeed the matron and had been since the asylum's founding.

I thought we might exchange pleasantries, but her sharp tone and first comment to me dispelled that notion. "Rachel Poncet was not allowed near the river—none of them are. But *you* found her there." Did that make me responsible? I was tempted to ask.

"A sad business," Kingston said smoothly. "And one soon to be resolved. I shall go to town in the morning and notify the authorities of this unfortunate accident."

"Will her remains be sent to her home?" I asked.

Kingston winced, wrinkled his nose, as if he once again smelt decay. "Oh, no, not all the way to New Orleans."

"It wouldn't have happened on my watch," Matron informed me.

Brusque and hard-faced, Lila Fentroy impressed me as the sort of commanding officer her troops—staff and patients—would obey in fear and quietly despise. But Kingston sang her praises. Tirelessly, she had nursed his late wife during her final illness. "And now Matron is indispensable to the order of the wards," he added, as she left us for her nightly rounds.

Ascending the stairs and still within earshot of his resonant voice, Matron lifted her head high and squared her heavy shoulders. I was glad to see the back of her, though not for the view she afforded.

"The upper floors are divided into wards, a few private chambers, and treatment rooms," Kingston continued. "You will see them tomorrow when you meet the patients. This way, please."

He led me across the hall to a pair of ornately carved doors.

"At the back of the house I keep a suite of rooms for myself—study, consulting room, and a bedroom converted from the back parlor. But here," and he thrust open the double doors, revealing a sanctum of gold and royal blue, "is the front parlor, fully restored to the beauty of another time. We reward the better behaved patients with the use of this room and the larger of the two dining rooms."

"Was the house much damaged during the War?" I asked blandly, refusing to exclaim over the opulence now before me.

"I should say!" Kingston replied. "The Federals confiscated the house for a barracks and hospital. Ate, drank, or smashed everything they laid hands on. By the time the previous owner regained possession, he hadn't the money or the mind to take care of the estate."

"But you did."

"Yes. As you see." Kingston gestured with a sweep of the hand.

The house was grand indeed, and, with its sixteen-inch-thick outer walls, was built to last despite mistreatment. The interior walls, covered with enameled molding and embossed wallpaper, supported fourteen-foot ceilings, which were themselves decorated with plaster rosettes encircling chandeliers. Reaching nearly the full height of the parlor walls were the gilt-framed pier glass mirrors and the French windows, whose blue velvet curtains cascaded from broad cornices to puddle on the floor in proof of luxurious excess.

I had seen such houses before—seen them lived in by the self-appointed aristocracy, seen them abandoned or converted into hospitals, seen them defaced or gutted or burned to the ground. Ostentation was built on the backs of slaves and defended by the sons of yeoman farmers who had not a prayer of gaining such a style of life for themselves. How cruelly we can be coerced or duped into doing someone else's bidding.

"Have you ever courted a girl in a room equipped with one of these?" Kingston indicated a circular convex mirror mounted high on the wall at a right angle to the doorway. "Very helpful to the chaperone who must step into the hall for a moment. Of course, we use it to observe patients."

I refused Kingston's offer of bourbon, but submitted to his questioning, while he downed one glass and poured himself another.

"You were east when the war broke out, were you not?"

"Yes, sir. I was finishing my training at Jefferson Medical College in Philadelphia."

I did not tell him that an established doctor and lecturer there had offered me a chance to stay on after graduation and assist in his private practice; after Fort Sumter, the offer had been brusquely withdrawn. My disappointments were none of my employer's concern.

But as if reading my mind, Kingston added, "When suddenly you found yourself no longer welcome in that part of the world."

"And I began my service with the Army of Tennessee, doing battle with measles." I recalled how an epidemic had swept through a regiment of young men, fresh from the farm and never before exposed to the contagion in a crowded barracks.

"Your father told me you turned down a commission and remained a contract surgeon. Why was that, Robert?"

Kingston's paternalistic tone and use of my given name irritated me. I had never considered a military career before the country tore itself in two and saw no reason to consider it afterward. Besides, my ambiguous status proved an asset at times when dealing with civilians, whose sympathies varied, enabling me to better negotiate for bed space in homes, warehouses and hotels and to obtain supplies from difficult purveyors.

"The work consumed me, sir," I replied. "Rising in the ranks seemed unimportant."

"Your attitude will be a great comfort to Dr. Hardy, I'm sure."

"Dr. Hardy?"

"Your predecessor. He has retired to a cottage overlooking the river, but still joins me here for supper. I'm sure he'll tell you about his grandson's entering the medical profession, and that he wouldn't mind having the boy out here one day."

So, my position at the Magdalene Asylum was likely as temporary as any other I had held.

Kingston finished his second bourbon, then asked, "What have you done since the war, Robert? You didn't go into practice with your father."

I thought a moment on how to answer him, not knowing what my father might have said to him or written to him. How much did Kingston know of the estrangement? As my parents, Father and Mother would speak of it to no one, but perhaps Father, as one physician to another? No. He had whispered his accusation, refusing to fully articulate my misdeed, as if to emphasize its unspeakable nature.

"Robert?" Kingston repeated my name.

"Yes, sir. The hospitals and prisons didn't empty themselves on the day General Lee surrendered," I began. "Sick and wounded soldiers kept me busy for over a year. I took my time coming home. And then, when I arrived, things were different."

Kingston arched one silver brow. "Your dear sister…"

"Yes, sir. Lucinda was dead on the eve of her wedding to your nephew."

"If she had been here, perhaps I could have helped her."

Something in his voice—that quick assumption of superiority—made me want to ask him just how much help he had been to Rachel Poncet. But I held my tongue. I needed a salary. And I wanted to practice medicine again, to do more than mix tonics for a druggist or run a shopkeeper's errands, as I had done on my return to Baton Rouge.

"Hasn't your nephew since married someone else?" I asked, knowing the answer.

Kingston nodded and led the way to the small dining room. There Dr. Joshua Hardy awaited us, seated at the oval-shaped mahogany table, decanter close to hand.

Dr. Hardy was old. His paper-thin skin was spotted with age, his gaunt frame lost in a cream-colored suit. Only a few long white hairs lay over his mottled scalp. But his whiskers were his compensation. A broad growth of side-whisker began near each pendulous earlobe and continued outward from each cheek a full six inches, tapering to a sharply waxed point over each shoulder. His wizened face was effectually dominated by a pair of white cones made of hair. Oh, for the dignity of my elders! Perhaps it was the strain of an exhausting day, but I found it impossible to suppress a burst of laughter. Quickly covering my nose and mouth, I hoped the sound might be mistaken for a sneeze.

Kingston and I took our seats at the table.

"Had a dip in the river, young man, so I hear," Dr. Hardy remarked, as if he were chiding me for wasting the afternoon in a spring pastime. "Water's cool yet—better put a plaster on your chest before bed, or you'll wake up ill and be no good to us at all."

"I appreciate your concern, sir," came as easily to my lips as "to hell with your advice" came to my mind.

Gaston entered, carrying a porcelain tureen in his gnarled hands. Carefully, he ladled out cream of tomato soup, slopping only a few drops on the white linen tablecloth, then left us.

During the first course, Hardy warmed to the notion of my poor health. "Your father wrote us that you suffer from malarial fever. I suppose I'll be forced from retirement when you're stricken."

"There's nearly always quinine in our dispensary," said Kingston.

Hardy wagged a bony finger in my direction. "My grandson, Bertram

Joshua Hardy—who, by the by, is nearing completion of his medical training—has never known a sick day in his life. No fevers, no measles, no smallpox—none of that!"

"Poor fellow," I murmured between spoonfuls of soup, "has it all ahead of him."

Kingston changed the subject. "Robert, I shall find it difficult to think of you as Dr. Mallory. That's your father's name, and not an easy one to live up to."

If he had paused to hear me say "I'll try my best, sir," he would have had a long wait.

Gaston returned with a tray of covered dishes, set a plate before me, and lifted the lid with an awkward attempt at a flourish. I stared into a single glistening eye of a poached mullet. "The catch of the day," my host remarked.

"From the river?"

"Of course. Wine?"

"No, thank you, sir."

"You don't drink, Robert? Is that your mother's influence?" Kingston proceeded to pour full glasses for himself and Hardy.

"I drank some, during the war. I don't now."

"Ah. Then I'll not offer again." With a gentle clink, he replaced the stopper in the mouth of the decanter. Let him assume, if he liked, that I'd once been a hopeless drunkard, sworn at last to sobriety. I had seen the depths of a bottle although it was the fever that taught me to value lucidity.

As we ate, Kingston and Hardy questioned me about my studies in medical school and my travels with the army. Tiring of their interrogation, I asked my employer about his own wartime experience. "My father said you were out of the country a good deal," I remarked.

Kingston cleared his throat. "Oh, some. I spent time in Europe, studying and pursuing my profession. But you may be aware that I also interested myself in hospital administration on this side of the Atlantic—the gathering and distribution of supplies for our forces."

"No, sir, I was not aware."

"Well, you were in Tennessee. My activities were concentrated in the port cities, New Orleans and Galveston in particular."

Kingston's refined, well-modulated voice could make profiteering sound like philanthropy. He began to offer his views on the women of his asylum.

"I am well aware of the tragic changes wrought by the last decade. You, Robert, have seen war's devastating effect on the menfolk. But at Magdalene Asylum you will see its lingering and profound effect on the women. Woman is naturally passive; her proper sphere is the privacy of her home. Many ladies, such as your mother, managed well enough in extensions of their maternal roles, performing some limited nursing duties, preparing bandages, sewing or cooking for the soldiers. But some..."

Here Kingston paused to exchange a knowing look with Hardy, who had been sucking a fish bone.

"Some unnatural creatures used the turbulence of the times to overstep the bounds of decency, involving themselves with the anti-slavery movement and agitating for women's suffrage. We have had a few of that type here," Kingston said with a curl of the lip, but his expression softened as he continued, "and there are some delicate ladies who were cut adrift in the world—a man's active, public, dangerous world—without a man's guidance. No wonder madness overtook these gentle beings."

Hardy spoke up. "We humor women with the notion that they are our moral superiors, but they are weak. Married off young, motherhood may bolster what strength they have, but even then… My advice is keep your wife at home and chaperone your daughters."

"He's right, Robert," said Kingston. "To be born a woman is in itself to suffer a precarious condition."

"Precarious for Rachel Poncet." I think Kingston flinched slightly when I said the name. At the very least, the tightening of a muscle in his cheek momentarily disturbed the placidity of his face. Was his conscience pricked by the failure of her treatment? I pursued the subject. "I noticed what appeared to be bruising around her wrists. I wondered—"

"How very observant you are," Kingston interrupted. "Of late Mrs. Poncet had become violent, a danger to herself and everyone around her. At times, we were forced to restrain her, even tie her to her bed."

"Could her hands have been bound when she wandered off and fell into the water?"

"Her wrists were not tied when you found her."

"She was disintegrating when I found her."

Kingston cast his glance toward the far reaches of the chandelier. "Young man, I wonder you find this an appropriate subject for dinner table conversation."

Reproved, I turned my attention to the remains of fish on my plate. Scrapping away at the white bits near the head, I uncovered a human tooth, a bicuspid, lodged close to the fish's jaw. "The catch of the day," Kingston had said. I pushed my plate aside.

Gaston cleared away dishes and brought more, which I refused. When he left the room, I asked Kingston about the girl who had washed my clothes.

"Yes, Effie Rampling is a patient," he replied.

"Why is she here, sir?"

He smiled benevolently. "She is one of those gentle beings of whom I spoke, changed by tragedy. Her ancestral home was raided by a band of marauders. The girl hasn't spoken since, and her family could do nothing with her, so they sent her to me."

"Do many of the patients work as she does?"

"I encourage them to do a little gardening or needlework, only to keep themselves pleasantly occupied, you understand. Our staff does the heavy work."

"Doing laundry looks like heavy work to me."

"Miss Effie *likes* it," Hardy interjected, and winked a bleary eye. "But I don't have to tell you about those laundresses who followed the troops. Dirtied the sheets as well as washed 'em, didn't they?"

Kingston shook his head, but he was still half smiling. "Now then, Joshua, we all know cleanliness is next to godliness."

Hardy snorted. "But she won't speak. She won't tell us what she's washing away."

"How long has she been here?" I asked.

"Nearly five years," Kingston said. "She came not very long after we opened the asylum at the close of the War."

"She must have been a child."

"Fourteen or fifteen. Some girls are married by such an age. But," and Kingston rose to indicate the meal was ended, "we have many interesting cases here. And tomorrow is soon enough to discuss them."

Kingston entrusted me with a lantern and the duty of escorting Hardy to his cottage. Despite the wine he had consumed, Hardy managed well enough to cross the lawn, leaning on his cane. I walked close by and could have caught him if he stumbled. But there was something repellent about him that made me refrain from offering my arm.

Joshua Hardy was vulgar, and in a way that had nothing to do with social rank or educational achievements. Everything he said, even when I could not see the glint in his pale eyes, confirmed this impression.

"I'll show you around tomorrow, young fellow. Tell you a thing or two about these madwomen, their vague aches and pains, their rashes and inflammations. Mark my word, some of 'em will do anything to provoke an examination."

In such a place as this, what could they do to refuse one?

When we reached Hardy's cottage, situated on a rise above the tributary, I remarked I thought we weren't far upstream from the place where I had waded in after Rachel Poncet's remains. "Did you notice anything unusual, Dr. Hardy? An odor?"

"At my age a thing would have to be under my nose for me to smell it." He fumbled with the door latch, while I held up the lantern.

"Perhaps you saw something?"

"Through these trees and underbrush?"

"Why was Mrs. Poncet brought to the asylum?"

Impatience entered his voice. "You just concern yourself with the live ones. They'll worry you enough."

Hardy shut his door, and I returned to the footpath, noticing this time that it not only curved toward the broad lawn, the route we had taken, but also branched. Following this narrower path led me down toward an embankment. There I discovered how near I was—and how near Hardy's house was—to the periphery of the estate. Ahead of me, the brick wall surrounding the lawn stopped abruptly at the height of the bank, and a wooden stockade fence followed the incline to the water's edge. I was left to assume the broad stream formed the east boundary of the asylum, and, indeed, crossing it might be difficult—dangerous when venomous snakes were active. But falling into it would be simple, particularly for an unsupervised and agitated patient.

My senses were not so dull as Dr. Hardy claimed his were. I watched the lantern light glitter across damp leaves and exaggerate shadows of tree trunks and hanging moss. I inhaled the pungent odors of fish, mud, and rotting vegetation that rose and mingled with the sweetness of flowering jasmine. The whir of cicadas throbbed in my temples. Running my tongue over my lips, I tasted warm, liquid air. But inside me crept a chill, the chill that precedes a fever.

Perhaps the peculiar coldness had been with me all afternoon, while I had been too distracted to recognize it, losing it among other sensations, as I immersed myself in the brisk current or sweated with exertion carrying the corpse or bathed in tepid rainwater. Now it demanded attention. I turned around, retraced my steps, and hurried across the lawn toward my new quarters—toward the consulting room with the bottle of quinine on the shelf.

Leaving the lantern on the desk, I reached for the brown glass bottle, but it was not where I expected it to be. The bottles and vials looked jumbled, the quinine shoved back behind an ointment jar. But was the disorder on the shelf or in my blurring vision, my fumbling hands? Had I waited too long to circumvent a bout of malarial fever? With the bottle nearly slipping in the grasp of one clammy hand and a tin cup shaking in the other, I poured a dose and drank down its bitterness.

# Chapter 4

Early next morning I approached the asylum through fog that lay over the lawn as heavy as smoke on a battlefield. But my head was clear, benefiting from the draught of quinine and the semblance of a night's rest. The bed slats had left a few bruises across my back; I would ask Gaston to stuff more Spanish moss into my mattress tic. Still, any sort of bed was an improvement over sleeping on bare ground, and at least I was not so footsore as I had been during my march from Baton Rouge.

Nearing the veranda, I saw Effie Rampling, sitting on the steps as she had yesterday, this time sweeping the loose sheaf of her chestnut hair over one shoulder and plaiting it with quick fingers. The sight of her reminded me of something I had read long ago in one of my father's old religious tracts: a warning that a witch might braid a man's fate into her hair. Such medieval superstition had once provided priests with an excuse to shave the hair from every part of a woman's body.

As I passed her, I smiled and wished her a good morning. She looked away, eyes downcast, more shy than wary of me, I hoped. But how could I know? How could I know what any of the women of the asylum would think of me?

I joined Dr. Hardy in the small dining room for weak coffee, corncakes and molasses. The old man seemed no worse for all the wine he had consumed last night, his eyes just as dull and his side-whiskers just as sharp.

"Kingston's gone into Lorraine," Hardy said, referring to the nearest town.

"To report Mrs. Poncet's death?" I asked.

"That business." He shrugged narrow shoulders. "Supplies expected. Took the wagon. Not due back 'til supper."

Hardy's verbosity increased after breakfast when he made good his threat of the night before to show me around the asylum and tell me "a thing or two" about the patients. With unsurprising boorishness, he described symptoms to me and passed judgments right in front of the patients concerned. They might have lost their reason, but these women did not appear to be dumb beasts. And the previous day, Effie Rampling had acted quite sensibly and practically to aid me when I arrived in a filthy suit. Touring the wards, I could see in many patients' faces the effects of Hardy's careless words. Eyes flickered with pain, narrowed with anger, closed with humiliation. An elderly woman flinched as if struck when he remarked what an embarrassment "the unmanageable and incontinent wretch" was to her politically successful husband. The woman in the next bed spat at him, splattering the tips of his boots.

Hardy stopped and laid a skeletal hand on her round shoulder. "Kneel, Veronique. Lick them clean," he snarled at her. I had never heard a doctor speak so to a patient, certainly never to a woman, and I started to protest, when she herself came back at him. "I could have you beheaded!" Then the corners of her generous mouth curved in a smile. Hardy drew back his hand, and I caught his sleeve. He snapped at a stout attendant, ordering her to take Veronique to the solitary room.

The patient made no protest, but rose and fixed me with her eyes. "Is this your replacement, Dr. Hardy? He'll make a change, sure 'nough."

While the inmates around her appeared disheveled with their unpinned hair and gaunt in their shapeless frocks, this woman's tangles gave her a wanton look, and her shift was immodest covering for a figure so endowed. Unflinching when the attendant gripped her arm, she turned and strolled away toward the door.

"Dr. Kingston will deal with you, missy," Hardy called after her.

"That's right, old man," she said without looking back.

"Trollop!" he muttered, then spoke up for, I assumed, the benefit of all present. "Veronique Beaulieu is a new arrival, only been here a few weeks. She won't stay incorrigible for long."

I waited until we left the ward before asking Hardy why Miss Beaulieu had been committed. His answer was simplistic and unsatisfactory. "Same reason as all the others. Madness."

We continued my tour. I had found the second floor of the mansion not so pretentious as the first. Formerly spacious bedrooms, once occupied by one or two persons, had become the wards, filled with rows of eight or ten narrow beds. Dirtied and patched wallpaper, chipped woodwork, and an absence of carpets reminded me of other houses converted to hospitals. The occasional feminine scent of lavender eau de cologne, however sweet and cloying, failed to mask the common odors of institutional life, of sweat and urine, of sickness and bitter medicine.

The third story was brighter and better ventilated by a cross breeze moving through long barred windows. What had been a large nursery now served as a day room for patients engaged in sewing and handicrafts. Unlike the patients below, still in their beds and shifts, the women here were up and dressed, mostly in plain frocks, their hair combed and secured under snoods or crocheted caps. A memory of Mother's sewing circle crossed my mind. But not all of these middle-aged women before me were dedicated to their embroidery.

One patient whispered rapidly to herself while stabbing a needle again and again into a red, apple-shaped pin cushion. Another rocked and cradled her embroidery hoop. A third stared down at a tangle of thread in her lap and wept, a hopeless, miserable sound. The attendants took no notice of her.

I left Dr. Hardy leaning in the doorway, where he still struggled for breath after our climb up the stairs, and went to the crying woman. "Are you hurt?" I asked. "Can I help you?"

"It'll never be right, never be right," she murmured without lifting her face, thin fingers pulling at the many colored threads. Then she cocked her head, and her eyes slid to look sideways at me through her welling tears. "You carried the body. I saw you from the window."

Another patient, who had been busily stitching, dropped her work and hurried to me, smiling eagerly. "Don't pay her no nevermind. You've come to take me home, haven't you?" She reached for me, grasping my lapels and chattering, "How wonderful to see you! I knew it was all a mistake. I knew you'd come. I told them…"

A haggard-looking attendant pulled her from me and plopped her into a chair with the grim efficiency of one who performs the same task countless times a day.

Though I pitied them, patients and attendants alike, what could I do? I had not come to take any of them home.

Denying Hardy an opportunity to hold forth on the conditions of the occupants in the day room, I started down the stairs. He came after me, gripping the banister with one hand and brandishing his cane with the other, prodding me in the back. "No easy job," he panted. "They're not like soldiers. They wheedle and lie. Can't trust any of them."

When we reached the front hall, I allowed him to catch his breath before asking, "Does anyone require my services today, sir?"

"Matron can tell you that. You'll treat most of them here, but some will be brought to your consulting room by a caretaker. Makes a little outing for them."

I went out on the veranda, Hardy still at my heels, seeking Lila Fentroy, whom I had not seen in the wards. At the front of the house there was only a servant girl sweeping the steps. Following the veranda along one side of the house, Hardy in pursuit, I came upon a woman sitting in a wicker armchair, gazing at a tall wire aviary filled with cooing doves.

"Why, there's Miss Cynthia Ann," Hardy yammered from behind me.

The doves fluttered in agitation at his approach, but the woman only turned her serene face toward him, her complexion fair as dogwood blossom. She was one of my mother's generation, her gray-streaked, faded brown hair center-parted, coiled, and neatly pinned on each side of her head, her pale yellow three-tiered skirt worn over a crinoline, reminding me of a style my mother favored years ago. She was different from the women I had seen upstairs. My first impression of her was not of a soul lost in madness, but of one simply caught in another time.

Hardy made a stiff bow and continued his show of patronizing familiarity. "Yes, siree, here we have Miss Cynthia Ann. Comes to us all the way from Virginia. Isn't that right, Miss Cynthia Ann? Isn't that why you're above sitting with the other gals in the day room?"

The woman ignored Hardy, but extended a blue-veined hand to me and spoke in a soft, cultured voice. "I am Mrs. Hugo Glover of Richmond. And you, sir?"

"Robert Mallory, ma'am, from Baton Rouge. I'm the new general practitioner."

When her face suddenly brightened, I felt an odd lift in my own spirits. I thanked Dr. Hardy for showing me the asylum and introducing me to the patients. "But I wouldn't want to exhaust you further now that your retirement has begun," I added and waited for him to stump back into the house.

Kingston must have known of Hardy's contempt for the patients. Did that mean he condoned it?

Mrs. Glover granted me permission to join her, and I pulled up another wicker chair, commenting how pleasant it must be to watch the doves.

"Yes, very pleasant indeed," she replied. "On the day I arrived here, Dr. Kingston promised them to me as companions. No squab is served in this household. Of course, when the aviary becomes crowded, I let a few of the doves go, younger ones that might find an interest in life beyond the veranda."

Two birds disputed a perch, and Mrs. Glover tapped a warning finger against the wire, then, peace restored, settled back in her rocker.

"I'm never ill," she said, "thank the Lord. But I worry about these birds. Look at them, if you please, Dr. Mallory. They're fat and sleek, but look at their little heads. A head like that couldn't hold a brain any bigger than a new pea. Can you imagine having a thought in such a tee-niney brain?" She sighed and folded her hands across her waist. "Sometimes I don't believe doves think at all. They lay eggs bigger than their brains."

"The wild ones were always easy prey for my mother's cat," I remarked.

"A cage doesn't make these tame."

"No, I don't suppose it does."

She smiled at me. "I hope you don't find this presumptuous, sir, but you do so remind me of my son, my eldest child. Must be your dark hair and your eyes. Gray, aren't they? Arthur will be a man by now. Can you imagine not seeing your loved ones for six years?"

Or never again—my sister gone forever.

"My daughters won't know me when we meet again. Oh, but forgive me, Dr. Mallory. Of course you understand separation, you must have been in the war."

"Yes, ma'am."

"And you served with?"

"The Army of Tennessee. I was a surgeon's assistant."

"Your people must me very proud of you."

I could make no response to that pleasantry.

She chatted on, showing a gracious interest in me and telling me a little of her home and family in Richmond, but never referring to her husband or to her reason for commitment to the asylum. Later, I gently introduced the subject of Rachel Poncet.

"Yes, sir, I was well-acquainted with the late Mrs. Poncet. She was a handsome woman from a good family. Indigo or cotton, I believe, with a house in New Orleans and one on Bayou Teche."

"Do you know why she was here? Was she melancholy, perhaps?"

"Oh, I shouldn't like to say, sir." Mrs. Glover hesitated a moment, then added, "For a while she seemed to have had the idea that she had improved her lot. But I believe she was mistaken. And then, these last months she was not so—polite—as previously."

"Mistaken in what way, ma'am? Would you explain?"

"When we are better acquainted." She looked past me, and I turned to see Lila Fentroy approaching us.

Rising to leave her, I thanked Mrs. Glover for her conversation. In parting she said, "When you write to your mother, Dr. Mallory, please give her my regards." I nodded. Hers was the sort of comment ladies made, generously including a gentleman's absent mother in their circle of civility. I could not share with Mrs. Glover my doubt that Mother would welcome a letter from me. My part in such an exchange was to pretend family harmony.

Mrs. Glover's manners carried her like a life boat on a lonely sea. In our first conversation, I might have detected a little eccentricity, but nothing of particular derangement in her thinking. I had heard only how sad she was, how she missed her children, longed for her home. But I was not an expert in such matters. All I could do was resolve to bring as much ease and comfort to the patients of Magdalene Asylum as my skills allowed, though for some things I had no remedy. I had no power to reunite Mrs. Glover with her children. Nor had I any means to bring my mother's lost daughter back to life.

I had not seen my sister die. No one wrote to me. I didn't see her buried. Only when I returned to Baton Rouge after the war did Father tell me how things were. But I always see her in my mind's eye, the way I never saw her. I follow the thread of any memory of her, some incident in our shared childhood perhaps, and then quite beyond my control, the memory veers away and finishes with the image of Lucinda, hanging by her neck from the balcony rail. I cannot cut her down.

# Chapter 5

The asylum housed fewer than forty patients, and, although trained medical workers were few, attendants and menials were numerous. Certainly the war had impoverished and displaced many individuals of both races, who were now desperate for work and sustenance; the caretakers, most of them former slaves, might work for pitifully low wages. Still, wealth had to exist somewhere to finance such an establishment, for the big house and outbuildings appeared in good repair, the lawn and gardens lush as Eden. I guessed Kingston must charge his patients' families exorbitant fees.

My first day on duty, Lila Fentroy showed me the small treatment room and dispensary, once the butler's pantry, warning me of pilfering by the staff. "Some of the hired help have tried to make off with medicines and ointments for themselves or their kinfolk. I keep the keys to the cabinets and will unlock them when you're here. Gaston can bring you a little chest with a lock and key for the remedies you keep at the cottage."

As Matron explained procedures to me, I noticed she rarely called me "doctor," and never "sir." Apparently, Matron had placed me in her mind only slightly above the staff and far beneath Dr. Kingston, to whom she referred in reverential tones, as a nun might to Jesus Christ.

"These mad women would worry Dr. Kingston to death with their trifling ailments if they were allowed. It's your responsibility to attend to their complaints. I won't have the Doctor pestered."

Then, in succession, she brought me my first patients. Their "complaints" included a case of severe dehydration brought on by a pernicious digestive disorder, a suppurating wound from a spider bite, and a lacerated back. For the first patient, I administered a tonic and prescribed a diet of broth and rice. For the second, I cleansed, salved, and bandaged her wounded arm. For the third, I was at a loss not as to the treatment for the bands of cuts across the woman's bare back, but as to how they had occurred. Matron enlightened me.

"Hannah's been bolted in the crib for most of two days. Slats leave the marks you see—they wouldn't, of course, if she hadn't squirmed and struggled."

After some prompting from me, Matron further described the crib and its uses. "Oh, it's like a bed with no mattress and a lid that locks down tight, so as the patient can't turn herself or lift her arms to thrash about. It's a powerful remedy, I promise you, for driving out demons."

The patient swayed a little where she stood, gathering the smock Matron had moments before yanked down to the young woman's waist, clutching the shreds of bloodstained cloth to her breast. Hannah, who looked no more than twenty years old, was sallow, malnourished, and vacant of expression. Her filthy skirt stank of urine and feces. I had never before seen a woman in such a degraded condition. Had she been a man, she would not have looked far out of place as a prisoner in Andersonville.

She trembled and winced when I approached her, though I had not laid a hand on her. I turned away from her and toward Matron. "Are the demons out of her now?" I asked.

"For the time being."

"Then be so kind as to bring warm water, soap, towels, and clean clothes for the patient."

Lila Fentroy regarded me disdainfully, then made an effort to flounce from the examining room, a maneuver impaired by the breadth and stiffness of her starched skirt. She did not return, but sent an attendant, bearing a worn, shapeless smock, a hand towel, a sliver of lye soap, and a pail of cold water.

I enlisted the attendant to bathe and partially dress the patient behind a screen. Then I set to work on Hannah's lacerations, applying ointment and strips of gauze with as light a touch as I could manage. Throughout the procedure, she remained docile and uncomplaining. Or was she merely listless?

"The wounds may drain," I told her. "Don't lie on your back until I've seen you again and changed your dressing."

"He'd have 'em put me in the crib face down," she muttered over one shoulder.

"No, of course not. That's no place for you."

"He's something worse in mind," she whispered, as if to someone else, some invisible listener.

"Trust me, I don't," I said.

Hearing her breath quicken, I rattled on, trying to reassure her. "I'll speak to Dr. Kingston on your behalf. Surely this crib device is unnecessary. Miss Hannah, you're fatigued and undernourished. You need comfortable rest and a fortifying diet."

I didn't see her hand move—didn't see it at all—till it appeared beneath my chin, gripping the pair of surgical scissors she had jabbed at my upper chest. My coat and shirt offered me some protection, but she had succeeded in rending the fabric and making an impression on my flesh. I couldn't speak for the shock and sudden pain of it. But unasked, the attendant wrenched the scissors away from my chest and Hannah's grasp, throwing them to the floor, where they spun to rest on the polished boards.

The moment before Hannah stabbed me, I would not have believed her capable of such violence or of the vigorous, piercing screams she unleashed as the attendant hauled her from the room. My gullibility provided Dr. Hardy much amusement at supper.

"You never put a sharp instrument near Miss Hannah. Matron could've told you that." The old man chuckled into his brimming wine glass.

"But Matron didn't tell me."

"You're fortunate the girl aimed no higher," said Dr. Kingston. "A caretaker nearly lost an eye to one of Hannah's outbursts."

"She looked so weak, helpless, really," I began, but Kingston interrupted me.

"You must never let down your guard, Robert. Sane or otherwise, all women are full of guile. Oh, some call it charm if the woman is beautiful, but I call it what it is. Without a man's intellectual and physical resources, what have they but cunning?"

"And spite," Hardy chimed in. "It's man's duty to manage woman, just as he holds dominion over the livestock, though brood mares and dairy cows are often better tempered than our God-given helpmeets."

"How true," said Kingston, touching his napkin to one corner of his mouth. "And Robert, if you should have another dangerous encounter with a patient, don't wear your bloody frock coat into the dining room."

It seemed to me that Kingston was hardly put off his feed by a stain on my lapel, and Hardy gobbled and drank everything set before him. During the meal, I continued to express doubts that punishment and deprivation could restore reason. But my employer informed me these were not his only methods and reminded me, as did the aching puncture wound in my chest, of my inexperience in the art of assessing madness. Still, I insisted on being shown the treatment rooms omitted from my first tour of the asylum and on seeing this contraption—the crib—in which Hannah had been confined.

"Of course, my boy, we must satisfy your curiosity," said Kingston.

"Perhaps, as you say, the staff was overzealous in the treatment of Miss Hannah. But you, yourself, have discovered how troublesome the woman can be. I'll have a word with Matron."

Kingston went on to leave me with the impression that Matron, not he, favored certain methods of restraint and discipline. He merely indulged her out of gratitude for her tireless service during his wife's final illness. His hands were always clean.

But I was to believe in the weeks to come that, although conditions of the inmates varied widely, treatments followed some scheme devised and ordained by Dr. Kingston alone. And, although he allowed Matron her odd predilection, he had little interest in any suggestions or recommendations of mine for change.

In parting that night, my employer invited me to witness a gentle form of treatment at what he called a soiree, to be held on the following evening as a reward for his more compliant patients. Then I was excused and took my time walking from the big house to my quarters, clearing my head of cigar smoke and tedious conversation.

Entering the house, I lit a lamp and carried it to the bedroom. On the top of the bureau I saw my laundered shirt and undergarments folded and neatly stacked. The minister's robe was draped over the back of a chair. But my second-best suit was oddly laid out, trousers and coat lengthwise on the bed, the sleeves crossed over the jacket front, giving the momentary impression that a faceless man lay outlined on the counterpane.

Nearing the bed, I noticed that beside the suit were indentations in the mattress and pillow, as if someone had lain there for a time, alongside my clothes. But perhaps what I saw, the incurved impression and shape, was only a trick of lamplight and shadow and wishful thinking.

# Chapter 6

Early next morning, Gaston shuffled into my room, bringing a mug of coffee and a message that Matron wished to see me in the wards immediately.

"Miz Ryder's still breathing, Dr. Mallory, sir, but she ain't waking up. I declare, she be limp as boiled greens."

I scalded my mouth on a swig of coffee and hurried to the big house. There, I found my first patient of the day lying stuporous on her cot, her pulse thready, her breathing fitful. Lifting her eyelids, I saw her pupils were contracted to pinpoints. And despite the humid warmth in the room, the woman's skin was papery and dry.

"Has she been drugged?" I asked Matron.

"She's difficult to quiet at night and requires a dose of laudanum. We couldn't run the place without it."

"Can you run a hospital by killing the patients?" I muttered, while bathing the unconscious woman's face with a solution of witch hazel and cool water. "Was her dosage administered by Dr. Kingston?"

"On his instructions," replied Matron.

The patient was barely able to wrinkle her nose and moan in response to salts of ammonia. Then, as I made an effort to raise her to a sitting position, her head lolled back against my shoulder, pale hair falling over her ashen face.

"That rag doll of a creature is the Lady Phillida Ryder. Would you believe it?" said Matron. "Sent to us by a lord, all the way from England."

"For what reason?" I asked.

"Possession," Matron answered matter-of-factly.

"Possession?"

"You heard me. She couldn't sleep without her laudanum long before she came to us."

Lady Ryder's eyes blinked open. A spasm seized and released her torso. She turned her face to one side, and I caught her vomit in the water basin.

After seeing that she was sufficiently revived, I moved on to other patients, who, though wide awake, suffered from other ill effects of too much laudanum; constipation and slight dehydration were common symptoms. I could voice my concern to Dr. Kingston, but I could also predict his answer—that he knew better than I how to administer a madhouse. With access to the dispensary, I was more tempted to dilute the supply of opiates.

At the end of my rounds, I left the wards feeling downcast. This had not been a day of performing amputations in a field surgery tent, leaving me exhausted almost beyond pity. It had been a day of witnessing and ministering to the sufferings of human beings already missing pieces, not of their bodies, but of their lives.

All day I had not once seen Kingston among the patients, and this was to prove usual in the weeks to come. He was in his study busy with the accounts, one attendant told me. He had ridden off, another said, to keep an eye on the tenants who farmed his land outside the asylum walls. He had gone to town, still others reported, to see his banker, his lawyer, his broker, or perhaps his tailor. A man of Dr. Kingston's importance hardly had time to waste upon his supposed professional calling.

In the late afternoon, a drowsy melancholy settled over the fitful patients, who at last languished on their cots, spent from screaming or weeping. I moved quietly down the hall toward the main staircase, hoping the peace would hold until I made my escape from the big house.

But halfway down the stairs I met a new onslaught of frenzied women. These, I soon learned, were the patients invited to the evening's soiree. Ascending the staircase, they surrounded and chattered all at once to a grinning Negress in their midst. She was small of stature, nearly as round as she was tall. As the demands for her attention increased, she laughed and shooed the women ahead of her as if they were a flock of noisy starlings.

I stopped a young maid who was following after them and asked her what the excitement was about, silently hoping the furor would not provoke any outbursts upstairs.

"That Charmaine they's all after, sir. She fix 'em up pretty for the party," the girl told me. "Nobody do hair better than Charmaine. She know all about painting faces and dressing fine. She learning me how, too."

Among the women vying for Charmaine's skills, I caught a glimpse of Veronique Beaulieu. Apparently her misconduct toward Hardy had not put her too far out of favor with Kingston.

Outside, the early evening was hazy and warm, but a light breeze hinted at a cooler night. I took the long way round the big house, walking past the outbuildings and the clotheslines. Effie was there, taking down the last of the washing. Intent on her work, she took no notice of me. Though passing at some distance, I could have called out "good evening" to her, but I hesitated and let the opportunity go by.

While I was washing up and applying a fresh bandage to my chest, Gaston arrived with a black frock coat for me, compliments of my employer.

"You mighty hard on your clothes, Dr. Mallory, sir. Miss Effie no sooner wash the river out of one suit than she washing blood out of the other. You better take care of this one."

As he held the coat for me to slip on, I caught a whiff of musty wool. I was surprised by the generous fit; the sleeves were sufficiently long, the waist far more than ample in both length and breadth. "This couldn't be Dr. Kingston's castoff," I said.

"Oh, no, sir. This here coat belonged to Colonel Cordelay. He owned the plantation back when it was called Magdalena after his bride. I work for him from day I's born 'til Dr. Kingston take over. The Colonel always had things nice and stylish, and more clothes than he could take with him. Many's the time I worn his old coats and trousers, too."

With a flourish, Gaston brushed the shoulders of the frock coat and adjusted my cravat at a devil-may-care angle—perhaps it looked straight to him—then sent me off to the big house.

There I was admitted by a servant who directed me down the broad front hall. Before reaching the parlor, I could hear the party in progress, the rustle of silk, the clink of glasses, the brittle notes of a music box waltz, and the trill of feminine laughter.

I paused before the open door and looked up at the convex mirror that reflected the candlelit parlor's occupants. I saw a room full of white shoulders—some rounded mounds of flesh buttressing the short column of a neck, some no more than translucent skin stretched over chalky bone. Then I saw Dr. Kingston in the center of the swirl of crinolines, mauve, pale blue, and primrose. Around him, ladies fluttered lace fans, pouted rouged lips, shook glossy ringlets. All were curved in the looking glass, all distorted.

Spinning round where she stood near the doorway, Veronique Beaulieu fixed me with her over-bright eyes and pulled me into the room, into the close press of pre-war fashion and affectation. Miss Veronique herself, apparently laced to a rib-cracking tightness, the extent of her décolletage far exceeding her ability to draw breath, looped her arm under mine and swayed as if fainting were imminent. "Sup with me, won't you, Dr. Mallory?" she whispered. "There's quite a spread—cold chicken, salads, wine, creme caramel. But we must hurry, before the vultures pick the table clean." Then she led me forward, past the other ladies, keeping a firm grip on my sleeve.

For a moment, I was reminded of the last time I saw my sister at a supper party, color and excitement burning in her cheeks as she flirted with her companion, Kingston's dapper nephew, Edgar. Lucinda had seemed frantic to convince us all, family and guests, that she was happy, that she was falling in love. But I knew differently.

No more was Miss Veronique falling in love with me. Repeatedly, as we threaded our way across the room, she cut her eyes toward Kingston, whose narrow gaze appraised her coolly in return. It was a hazard of the profession, I'd been told, that a doctor sometimes became the object of a patient's infatuation. I had yet to face such a predicament, though, for the elegant director of Magdalene Asylum, the occurrence must have been commonplace.

The air was heavy with gardenia perfume vaporizing from the warmth of bare wrists and throats. Patients I had met earlier I hardly recognized now, seeing them through a flickering sheen of candlelight, through their masks of beeswax, with their lamp-blackened lashes and carmine lips. They fawned on Dr. Kingston as if he were not their physician at all, but the catch of the county. I thought of sensuality gone mad, alluring and grotesque, the kind one finds when stumbling drunk into a New Orleans bawdy house. But I was sober, and this was a lunatic asylum.

Oh, I was not immune to women, softened by silk and lace, inviting in word and manner. But I knew my place. I did not put myself forward in the ranks of society ladies, nor did I take advantage of those in reduced situations. And patients were inviolate. Some other men, soldiers in particular, told me that I was too circumspect, though that was not how they had phrased it, and that I'd left myself no relief except what could be bought.

At Veronique's insistence, I sampled a little of the refreshments, then stood back as the women flocked around the table, devouring the victuals with such relish that I guessed this was not their usual fare. Briefly, as they ate, the patient's high pitched chatter dropped to a hum, then rose to new heights, as the food and drink disappeared. Veronique, who had left me by a window and moved across the room to Dr. Kingston, was soon the subject of conversation.

"Rachel Poncet all over again."

"Miss High-and-Mighty."

"She won't last any time at all. I've seen the likes of her come and go."

"Someone said she killed her baby."

"She would do anything."

Then the same women who had gossiped about her fluttered to Veronique's side, smiling and putting themselves between her and Kingston.

An elderly woman in antique finery waved her ivory-handled cane at me, summoning me to where she sat in state on the divan, flanked by two attendants. "I can see nothing close," she said, "but I can spot my husband's suits across the room. Have you an explanation, young man?"

"Gaston brought me the suit."

The stiffness in her shoulders seemed to ease slightly. "Oh, well, then it's a castoff."

"Yes, ma'am."

I introduced myself and felt oddly disturbed when she confirmed my suspicion of her identity. This, the only very old woman in the room, was Mrs. Cordelay, wife or widow, I was unsure which, of the estate's previous owner and now an inmate of the asylum that had been her home. Satisfied that I had not stolen a suit of clothes from her husband, she held me in conversation for the rest of the evening. Mrs. Cordelay pursued one topic of discourse, and only one: the assassination of President Lincoln.

"I was in New Orleans, you understand, when the news reached me that Mr. Lincoln had passed over." Mrs. Cordelay pressed a lilac-scented handkerchief to her temple. "Such a trying time! Oh, the commanding general told us what we must do—toll the bells, hang black crepe from every window, close the shops and offices, gather to hear eulogies, wear the face of grief—as if we had not worn it long enough to suit our captors."

"I've heard it said Mr. Lincoln might have been kinder than his successors," I put in.

A glint came into Mrs. Cordelay's watery eyes. "And I've heard tell that Mrs. Lincoln is a madwoman." Then she clutched my wrist and fired a question at me as if I were on trial for murder. "Where were you, sir, when you heard of the assassination?"

Without hesitation I answered, "I was in an army hospital, changing the dressing of a bullet wound." But I did not share with her the thought that had run through my mind: So, another man has been shot dead. Hadn't I seen thousands who had met the same fate? And we were asked to mourn for him as if he had been all of them.

One by one, the women became tired or querulous, were excused by Dr. Kingston, and led away by attendants. Veronique was the last to go.

Alone with Kingston, I remarked that I had not seen Mrs. Glover at the party. Kingston shrugged, saying, "I only issue invitations. I do not coerce the ladies into acceptance."

Then I asked what had become of Mrs. Cordelay's husband, wondering also how he managed to keep his wife in the asylum.

"I believe Colonel Cordelay is somewhere in Mexico," Kingston replied. "As you know, he couldn't afford to stay on here. And he couldn't quite bring himself to swear allegiance to the Union."

"He doesn't write to you or—"

"Or send me payments for the upkeep of his wife? No. Mrs. Cordelay, the former mistress of Magdalena Plantation, is my one and only charity case."

Kingston had taken up a lamp and started off toward his suite of rooms when I prevailed on him to answer one more question. "Why didn't Matron attend the soiree?"

Without turning back to me, he replied, "Oh, she never attends. That would undermine her discipline. Good night, Robert."

# Chapter 7

The next morning I came earlier than usual to the big house and caught Kingston before he left for the day on some pressing business or other. I reminded him of our agreement that he would show me the treatment rooms at the top of the house. Later, he said, evening would be soon enough, when the patients were settled down, the wards quiet. Later, whenever it suited him.

After finishing my rounds that day and being told by Matron that Dr. Kingston had still not returned, I took a stroll on the veranda. There I found Cynthia Ann Glover, standing near the wire aviary, poking bits of cornbread through the mesh to the doves perched inside. As I neared her, she glanced at me and nodded.

"Good evening, Mrs. Glover," I said. "I missed seeing you at last night's soiree."

"You're very kind, Dr. Mallory. But I do not attend such gatherings."

"More's the pity. You would be an asset."

"I prefer the company of my doves."

The birds, which had retreated along their perch at my approach, now maneuvered close again to the mesh and to Mrs. Glover's handouts.

"Can you imagine, sir, why Nature would give these lovely gray doves red feet?" Mrs. Glover's voice remained soft and pleasantly modulated, regardless of what she said. "It disturbs me, Dr. Mallory, wakes me in the night and robs me of sleep. I think of our soldiers in worn out boots, marching till their feet bled. Gray coats, red feet."

"That's all done with now, ma'am."

"Is it? Is everyone satisfied?"

She offered me a wedge of cornbread to feed the birds, but the creatures were too timid to take it from me.

I cleared my throat before changing the subject. "Miss Effie Rampling— does she ever attend those evening parties?"

"I think not. Dr. Kingston says the parties are treats for the best behaved patients, but I know for a fact some well-mannered ladies are never invited."

I recalled Kingston had not actually said he had invited Mrs. Glover.

"Besides, what would Miss Effie gain by attending?" Mrs. Glover continued with dignified authority in her voice. "It would hardly advance her social position. Oh, no. It's the ones who give Dr. Kingston what he wants who are allowed to come, the ones who smile and flatter and fawn on him. I ask you, sir, what good is it? It's nothing but humiliation."

"Did Rachel Poncet go to the parties?"

"You might well ask. That's how Rachel Poncet thought she had bettered herself, don't you know? She went so far as to forget her place and his—forgot he was her doctor and imagined him her suitor. Told us all as much. Poor creature thought Dr. Kingston had some power to send her husband to the front lines and make her a widow, so that he might marry her. Like David and Bathsheba, don't you see? Never mind that the war is over, and Dr. Kingston is neither a general nor a monarch."

"Would you agree with Dr. Kingston that toward the end she had become violent?"

"I never knew her to hurt anyone," said Mrs. Glover. "But at the last she seemed to have forgotten she had ever been a lady. I am ashamed for her sake to say it, but Rachel Poncet became wild, rather like an animal. I could have no more to do with her."

Resolutely, Mrs. Glover brushed the bread crumbs from her hands, and the startled doves flew upward to the far reaches of their cage.

I gave up seeing Kingston that evening and started for my cottage, still a strange phrase to me after years of tents and boarding houses. On the way I met Gaston. He was lugging a varnished pine rocking chair and didn't object when I offered him a hand with it.

"This here chair for yo' front porch, Dr. Mallory, sir. A gentleman needs a place to set in the evenings."

"You think of everything, Gaston."

"Ain't got nothing else to think of," he replied.

Effie Rampling was waiting on my porch, silent as always, while Gaston and I brought the rocking chair up the steps. Then she held out to me what she had brought: my best white shirt and black coat, mended and laundered. She touched the stitching where the rents had been, then looked up at me with a question in her eyes. Did she wonder how I had come by the tear and the bloodstains? Surely by now the tale of my stabbing was common knowledge in the wards. I thanked her, complimenting her work; the seams were even and the stains gone.

I wanted to say something else, something more, something that would keep her there a little longer. How can I explain, even in retrospect? I knew the blue of her eyes had simply caught the lowering sunlight, that it was mere illusion that the light came from behind her eyes, shining through the color as if through stained glass. She turned away, so I let her go without a word.

Gaston rattled on, fussing over the placement of the chair, delaying his departure. "You want to see the clouds and the colors when you sets out here. But then again, you don't want no sun glaring in yo' eyes."

I think he was lonesome. There were no other old men around here who'd lived so long, lived through so much, with whom Gaston could reminisce. Only Dr. Hardy might match him in years, but I doubted my predecessor would admit having anything in common with a former slave.

At Gaston's insistence, I tried out my new rocking chair, while listening to him talk and asking a few questions. He admitted to seeing little of his own people since Kingston had taken over the plantation.

"We don't mix much outside the wall. Oh, the gals go home from time to time, bringing they folks some money, maybe toting a little something from the kitchen. But out there they don't fit in so well no more. Me, I done outlived my kinfolk, what I knew of 'em. I reckon I wouldn't leave now if I could. After while, craziness kinda rub off on you."

A few days later Gaston's sentiments were echoed by the Reverend Mr. Jonas. I had delayed long enough returning his minister's robe, and after asking Gaston for directions, found the minister alone in his cabin on the wooded outskirts of Lorraine.

Some ways off, closer to the town, was a collection of hovels and shanties occupied by his parishioners, former slaves and their offspring. But Jonas lived apart in a snug log cabin, no bigger than ten feet by twelve, with a dry dirt floor, tightly plastered walls, and a sleeping loft a few feet shy of the rafters. The room was smoky and smelled of grease candles and pipe tobacco.

"You could've sent my robe by one of the girls working up there."

"I wanted to bring it myself, Reverend, and thank you again for your help with… well, your help down by the river."

"Oralia told me you was some gentleman."

Her name sounded vaguely familiar, but I couldn't place it.

"You don't know who she is, do you, sir? But she seen you being kind to a madwoman who done stabbed you with a pair of scissors."

"Oh. She's a caretaker then?"

Jonas nodded. "I was baptizing her little brother, Asa, the day your patient come floating by."

I didn't correct him that Rachel Poncet had never been my patient. Instead, I asked him if the women working for Dr. Kingston talked much about the asylum and its inmates on their visits home.

"Not much." Jonas shrugged and filled his pipe. "Maybe they be tired of that place when they comes to Lorraine. Maybe most folks don't want to hear, too busy with their own troubles."

I asked him to explain.

"Dr. Kingston keeps the women working real steady like, but the men don't get much. Men who years back never took a rest are sitting idle now, letting their wives and daughters support 'em. Maybe drinking a little too much corn liquor. It ain't like it was—everybody working together. The women are separate now. It don't set well, but folk's got to live."

"But isn't Kingston's land farmed by tenants? Surely the men…"

"He don't rent land to my people. Whether he's a mind to or not, I don't know. But there's those round here wouldn't tolerate it."

I asked him about Oralia, how she came to speak to him of me.

Though Jonas was a minister living in poverty and Kingston an asylum director and a landholder living in luxury, there was something about the Reverend's way of speaking that reminded me of my employer's. Jonas, like Kingston, held a position of authority in his own community that gave him assurance in leading a conversation, doubtless that the final point made would be his. Although his tone was not so condescending as Kingston's, Jonas addressed me as if there were much I did not know, as if what he chose to tell me might be intended to shock me, just as I believed my employer's comments were sometimes designed to provoke.

"Well, you're something different up there, Dr. Mallory—something for Oralia to talk about while she be keeping other things to herself."

Jonas told me Colonel Cordelay was not one to encourage family ties in the quarters, but the Reverend had taken it on himself to look after orphans, including Oralia and her brother.

"Their parents are both dead?" I asked.

Jonas drew on his pipe, nodding as he slowly exhaled. "Mother be dead for sure. Father—don't know. He was a buck up at the plantation. Later on, Cordelay took him as his body servant in the army. Oralia and Asa, they was both begot in the breeding shed. I took 'em in during the War, and Lord knows, they be preacher's children now."

"A little wild?"

"More than once I done dipped that boy in the river. And Oralia—she's a hard-working girl, but she don't come to prayer meeting no more."

Oralia's name had meant nothing to me the first time I heard it, on the day of my arrival at the asylum. But I recalled then that Gaston had linked it with Rachel Poncet's.

"Has Oralia said anything to you about the woman whose body we pulled from the river?" I asked. "Does she think it was an accident or a suicide?"

"Well, Oralia talks to me. But she don't necessarily tell me what she thinks."

"Then what do you think, Reverend? You saw the body."

"All kinds of sin wash down that river."

"You think she drowned herself?"

"I think those women be mostly dead the day they goes inside. No healing going on there, no saving bodies or souls. And then Dr. Kingston brings you in—for what? A case of head lice? A few bedsores? You ain't saving lives up there, no, sir. You just killing time."

With that thought, the Reverend Mr. Jonas saw me on my way, once again to pursue my chosen profession, however ineffectively.

I soon noticed that Sundays at the asylum were much like any other days, except that the staff was reduced and meals were simpler. The workers were not discouraged from observing the Sabbath, and most who did so joined the Reverend Mr. Jonas's congregation. But Kingston offered no worship services to his patients, invited no itinerant preacher or priest behind his gates. And though Matron allowed grace to be said at meals, she did not encourage it in any formal way; patients might simply bow their heads or murmur words according to their own personal customs.

When I questioned Kingston on the reason for the absence of religious rituals at Magdalene Asylum, he answered with customary authority. "It has been my experience that religion only confuses the patients. Theology, of course, is beyond the understanding of most sane women. So, you can well imagine how such ideas would exacerbate the chaos in already disordered minds. No point in filling madwomen's heads with the foolish notion that God will answer their prayers—for what grotesqueries might such creatures pray?"

My employer's reasoning reminded me of that of some slaveholders of old who had discouraged their human property from thinking too much about the compassion of Jesus Christ—for then those slaves might pray for it, expect better treatment from their Christian masters, or even go so far as to imagine that they, like their masters, possessed immortal souls.

# Chapter 8

Certainly general practice at the asylum did not inspire the rush of energy or the pulse-quickening horror I had felt when battle casualties crowded the surgery tent. The ailments I treated were, for the most part, routine, and the horror had been replaced by a nagging unease. Regarding the illnesses, most were genuine, but sometimes I found it difficult to distinguish the effects of a fever from those of a fevered imagination. As for the patients' injuries, while a few were the result of mishaps, some were self-inflicted, some were, I suspected, the evidence of cruelties inflicted by other patients or by attendants, some may well have been the result of Kingston's treatments gone awry, though I never saw him in the act of any physical cruelty.

Indeed, Kingston apparently provided a far more humane environment for his patients than any he described having seen on his visits to asylums in other parts of the country or in Europe. In his facility, all patients were given plain, wholesome food and were allowed to use eating utensils rather than fingers, if they could be trusted with spoons. Patients who were in the least tractable were permitted to walk in the gardens or to occupy themselves with needlework. Magdalene Asylum was no dungeon, crowded with naked inmates, chained and cringing in their own filth.

Some weeks after my first request to see the upstairs treatment rooms, Kingston showed me three small, windowless, musty chambers—padded cells with mattresses nailed to the walls. A fourth room contained the narrow "crib" and "tranquilizing chair"—a heavy wooden armchair with leather straps attached which could be buckled around the wrists and ankles of the occupant. Neither device was presently in use. Nor were they likely to be, Kingston assured me, except for cases of extreme derangement.

"Any gentleman," said Kingston, "is appalled by the thought of a woman turned wild as a beast. Yet something must be done with them. In other establishments I have witnessed such creatures not merely restrained, but shackled and beaten. The public—for a price—is allowed to tour these corridors of hell to be titillated by the lurid acts of demented souls and their keepers. Can you imagine that, Robert?"

"Yes, sir, I can. People will bring a picnic lunch to a hillside and watch men kill each other on a battlefield. Do you think there is any cure for madness?"

Kingston sighed. "Experience has made me doubtful."

"But do you attempt to cure it?"

"I protect my patients—and their families—from the shame of their affliction. I make it possible for fathers, husbands, brothers, and sons to rest assured that they have done all they can."

It followed naturally that any suggestions of mine for improvement in the running of Magdalene Asylum, model of humaneness as it was, or the treatment of its patients, were seen as unnecessary and unwelcome by its overseer.

From further discussions with Kingston, from remarks made by Matron and the attendants, and from conversations with some patients themselves, I began to discover the individual designs of madness. One patient believed she was in hiding, that the asylum was indeed her sanctuary from a nameless beast that waited outside the gates to devour her. One believed herself to be a house guest, staying on only to give her mad former slave woman an occupation. Kingston told me the servant was actually retained by the patient's family to wait on her mad mistress. But overhearing mistress and maid servant whispering together, describing fantastical imaginary events and plotting impossible futures, left me with the impression that theirs was a madness for two.

Many inmates were melancholy. Some heard voices. One had killed her child.

Matron confirmed the gossip I had heard at the evening party: Veronique Beaulieu had wrung the life out of her newborn baby at the Devil's bidding, so Matron claimed. But Kingston, who had been consulted by the Beaulieu family several times in the years prior to Veronique's commitment, told a different story of her emotional collapse shortly after giving birth.

"For many women, of course, motherhood is a fulfilling, perhaps even a morally fortifying experience," he had told me. "However, for some, the very condition of being with child acts to destroy an already fragile temperament. Matron may call Veronique's action the work of Satan—Matron is a hard worker, not a deep thinker—but I will give you a different explanation, a scientific one, based on my careful study of the nature of woman…"

And not for the first time my employer had patronized me with his theories.

"Woman is a vessel," he concluded. "Her purpose is to receive man and to bear his children."

"Woman is also a cognizant being," I asserted, "self-aware, capable of learning and creative thought."

"Oh, you misunderstand me, Robert. Of course, serving a man and caring for children require some modicum of intelligence. But if ever a woman deviates from the proper guidance of father or husband, she takes her first step toward the precipice of madness."

For one thing I thought then I should have been grateful: Dr. Kingston allowed me more idle time than had any of my previous employers. He even went so far as to discourage me on some days from going my rounds, suggesting that I instead avail myself of his library or try my hand at gardening alongside some of the more docile patients. I enjoyed the occasional respite, but needed—longed—to be more fully employed. Hadn't my parents taught me that industry was safer than idleness? Straying thoughts put one in danger of straying actions.

One day I approached Kingston in his consulting room on the subject of offering my services to the caretakers and their families.

"They have their own people," he replied dismissively.

"But have they surgical skills and medicines?" I asked.

"You'd be surprised what they have and do for their own. But what are you suggesting, Robert? That we run a hospital for the indigent?"

"I would go to them and give my time, not yours, sir."

"But you'd give away my ointments and medicines? Such things must be purchased by someone. And these folk are poorer than even you have ever been."

"Perhaps we could barter with them, medicines in exchange for labor or such goods as they have—a clutch of eggs, a bundle of firewood."

"I didn't hire you to start a new order in my territory. Do you understand that, Robert?"

"Yes, sir. I only hoped to do some good in the community."

"You think I don't?"

"Pardon me, sir. I never meant to suggest—"

"Why, I employ half the Negresses in the parish," he interrupted. "I don't need you coming in here telling me how to play the benefactor."

"Of course not, sir." I turned toward the door, suddenly weary of him. I could be subtle or blunt, civil or rude, it made no difference. Kingston would take offense when he would take offense.

"Just what surgery skills do you intend to offer at large? Tell me that, *Doctor* Robert Mallory. Will you generously lop off dusky arms and legs? Or ease the poverty of Lorraine's environs by kindly aborting the next generation of nappy-headed babies? You go on, then," he called after me. "Practice your interference in the name of charity and see what gratitude it brings you."

Not long after, I did go, walking among dilapidated shacks and past drafty cabins on the periphery of the town and in the neighboring woods. I encountered poor white folk, who had always scratched a meager living from the ground, and former slaves, who struggled to survive under a new system no more welcoming to them than the old one. Poverty did not surprise me, here or anywhere else in the South, populated as it was by broken men, worn-out women, and bedraggled children. The disadvantaged and distressed, with their tattered clothes and bare feet, their teeth rotten and their bowels worse, were commonplace. So too were their attendants: hopelessness and lethargy. But there was something else present in Lorraine, something more, a dreaminess, heavy, hanging like mist even on a clear afternoon.

Many of the young women must have been away for the day, working at the asylum, while the old women washed clothes or cooked over open fires in the yards. A few half-naked children played tag, running through the mud and filth that collected between the shacks. But the children did not shout or squeal when they caught one another, and the women conversed only in low tones. Perhaps they feared disturbing the menfolk. The men, both young and old, were silent, leaning in the open doorways or dozing under the trees, as little affected by my passing as by anything else, dull as patients of Magdalene Asylum when pacified with opiates. The scene reminded me of the Reverend's comment about corn liquor; looking at the squalor around me, I'd no doubt how tempting it would be.

I encountered much suspicion of my presence and little interest in my services. An old *traiteuse* named Velmina, steeped in remedies omitted from my medical training, already attended to most of the ailing, who had few complaints of her ministrations. I could hardly expect to compete with her for the loyalty of her patients. Beside Velmina, I was nothing more than a narrow, dour shadow in a black suit, carrying a scuffed black leather bag. But she was a sunburst in a yellow and scarlet turban, wearing her diverse and aromatic pharmacopoeia in string bags and many-colored pouches hung round her thick neck and broad waist.

Whereas Kingston had scorned my efforts to practice medicine among the poor, Velmina openly laughed at my attempts, but good-humoredly. She even allowed me to assist her on one of her cases. With her permission, I amputated an old man's gangrenous big toe, while Velmina, the patient's true healer, distracted him with her incantations. And she, not I, collected the fee of a bit of fatback and a bunch of greens. For reasons she did not share with me, she also took away with her the severed toe.

On my way out of town I saw Oralia Wilkins walking ahead of me, on her way back to Magdalene Asylum, I supposed. But she seemed in no particular hurry. With a straw basket on her arm, she ambled down the dirt road, the hem of her dark blue skirt stirring the dust. She was passing a shanty on the edge of town. In the yard stood a tall black man, shirtless, back beaded with sweat, swinging an ax down to split a log on the chopping block. A woman with a baby on her hip shooed two older children and a mongrel dog out the doorway, then retreated inside the house.

The man paused in his work to wipe his brow with the back of one hand and in doing so, slightly turned his head, catching sight of Oralia, who was watching him. For a moment the look that passed between them became a tangible thing, a thing that I could witness, though I knew even then that I was never meant to see it.

The baby cried, its bellowing sounding in the yard and down the road. Oralia went on her way, and I quickened my pace to catch up with her outside of Lorraine as she passed under a giant cottonwood tree.

She declined my offer to carry her basket; it was empty now, she said. And she was cautious of my conversation, until I described my attempts to practice medicine alongside the *traiteuse*, and our successful amputation of a man's toe.

"Folks just meeting that old man gonna figure he be smarter than he is," she said.

"Why do you say that?"

"Used to be, master would cut off a nigger's toe if he thought he'd learnt to read."

"Colonel Cordelay did that?"

"He done what he pleased."

Oralia didn't attach a "sir" to her remarks, something she might not dare to omit when answering Kingston. But I chose to interpret her omission as a sign that we were both off duty and perhaps a little off guard. Telling her I'd had a recent visit with the Reverend Mr. Jonas, I led her toward some revelations of her past as a slave's child on Magdalena Plantation. Her mother had died of a fever, she said, when her brother Asa was little more than a yard baby. Her father might be in Mexico with Colonel Cordelay.

"And what about you?" I asked. "Will you ever leave Lorraine and the asylum?"

Oralia shrugged. "Them Cordelays owned my people for so long—hard to believe I could just up and move. I don't know no other place."

"It can't be easy, watching over madwomen."

"Oh, some's moody, some's mean—you seen 'em. But they just a job. I be working for wages."

I, too, was working for wages, but I could not view my patients with such detachment.

Once, when I found Effie sitting alone on the front steps, I offered her pencil and paper, suggesting that she might wish to draw or write. Hoping to learn more about her, I went so far as to propose that she might write something to me or perhaps begin a diary. She shook her head in adamant refusal, and I didn't ask again.

There is always the risk in writing down one's life that with the same stroke of a pen one may encircle another's life and cross it out. Still, from the beginning of my employment at the asylum, I kept not a diary but a sickbed journal, much as I had done during the War, when time permitted. I catalogued patients' symptoms, described treatments, recorded clinical observations, striving to understand more of the science of medicine and surgery, trying to learn from my mistakes and not repeat them. I sought most in the art of medicine what I would seek if practicing any other art. I looked for pattern, hoping to find and follow a thread in Nature's fabric.

In ways I never could have anticipated, I was drawn in by the women of Magdalene Asylum, caught in their webs of remembrance and delusion, entangled.

One morning, after I had revived her from another near overdose of laudanum, Lady Phillida Ryder described her situation to me, which was so like that of many of the other patients, and not so very different from my own. "At first, family and friends are sympathetic," she said. "One is fatigued, one has a delicate disposition, they say. One is unbalanced, they whisper behind one's back."

As she spoke, Lady Ryder paced the ward, empty now except for the two of us. Only from time to time she paused to examine the fraying hem of a curtain or a brittle curl of peeling wallpaper.

"But then, life and duty call to them. They become bored with one's illness. Sympathy cannot be sustained forever. Believing they replace themselves, the family and friends send in paid attendants. Or send one *away* to those paid attendants, who provide, at best, indifferent care. Soon, quite soon, the indifference is mutual. In the end, the patient's only real companion is the illness itself. The pain reminds one that one is not alone, one is occupied. The fevers bring dreams. The voices, when they come, fill a void the loved ones left behind."

I don't know what lies on the other side of our passing. I don't know if the dead denounce us for living on after them, the dead we've touched and have not healed. But if we feel their reproach, whether or not they wish it upon us, is not our guilt just the same? And if the horrors I had seen and done, the pain I had inflicted and sought to allay, ever receded in my mind, if my conscience ever allowed me a respite, Kingston's voice was there to fill that void.

One day Kingston called me to his office to announce his decision that Battey's operation was the thing to cure Hannah of her violent outbursts.

"But do you suspect her ovaries are diseased?" I asked.

"That's of no consequence," he said. "The procedure has been repeatedly successful in producing more docile patients. You have performed the operation yourself, have you not?"

"Yes, sir, once. But the circumstances were quite different. The senior surgeon at the teaching hospital had ordered an emergency appendectomy. When I opened the patient's abdominal cavity, I discovered her appendix healthy, but her right ovary a mass of infection."

"So you knew best."

"I'm stating facts, sir."

"Well, I'm sure you wouldn't mind a chance to brush off your surgery skills. I have ether, so you can take your time, slice and delve and stitch as meticulously as you desire. No screaming. That should make a change from your hack and slash days."

I ignored his sneering tone and stated my own position. "Hannah has developed a chronic bronchial inflammation. The surgery you propose is an unnecessary risk to her health."

"Unnecessary?"

"If you have no respect for my professional opinion, Dr. Kingston, why do you employ me?"

"Why, indeed? I employ you, Robert, because I can. I use your services, your skills, such as they are, because I can. Don't forget I took you on as a favor to your family. Who else would have you? Where else would you go?"

What had my father told him? Was my employment a punishment they, together, had devised?

"I won't perform the operation."

"Shall I call Dr. Hardy from retirement?"

"No! Sir, you isolate the woman, restrain her, drug her. Isn't that enough?"

"Very well." Suddenly Kingston smiled, his tone and manner changing so dramatically with the two words he had spoken that I was left with the impression he had never intended me to operate. This was only another instance of his baiting me. "Very well," he repeated. "There will be no operation on Miss Hannah. But your insubordination has been noted— and your self-mastery. I wonder, Robert, what I would have to say to you before you'd tell me to go to hell."

I need never tell him, I thought; I would not be the one to send him there.

# Chapter 9

Sometimes when approaching the big house to go my rounds, I took the long way, passing the back of the house, where Effie Rampling busied herself with the laundry. On the bright summer days, she wore a broad-brimmed straw hat that rarely allowed me a glimpse of her face. But I could see her arms, thin but strong, encased in the long, tight sleeves of her brown dress, as she lifted damp gowns, bath towels, and bed linens from her basket and hung them on the clothesline.

I had examined or treated nearly every other patient at the asylum for one thing or another; each time the only threat to my professionalism had been pity. Effie was never ill, so I never touched her. If she had needed the services of the resident physician, perhaps I could have forced myself to view her with the necessary clinical detachment. Perhaps my more intimate thoughts of her would disappear. Perhaps not.

I didn't understand the workings of her mind. I could only observe the intensity with which she toiled and the consideration she showed to others. It was my own choice to believe her silence was not evidence of madness, but of self-possession.

Kingston and Hardy had their opinions of how women bewitched men, holding forth on the coy, who appealed with pretended modesty, the sly, who lured with feigned helplessness, the seductive, who entrapped with tantalizing possibilities. But what wiles had Effie ever practiced upon me? None. She never spoke, she hardly glanced at me. Perhaps all she had done was simply braid my fate into her hair.

I did my work, I kept my vows. And I permitted myself, from time to time, to think of Effie Rampling—only think of her. It was not a privilege that would have been granted to me from the pulpit. "Whosoever looketh on a woman to lust after her hath committed adultery with her already in his heart." Whatever God knew of my sins, Effie would not know.

One summer evening I pulled up a wicker chair alongside Mrs. Glover's rocker and sent the attendant away with the assurance that I would see the patient safely to the ward. I found Mrs. Glover's voice always soothing, whatever she said, and I was comfortable in her silences. Our times on the veranda were the pleasantest part of a day, especially when she spoke of Effie, often praising her, even without my prompting.

"Miss Effie is a sweet, thoughtful girl. You sense that, too, don't you, Dr. Mallory?"

"Yes, ma'am, I do."

"She launders my lace handkerchiefs so very carefully that they've lasted for years. My things will not be replaced and must be made to last. But I've no need to remind Effie of that fact. She knows."

I wondered what else Effie knew besides how to be careful with lace. What intimate knowledge had she of all of us at the asylum simply by doing the laundry? I imagined her touching my clothes, taking them away from the cottage, scrubbing out the sweat stains on her washing board, hanging my shirts and trousers to dry, ironing and folding—and never touching the man who wore those clothes.

Mrs. Glover gazed at her cooing doves, settling themselves for the night behind their wire mesh. She sighed and slowly waved her palmetto fan to and fro. Near as I was to her, I felt the gentle stir of air.

"I am not mad, you understand." Mrs. Glover's words, though softly spoken, jolted me from my reverie. "I wasn't sure when they brought me here," she said. "I'd begun to doubt myself. There is always the possibility, isn't there, for any of us to go mad?" She never shifted her gaze from the doves. "But things have become clear to me, Dr. Mallory, and I wanted you to know. I am not mad. Love has saved me—love of family, love of Nature, love of God."

An outbreak of severe sore throat and fever swept through the wards, coinciding with two weeks of summer thunderstorms and incessant rain. At least a third of the patients and some of the staff were affected, though Mrs. Glover and Effie were spared. I hardly saw them during my time of slogging through the mud, back and forth from my quarters to the big house to take pulses and temperatures, apply plasters, and paint ulcerated throats with patent medicines. Because or in spite of my efforts—a physician could never be sure—all but one of the patients recovered. Hannah, with her weakened lungs and poor constitution, succumbed to the infection.

My own condition I did my best to ignore, as duty demanded. In some parts of the South, malaria—the ague—was so common as to be hardly considered an illness at all. But as my patients gained their strength, I found myself losing mine. One morning I woke an hour before daybreak, uneasy, unable to keep still. When I had gone to bed late the night before, the house was suffocatingly close; now I could find no warmth anywhere in it. My teeth chattered against the glass as I drank down a bitter draught of quinine. But the shivering in my body only increased, as if it must reach its own climax, spend itself, regardless of my efforts to control or quell it.

I dressed, even to my hat, coat, and gloves, and wrapped myself in a woolen blanket before going outside. A queer sight I must have been on a summer dawn, if anyone had observed me, bundled up as I was against my own internal winter. In the first pale pink and gray streaks of morning's light, I paced the lawn, impatient for the full heat and glare of the sun, paced unseen, I supposed, since the asylum ahead of me was dark and still, the lower floor completely screened in fog. At the upper windows not a lamp was yet lit nor a curtain parted.

The fog encircled the house, coiled among the trees, and swallowed me whole. I could not see the ground, but sensed when my feet left the spongy softness of grass for the hard packed earth of the driveway. The sun rose, yellow haze burning through white fog. Some ways ahead I discerned the convoluted pattern of the wrought iron gates, traced faintly as a soft pencil line. The pattern moved on silent hinges, was momentarily obscured by bolder, heavier outlines, then reappeared. I heard the chink of metal against metal, the gate shutting, the latch falling into place. I saw a woman running, not down the drive toward me, but veering off from the gate, passing beside the brick wall, and vanishing into the pecan grove. I glimpsed a smear of dark skirt, a blotch of dark hair, nothing more really. But I guessed I saw a Negress, an attendant or servant, certainly not one of the pale, white-gowned inmates.

Reaching the gate, I found it locked. Had the woman been coming in or letting someone else out? Hadn't I seen two figures when the gate swung open? It was difficult to be sure, difficult to be sure of anything. I continued to stand by the gate, not leaning against it for support, but simply frozen beside it.

The light increased, and still I was paralyzed with cold, unmoving, until

I heard a voice from somewhere to my left, sounding warm and languorous. "Every morning is a rescue from the night before."

I turned to find Veronique Beaulieu only an arm's length from me, yet, in her white shift, appearing little more substantial than the mist surrounding her. Or did she shimmer in a steaming heat that I could not share, that dampened her forehead and glistened across her upper lip?

"Rescue." I repeated the word.

"From the darkness, the secrecy, the stealth—the getting away with murder." Something in her voice, that trace of private amusement which hinted at an intent to startle, even shock her listener, reminded me of the tone Kingston sometimes adopted. She stepped close to me and with her fingertips touched the blanket I had pulled around my shoulders. "So cold," she murmured. I caught a scent of wet grass and sweat.

"What do you mean," I began, "getting away with murder?"

"Well, you could, someone like you. More easily than most. Call it surgery. The knife slips and—oops—it's done."

A spasm ran across my shoulders and down to my clenched right hand, as if I could feel the knife of which she spoke slipping and sought to stop it.

"It was not so easy to behead Holofernes," she said. "The blade was dull, and the act took all my strength."

So Veronique was Judith this morning. Kingston had mentioned to me her preoccupation with the characters of women noted historically for murdering men.

"What do you really know about murder?" I asked her. "Has it been done here, at the asylum?"

"Has it been done?" she said with a light laugh. "Why not ask me, will it be done?"

"And what would you answer?"

"You decide, you decide…" She was sauntering away, her voice growing fainter and more distant, until she disappeared. I continued to stand where I was, for how long, I don't know.

Then there came a space in my mind, like a page left empty in the middle of a closely written journal. Time passed, but I was absent. And then I lay in my bed, in a cotton nightshirt on a white sheet that still smelled of starch and fresh ironing. Running a hand over the stubble on my cheeks, I reckoned I had lain ill and unshaven for at least three days, but not uncared for. I became aware of Gaston, shuffling in and out of the bedroom, pushing a mop, bringing in a covered tray, carrying off the slop jar.

I heard a woman humming "Somebody's Darling," sweet and clear. I turned my head to see who was in the room. A tall glass pitcher, filled with water, blocked my line of vision, which was already blurred with fever and too much sleep. Then, through the water I saw her, saw Effie, tie up a bundle of laundry and take it away. The humming must have been in my imagination.

My head ached. I pressed the pillow against my ears and heard a woman weeping.

Lucinda, weeping night after night. I was home on leave that summer, after more than three years of following the army with my black bag and my amputation kit. For more than three years I had listened to the chant of pain, while transporting wounded men in a springless wagon to a surgery tent or a makeshift hospital that stank like a charnel house. And there I heard sounds only echoed in hell. But it was Lucinda's weeping I had found unbearable.

Father seemed oblivious to her suffering, and Mother chose to misinterpret it as heightened sensitivity to the wartime tragedies of others. But I heard Lucinda crying when I passed her door. Through the wall, when I lay in bed, I heard the sounds of her sobbing and retching. Night after night I heard her, until I was as fevered and exhausted as she. By day she brushed away my concern, admitted nothing to me, kept her distance as she never had when we were growing up, before the War. Then, on the last night of my furlough she came to my room.

The flame of my bedside candle wavered when she opened the door, the wax guttering and spilling. In her pale blue dressing gown, she crossed to where I lay. Kneeling at my bedside, pressing her forehead against the mattress, twisting the sheet in her hands, Lucinda wept inconsolably.

I reached out to her and stroked her tangled hair. "Tell me the man's name," I said wearily, resigned to doing a brother's duty. "Father and I will guarantee you a decent proposal."

"I can't, I can't." She choked on the words, wept them into the bed sheet.

"You must tell me his name and put an end to this before you put an end to yourself."

"I can't."

"Please, Lucinda."

"*He* can't."

"Is he dead?" I asked, assuming her seducer had been a soldier. "Was he killed?"

She lifted her face from the mattress. "He won't marry me, he can't. He's married already."

I sat up, swinging my legs over the edge of the bed. "Then I'll call him out." How ridiculous, as if at that moment I would stride off barefoot and duel in my nightshirt.

But my sister, kneeling before me, took the offer seriously. "No!" she cried, clinging to my knees.

"He must pay for what he's done to you."

"No! More likely you would pay, Robert. You're no sharpshooter."

"I'm your brother, Lucinda. I would die to defend you." Dying for politics was another matter to me, but I meant what I said to her. "Tell me his name."

"I can never tell you. I can never tell anyone." Then I understood that with her secrecy she was not only shielding me from a duel I might well lose, but shielding the man she had loved, still loved, from exposure.

For a time she rested her head in my lap, her sobbing rocking us both before it eased. At last, her fitful, rapid breathing became steady and slow. I wondered if she might be drifting into sleep, when suddenly she raised her tear-stained face. I shall never forget her expression, never forget the terrible and desperate conviction in that face.

"Robert," she whispered, "make it as if it never happened. You must know how."

For a moment I couldn't take in her words, her meaning.

"Make it as if it never happened," she said again.

"Do you know what you're asking me to do?"

Her wet lashes glittered in the candlelight as she stared back at me. "I know. There are women who do such things, but I'm afraid of them. I'm not afraid of you."

"I took a vow to save life, not destroy it."

"You're willing to kill this man. Why not rid me of what this man has done to me?"

"Lucinda." I said her name to remind myself this was my sister I looked upon. Though in that moment, I thought her changed past all resemblance to the little girl I had loved. "Lucinda."

"*Make me as I was before I met him.*"

"You will *never* be as you were before."

"But only you and I will know. I beg you, Robert. On my knees, I beg you."

And the weeping began again.

Perhaps I was seduced by her need of me, by the power I held, the knowledge. But for what I did and for what I did not do, I alone am responsible.

# Chapter 10

When the fever abated, I returned to my duties, with a vaguely disquieting feeling that I should have a word with Kingston about something, something that had happened just as I became ill. Days later at supper, my memory was awakened by Kingston's recounting of an incident that had occurred that morning. Veronique Beaulieu had stolen a silver platter from the butler's pantry and danced through the wards with it, demanding someone bring her John the Baptist's head.

"Virtuous young man that you are, Robert, be wary she doesn't cast you as the Baptist," said Kingston, smiling as if the idea amused him and refilling his wine goblet.

"Or Holofernes." Veronique's words came back to me. "Every morning is a rescue from the night before, she said. I remember now."

"What on earth are you talking about?"

"I saw her at daybreak, the day I fell ill. I was walking the grounds, unable to sleep, and she was there, in only her shift."

"Are you sure?" Kingston asked.

"Yes, sir. The fog was heavy, but she came close and spoke to me as if she believed herself Judith from the Bible story. I would have told you sooner, but—"

"Yes, I understand."

"Her appearance surprised me. I thought the patients were locked in their rooms at night."

"Those are my orders."

"And I saw someone else, perhaps two people. Someone was coming in or going out at the gate, I couldn't be certain in the fog and with a fever coming on. But I recall one of the figures in a dark skirt, running into the grove. I guessed she was an attendant or servant girl."

"And the other?" Kingston asked.

"Bigger, taller, if there was another. Perhaps I saw a shadow."

"Perhaps what you saw was a figment of your imagination."

"I spoke with Veronique Beaulieu. I'm sure of that. You can ask her yourself."

"Ha! I'd sooner accept your fevered account of things."

"My concern in telling you, sir, is for Miss Beaulieu and other patients like her, who might be distracted, wandering alone, and fall into the river. We know such things are possible."

"Will you never forget Rachel Poncet?" Kingston tossed his napkin beside his plate. "Rest assured, I will investigate the matter. And report to me at once if you notice any more odd happenings on your sleepless nights."

Later, walking toward my cottage, I glanced over my shoulder, noting that the sun still lingered behind the big house, at least half an hour away from setting. Perhaps this was the summer solstice. One long, hot day was much like another. Still, the evening air had at last begun to soften, and I felt in no hurry to leave it for the confines of my room. Circling back, I found Gaston locking up the outbuildings and asked him to show me the way to the graveyard. Kingston had not expected me to answer his question, but no, I could not forget Rachel Poncet. She had been buried quickly and quietly the day after my arrival, but I had yet to see her resting place.

Gaston led the way, shuffling barefoot over rocky earth, his feet tough as any shoe leather. He hardly looked around him, could hardly focus on anything a yard beyond his nose, but he knew where we were going. And he talked all the way there, his words occasionally whistling in the spaces between his teeth. "When I's young, Magdalena Plantation was the whole world," he said. "Cotton, sugar cane, corn and alfalfa far as sharp eyes could see. All divvied up now."

Gaston told me Kingston had bought back some of the land sold off by Cordelay during the war, then leased it to tenant farmers and sharecroppers. Seeing a few shanties ranged along the edge of a cornfield, I asked if they were the old quarters. "No, sir. They built since the War. Quarters be all burnt down now or tore up for lumber."

The graveyard lay far outside the walled grounds, on a rise shaded by elm and oak and bordered by pastureland, in a direction I had not yet explored. A low iron fence enclosed a few weathered wooden crosses and numerous moldering headstones of long-dead Cordelays. The stones recounted a family history of elegant names, the dates of births and deaths, the quality of relationships: "Beloved husband, cherished wife, devoted mother, precious daughter, and treasured son." The crosses were inscribed only with first names: "Marie-Claire, Charlotte, Julia, Elizabeth, Lillian, Suzanna."

"They was patients," Gaston said.

"I don't see Rachel Poncet's name. Or Hannah's."

"Oh, they be over here, sir." Gaston led me around the small fenced cemetery, past a curtain of grapevine, into a shaded clearing. There, as my eyes adjusted to the dimness, I made out perhaps another dozen whitewashed crosses with black lettered names, Rachel's and Hannah's among them.

"So many dead," I murmured.

"You seen enough, Dr. Mallory, sir?"

"Yes. Thank you, Gaston."

The summer wore on. The garden flowers dropped their last petals and ceased to bloom, exhausted by the heat. The patients, exhausted too, were given more to spells of languor than fits of hysteria. August was quiet. I regained my strength and was well enough to work steadily, though it worried me how little relief the quinine gave me.

In the hot weather the treatment of skin rashes, insect bites, and digestive disorders occupied much of my time at the asylum. Although I often lacked the means to cure complaints, I was persistent in finding ways to ease my patients' physical discomforts. Charmaine, the clever maid whose cosmetic skills could transform disheveled madwomen into belles, was flattered enough by my seeking her advice to show me her trove of preparations for the care of the skin: sweet-scented talcs and salves, essence of witch hazel, lavender oil, eau de cologne, rosewater and glycerin soaps. These items, she warned me, were not generally available to the patients. Dr. Kingston imported them for the special ladies who attended the soirees. But Charmaine kindly turned a blind eye and allowed me to pilfer a few supplies and relieve a few cases of prickly heat.

Adamant about the dangers of night air, Matron refused to allow patients' windows open during the summer nights, a rule disregarded by the sweltering staff, resulting in a bane of mosquito bites. I could not accept that the previous owners of the estate had suffered so in their grand house. Questioning old Mrs. Cordelay on the subject, I learned there had once been netting around all the beds—of course, she meant all those in which Cordelays had slept. I enlisted the help of several attendants to search the attic and storerooms, and we discovered enough netting to cover at least the bedroom windows. The house now held too many beds and cots for each to receive an individual gauze curtain. Dr. Kingston and Lila Fentroy, themselves, never complained of mosquitoes disturbing their sleep, so I assumed their chambers were already equipped with netting.

More problematic than skin irritations were the patients' recurring digestive disorders. During the war, such maladies among the soldiers had been more common than battle wounds. Here a general lethargy, lack of exercise, and use of opiates led to constipation. Spasmodic fits, erratic eating habits, and, I suspected, occasional ingestion of spoiled foods led to the other extremes, vomiting and diarrhea. I made the commonsense recommendations to Matron, hoping she would relay them to staff and cooks: be sparing in the use of laudanum, allow the patients to walk about, reduce the amount of lard used in cooking and, whenever possible, provide fresh greens and cracked corn or wheat. Still, despite my preventive efforts, I spent much of the summer dispensing castor oil and prescribing cathartics. But apparently, when some asylum workers went to Lorraine, they spoke well enough of my treatments that Velmina, the *traiteuse*, invited my assistance in curing village children of dysentery and worms.

One mid-morning in September, I descended the stairs after finishing my rounds of the wards, contemplating a walk to town to see my young patients, when I was struck by the activity in the front hall. Whimpering patients restrained by attendants were not out of the ordinary, except that today they were gathered in greater number than usual, and the source of their collective distress appeared to be Dr. Kingston's imminent departure. He made frequent trips to Lorraine, but the preparations now underway indicated a longer journey. Gaston shambled by, muttering and laden with luggage. Matron, clutching a stack of files and a pencil, followed Kingston about, jotting down orders he directed her way, when he was not otherwise occupied soothing distraught inmates with his beneficent smile or adjusting his cravat in the pier glass mirror.

He had had ample opportunity to tell me he was going away, where, why, and for how long. But as was his custom, Kingston chose not to explain himself to me. He rarely discussed with me or described to me his diagnoses and treatments, dismissing my questions and concerns with cursory replies. After my one brief tour of the third-floor treatment rooms, that I was discouraged—forbidden—to return to them was implicit in Kingston's frequent reminders that the mental disorders were his province, the physical were mine.

Not until he drove away did I learn from Lila Fentroy that our employer was off on a patient-collecting jaunt. More fees to support his way of life, I surmised.

I stood on the veranda and watched him go, feeling the subtle softening of an early autumn breeze on my face. Kingston's carriage was drawn by a pair of sleek bay geldings, perfectly matched in size and conformation. It was still uncommon to see such fine animals. So many of the best horses as well as the best men had fallen during the war and were yet to be replaced.

With our employer gone, Matron quickly took up the reins of command at the asylum with an assurance only rivaled by Kingston's liveried coachman. For the next week, she worked the staff harder than usual, supervising a thorough fall house cleaning—scrubbing floors, polishing fixtures, whitewashing walls, beating carpets. I hoped her new exertions gave the patients some respite from her customary vigorous efforts to drive out their demons. Fortunately, I remained beneath her notice and was able to go about my business.

# Chapter 11

Late one afternoon, when I could only assume Matron was unavailable, Oralia called me away from the wards with the news that a stranger had arrived at the asylum, demanding to speak with Dr. Kingston. She had shown him to Kingston's office, and there I met with him, a man so like myself that any other onlooker might take him for my younger brother. He was nearly as tall as I, quite as lean and long-faced, with dark brown hair and gray eyes.

As I entered the office, he strode forward, offering me not his hand but some sort of documents. In a voice determined, if a trifle strained, he announced: "I have come for my mother."

He thrust the papers toward me, shaking them until I took them from him. Perusing the first page, I found it was an authorization, drawn up by a firm of Richmond lawyers, giving the young man guardianship of his mother. I was more relieved than surprised to recognize two names on the page: the mother referred to was Cynthia Ann Glover, and Arthur Hugo Glover was her son. Mrs. Glover had told me more than once that I resembled her son. Looking again at the young man assured me the similarity was more than his mother's wishful thinking.

He stood rigid, fists clenched at his sides. His jaw was set hard, and his nostrils flared with the impatience of his breath. I must have looked much the same when confronting Kingston on some point of disagreement.

"Dr. Kingston is away, sir," I said, hastening to assure Arthur Glover that I was not my employer. "I'm Robert Mallory, the general practitioner. Perhaps I can help you."

"Release my mother," he replied, pointing to the papers I held.

Having received no instructions from Kingston on matters such as this, I was uncertain of what to do. Matron might be able to advise me, but in all my months at the asylum, I had never seen her question or override any of Kingston's edicts. Carrying out his orders in his absence suited her, but this situation might require independent initiative, perhaps even running contrary to Kingston's usual policy. I thought of Gaston's comment on the departure of patients: "Myself, I never seen one of them leave here, 'cepting for the graveyard."

Asking Arthur Glover to be seated, I assumed Kingston's chair behind the desk and carefully read the documents. Many of the details listed therein were already familiar to me from my conversations with Mrs. Glover: her former place of residence in Richmond, names of various relatives, the date of her commitment to the Magdalene Ladies' Lunatic Asylum on the authority of her husband and of Dr. Douglas Christopher Kingston. An affidavit, signed by Kingston, described Mrs. Glover in vague terms as temperamental and a cause of unspecified "distress" to her husband. Another page recounted a court hearing in which young Arthur Glover challenged his father's control over the fate of Cynthia Ann Glover. Then I looked again at the first document I had seen, the one legally granting Arthur guardianship of his mother.

"It's all in order and official," the young man said.

"I'm sure it is, Mr. Glover, but I must also consult Dr. Kingston's records. Each case is unique, and I would not want to overlook any important details that might bear on your decision to remove your mother from the asylum." I rambled, stalling for time as I pretended to know my way around Kingston's filing cabinets. "After all, though this document may allow you to take custody of your mother, it does not require that you do so. We should consider Dr. Kingston's latest notes on her condition." Several drawers were locked, but I found one accessible, before Arthur Glover became too restive.

"Ah, here we are," I murmured, thumbing rapidly through pages of descriptions of various patients, not recognizing any of the names and still finding no reference to Mrs. Glover.

Arthur reminded me that his carriage was waiting and that he would be obliged if I would send for his mother before dark.

I could let her go, I thought, simply let her go. But what if she *were* mad in a way I had not seen or could not understand? What if Kingston's records held some incontrovertible evidence of mad acts of which her young son—and I—knew nothing?

Continuing to search another drawer for some record pertaining to Mrs. Glover, I asked her son, "Do you know why your mother was sent here? Do you know in what way she distressed your father?" By my tone, I attempted to imply I knew the answer already and was merely testing his knowledge. Apparently, my dissembling tone failed me.

"Yes, sir, I know quite well," he replied. "Though I doubt you'll find the reason in that drawer. I was twelve years old when my beloved mother was torn from the bosom of her family and locked up here. I wasn't supposed to know why, but I knew, all the same. My mother distressed my father when she objected to his manners."

I shut the cabinet drawer and looked at the young man, who stood now gripping the back of the chair he had vacated. "Mother objected, in particular," he continued, "to Father's manner of keeping a mistress under the same roof as he kept his family. Oh, he brought her in with the pretense that she would be governess to my little sisters. But I knew what she was from the beginning, and what she was after."

"You were a boy of twelve."

"And she was a woman of no character. And still is. My father continues to live with her in a state of debauchery. Upon her he has squandered most of my sisters' dowries and my inheritance. The only money that woman allows him to spend on something other than her pleasures is the sum he sends here to Dr. Kingston."

"Then how do you live?" I asked. "How do you expect to support your mother?"

"I have apprenticed myself to the lawyers who advised me on how to free my mother."

"You are a devoted son, Mr. Glover, and I am in sympathy with your situation—" I began, but he cut me off.

"The only reason my mother is here, sir, and not in some graveyard, is that this other woman, for all she lacks of morals, sticks at the idea of murder."

Almost involuntarily I said, "Women have died in this asylum."

"But not my mother. I want to see her—now."

"And you will." I hoped my first impulse to simply let her go was also my best. Certainly it was my strongest.

Stepping out into the hall, I found an attendant, who fetched Oralia for me, and the arrangements were begun. Oralia already knew Arthur Glover was in the house, perhaps knew or guessed his business there. I hoped I could trust her to help me, without carrying the tale to Matron. I asked that Oralia gather and pack Mrs. Glover's personal possessions as quickly and quietly as possible, without drawing attention to herself or her task. My explanation to her was that I feared the departure of a patient might upset the other inmates. Oralia was to give the luggage to Arthur Glover, who was to wait on the drive in his carriage. I would bring his mother to him there and send them off, to make what they would of their reunion, beyond my sight and hearing.

From the front doorway, I watched the plan proceed. Arthur climbed into his closed carriage, and Oralia soon after handed in to him a tied cloth bundle and started back to the house. I came out on the veranda just as the girl mounted the steps and Lila Fentroy, rounding the corner of the house, stopped her.

"Oralia, what's that carriage doing here?" Matron demanded.

Oralia glanced at me before she answered. "Gentleman come to see a patient, ma'am."

"Well, I should hope he has not seen her. I must supervise all visitations. Dr. Kingston's orders. Is the person inside?" But without waiting for the girl's reply, Matron moved past her and in my direction. "You have not allowed a visit, have you, Dr. Mallory? You have no authority."

"The gentleman has not seen the patient," I said, and stepped aside, holding the door open and giving her wide berth as she advanced through the doorway. Then I hurried around the veranda to the side of the house, hoping to find Mrs. Glover sitting by the aviary.

Indeed, she was in her usual wicker chair, but not alone. Effie Rampling knelt beside her, holding in cupped hands a dead bird. Mrs. Glover opened a lace-edged handkerchief in the lap of her faded yellow silk gown, and Effie placed the dove there and wrapped it, as if in a little shroud.

"Mrs. Glover," I said softly, but with some urgency. "You must come with me now."

She looked up. "Oh, no, Dr. Mallory, not now. Effie and I must bury this poor witless bird. They do age and wither like the rest of us."

"You must come with me, ma'am. Please excuse us, Miss Rampling."

Effie rose and stepped aside, holding the dead bird to her breast.

"You will bury it in the garden, won't you, Effie?" said Mrs. Glover. "Of course you will. You wouldn't throw it in the river."

Taking a firm grip on Mrs. Glover's arm, I led her away, not daring to linger or explain myself to either of them. Perhaps my anxiety was unfounded, but I believed if Lila Fentroy knew I were releasing Mrs. Glover, she would more than object to my decision.

"Must we hurry so, Dr. Mallory?" Mrs. Glover asked with an unfamiliar catch in her voice. Always before, we had conversed while sitting or strolling slowly on the veranda, and until now I was unaware of Mrs. Glover's labored gait. She winced with each hurried step, perhaps suffering with arthritis, though she had never complained to me. "Pardon me, ma'am, and I'll help you," I said. She gave a little gasp as I swept her up in my arms, carrying her the last length of the porch and down the steps. Perhaps she was heavier than Mrs. Poncet had been, but easier to manage somehow, with her arms firmly around my neck.

I set her down beside the carriage and opened its door. Mother and son stared at one another—she at a boy grown to manhood, he at a woman grown old. Mrs. Glover began to tremble, and supporting her, I urged her to enter the carriage. Arthur was speaking, reassuring her that he had come to take her away, to take care of her forever. And then she was beside her son, laughing and sobbing. I started to shut the door, but she leaned out and kissed my cheek before I waved her away. Far down the drive, Gaston opened the gates, and soon Mrs. Glover and her son were gone.

The light was failing. I turned back to the house and started up the broad steps, not seeing Effie right away, standing as she was in the shadow of a column. Coming toward her, I saw she still held the bird wrapped in the handkerchief. "I'm sorry," I said, imagining how she would have liked to tell her friend a proper good-bye. Then I caught myself. Effie would have told Mrs. Glover nothing, but perhaps they might have embraced.

"Her son came for her to take her home," I said.

Effie nodded and walked past me, toward the garden, I supposed.

Then the thought struck me that Mrs. Glover had given up one of her prized lace handkerchiefs to be buried with that dove—given it up at a time when she believed her nice things would not be replaced.

At the front doorway I saw Matron in her starched cap, staring at me. I thought she would whip her words at me in the same way she reprimanded patients and attendants. But she didn't. Instead, she whispered, "Come with me," in a voice so dry and hard that the words nearly choked her. I followed her into the house, down the hallway, and to Kingston's office, where she shut us in.

She paced the room, her strong, big veined hands oddly fluttering in gestures of dismay, unaccompanied by words. Mrs. Glover had maintained more reserve at sight of her son than did Matron, surveying the scattered files and papers on Kingston's desk. Breathing heavily, shaking, muttering, she sank into Kingston's chair. "What have you done?" she cried. "Let that woman go? How could you? Dr. Kingston trusted me—me—and now you come in here and ruin things."

So amazed was I by her sudden show of vulnerability, that I found myself offering her a snifter of Kingston's bourbon and running through a string of comforting phrases. I was my mother's son after all, even with such a woman as Lila Fentroy. "I take full responsibility," I said. "I'll explain it all to Dr. Kingston on his return. You won't be in any trouble, Matron. I read Mr. Glover's documents and I made the decision. Kingston might very well have done the same. Please, calm yourself."

She wetted her words with a swallow of bourbon. "No one leaves here without Dr. Kingston's permission. *No one.*"

"Is anyone ever granted permission?" I asked.

Matron declined to answer, but began to tidy the files through which I had rummaged. The activity seemed to restore her composure. "We'll say no more about this, you and I. And you will take responsibility, Dr. Mallory."

Stacking Arthur Glover's legal papers and placing them on one corner of the desk, I commented on the disorderliness of the filing system, which had surprised me given how particular Kingston was about most things. I had noticed the names on several files referred to women no longer in residence at the asylum. And several patients had numerous files devoted to them.

"It's not your place to question Dr. Kingston's methods," Matron reminded me. "Our obedience is essential to the Doctor's work."

But why was it essential? Should not every man of science be questioned by every other, and be held accountable for his diagnoses and prescriptions?

Later that night I returned to the big house and, not surprisingly, found all the lower floor doors and windows securely locked. I remedied that situation the next evening, after finishing my rounds, by slipping into Kingston's office while Matron was still upstairs and jamming one window latch with a piece of folded blotting paper. My plan was to take advantage of Kingston's absence to acquaint myself as far as possible with the patients' files. I told myself that it was not unreasonable for me, as his medical colleague, to read the case histories of the women both he and I treated. But, though he had not locked away all of the files, I knew he would not have invited my curiosity. And, though I was driven in part by the desire to better understand the patients, I was also increasingly suspicious of my employer's methods.

Well past midnight I climbed through the window into Kingston's office, bringing with me my sickbed journal, a stub of pencil, and a lantern, which I lit after drawing the curtains. Then I set to work reading the files and making notes in my journal of patients' names, origins, dates of admission, and types of symptoms. The locked file drawers I did not pry into, but assumed they must contain information regarding fees and payments, since there was no mention of money in the files I read.

I thought some patients might be known to me by names other than those I found in the files; there were so many unfamiliar names here as well as mentions of patients from states far away, even some from foreign countries. A few old files contained first names I recalled from the grave markers, but some of those were common names appearing on more than one document and paired with more than one surname. Perhaps in my haste to review the files, make my notes, and be gone, I found it difficult to make sense of the papers before me. But the impression I had received when searching for Mrs. Glover's file occurred to me again: for one so precise and certain of his opinions, Dr. Kingston kept a random mess of documents.

Or perhaps the randomness was in my search for—what? Evidence of an error in judgment, a precipitous decision, or a momentary lapse of ethics? If I discovered some such thing, what would I do with the knowledge? Who was I to cast the first stone? And yet, someone must protect those who could not speak for themselves.

In one thick file, tucked between a lengthy series of entries regarding a woman of whom I had never heard and a few cursory notes about Miss Beaulieu, I chanced on a description of Rachel Poncet. She was committed in 1867 by her husband. Kingston listed her symptoms upon admission as auditory hallucinations, melancholia and a pernicious indulgence in self-abuse. More recently dated notations indicated she had begun to suffer from hysteria and had threatened to harm herself. At that point the file abruptly left off.

Continuing to shuffle through more papers, I chanced on a narrow file devoted to Euphemia Louise Charlevoix Rampling—Effie. Mention was made of her family members, and in my journal I jotted down their names and the brief description of Woodbine, her father's plantation near Lake Pontchartrain, and the location of her married sister's home in the Garden District. Kingston had written little regarding Effie's condition, but he had underlined the words "silent" and "obedient." Silent for what reason? Obedient to whom?

The floorboards above the office creaked under a heavy footfall. Quickly, I returned a stack of files to its drawer, blew out my lantern, and left the room as I had entered it by the window. I had no wish to explain myself to Lila Fentroy if she were on the prowl, or to one of her minions who might report my presence to her.

# Chapter 12

A week later at midday, Kingston returned in high spirits, bringing with him three new patients. One was a young, vacant-eyed wraith with a shorn head, one was a middle-aged woman, snarling and spitting, struggling against the bonds of the quilted straight-waist coat that secured her arms around her torso, and one was a seemingly well-mannered lady, her only obvious peculiarity an incessant murmuring. "Lord, I am not worthy that Thou should come under my roof," she chanted. "Speak but the word and my soul will be healed. Lord, I am not worthy... Speak but the word... Lord, I am not... Speak but the word."

After attendants led the new patients away to the wards, Kingston commented to me that the chanting woman, Adele Meredith, suffered from religious monomania. "Her husband, a distinguished professor living in New Orleans, assures me she is quite fanatical. Indeed, she goes so far as to refuse her marital duty and has been quite a trial to Professor Meredith."

"It must be worth a great deal to him to be rid of her," I said, watching for any flicker of conscience on Kingston's face.

He smiled, unperturbed. "I think we'll have old Hardy up to supper tonight," he said and retired to his office.

Unlike Matron, who followed closely on his heels, I did not hurry after Kingston to volunteer an account of what had transpired in his absence. Soon enough I was summoned.

My employer sat in his high-backed, red leather chair behind his broad mahogany desk, Matron standing at his right. A week earlier, when she had revealed to me her anxiety over Mrs. Glover's release and I had promised her she would not share the blame for it, I'd wondered briefly if afterward Matron and I might be on better terms. Her cold demeanor now assured me we were not.

"I understand that you took it upon yourself to release Miss Cynthia Ann into the custody of Arthur Glover." Kingston's voice was smooth, gently inquisitive.

"Yes, sir."

"You thought her well enough to travel?"

"She seemed so to me."

"Well, whatever she seemed, I suppose her son will take the consequences."

"Her son had the legal right to ask for her release. And I think she is well, physically and mentally."

"Oh, do you, Robert?"

I carefully worded my next remark. "Perhaps, sir, Mrs. Glover has been restored to health by your treatment and her rest here. Is that not the purpose of Magdalene Asylum, to heal diseased minds?"

Kingston took a chestful of air and expelled the words. "I never pronounced her cured."

"Doesn't anyone get better here?" I asked. "When the women are committed, must it be for a lifetime?"

Kingston didn't answer me directly, but first nodded to Lila Fentroy and dismissed her with a courteous "Thank you, Matron."

When he and I were alone, Kingston said, "My boy, your experience as a surgeon leads you to this simple view of success or failure—the patient survives the knife and lives, or he worsens and dies. The mind is more complex than the body. The body is the slave of the mind."

"But is there no cure for any of these women? Must they live for years in a kind of purgatory?"

"You consider their lives wasted because they no longer fulfill their roles as wife, mother, sister, daughter. Do they seem so useless to you, their existence so pointless? What would you have me do, Robert? Shoot them? Put them out of their misery?"

"I would have you treat them, sir, and cure them when you can and let them go."

"I do treat them. And I give them sanctuary."

"At a price."

"We live in the world, my boy."

Then he turned his attention to the new patients, giving me instructions to examine them and complete written reports on their physical conditions.

"Of course, the patients' mental conditions you will leave to me," Kingston added, a needless reminder.

I left his office for the consulting room, where I learned a little more about the devout Adele Meredith. She was well nourished and in fair health, but complained of severe headaches, recurring nightmares of damnation, and a painfully held conviction that her husband was a libertine. This information I gleaned from her in bits and pieces between refrains of "Lord, I am not worthy that Thou should come under my roof... Lord, I am not."

The other new patients were a mother and daughter. The middle-aged Hattie Judice, now exhausted from thrashing in the confines of her restraining jacket and firmly held by a pair of strong attendants, barely tolerated my examination of her. I found no obvious signs of disease, but attributed her rapid heartbeat and high color to the fierceness of her anger.

According to Matron, the woman was an East Texas lumber mill heiress, widowed and remarried. The frail seventeen-year-old Jane was Mrs. Judice's daughter by her first husband. The new husband had committed the pair of them, one for her violent outbursts, the other for her lethargy and refusal to eat. But I suspected Mr. Judice had found these two troubled women disposable in a transfer of property. Rid of bride and step-daughter, he had kept the lumber mill. And now my employer would share in the profits.

Later in the afternoon, when I delivered my reports on the new patients to Kingston, he assured me that Mrs. Judice's rages were a genuine danger to her community and necessitated her confinement. She had beaten servants and once struck a shopgirl. "Her first husband fell down the staircase to his death," said Kingston, "an event that may not have been accidental. The daughter came here because she will not leave her mother."

I asked if the girl had been recently ill, her hair cut off in a fever treatment.

"Oh, no. She did that herself," said Kingston, "on the day we came to collect her. But Matron took the scissors from her before any real harm was done."

Regarding Adele Meredith, Kingston remarked, "Her ceaseless chanting, however irritating to us, protects her from thinking evil thoughts. We must tolerate the chanting, Robert, for if the wicked thoughts are allowed to form in her mind, they may become wicked deeds."

That evening we were four for supper: Kingston, Hardy, myself, and, for the first time since my employment at the asylum, Matron, in a stiff, dark green taffeta gown cut to allow a glimpse, however undesired, of pallid bosom. During the soup course, Kingston gave a brisk account of his travels, commenting on the still oppressive presence of Federal troops in New Orleans, the difficulty of finding comfortable lodgings and decent food. Hardy muttered a few reminiscences of his own visits to the Crescent City before the war, and Matron, acting the lady, took the attitude that she had no idea what he was talking about.

After Gaston served the main course, a lull fell on the conversation. Hardy gulped wine to wash down heaping forkfuls of pastry crust and succulent fowl. Kingston and Lila Fentroy ate with more decorum, but evident relish. I took a few bites, then ventured a comment to Kingston, hoping the presence of the others might mitigate his reply.

"With Mrs. Glover gone, sir, do you think another patient might be persuaded to take an interest in the doves? Perhaps Miss Effie? She and Mrs. Glover seemed to have had a close understanding, a sympathy for one another."

"Oh, I hardly think so, Robert." Here Kingston winked in Hardy's direction. "The girl has so little appetite."

"Sir?" I said.

Then Kingston fixed me with his narrowed eyes and spoke in a voice laced with amusement. "Well, now. Just what do you think you've been eating tonight, my boy? *Chicken pie?*"

Involuntarily, I dropped my fork onto my china dinner plate. He laughed at me. Hardy joined him. Matron almost smiled. But when Kingston's laughter died away, he said in a tone devoid of mirth, "Without my permission, no one leaves Magdalene Asylum. Do you understand that, Robert?"

"Yes, sir." I also understood that I had been punished and everyone else at the table was party to my punishment. A pity Mrs. Glover had not kept a cage of rats.

Soon after, I excused myself from the dining room and took a turn on the veranda, drinking in the humid night air. Lamps, shining from a few windows, lit sections of the planking, but the aviary was in shadow. How quiet it was, not a coo, not a rustle of wings. Nothing. My eyes grew accustomed to the darkness, to the pale illumination of a half moon, and I saw the cage door standing open, a few remaining feathers scattered on the aviary floor.

I wondered if the scene would trouble Effie. Should I explain to her that I had nothing to do with the killing of Mrs. Glover's pet doves? Or that I had everything to do with it, and ask her to forgive me?

After that night I rarely took a meal at the big house, but asked Gaston to bring me something on a tray. My appetite was often poor, weakened by frequent bouts of malarial fever. And I was often troubled with a ringing in my ears, sometimes dull and clangorous as church bells rung in panic, without a pattern, sometimes sharp and piercing as calculated gunfire. Although I had increased my dosage of quinine several times, the medicine's effectiveness seemed to have inexplicably diminished.

Kingston outwardly accepted the polite excuse my ill health gave me for refusing to dine with him. But I think he understood that I was registering my disapproval of his behavior, and I was sure he did not miss my company.

I contemplated ways to protest the attitudes both Kingston and Hardy espoused and the treatments Kingston practiced on that houseful of unfortunate women. I had witnessed in wartime how men would convince themselves that their enemies were different from themselves, hardly the same species, in order to sustain their hatred, their fighting edge, although their enemies bled and died the same as they and their compatriots. Kingston and Hardy asserted much the same belief, holding forth that woman's natural inferiority to man justified his subjugation of her. It was a familiar stance struck throughout human history by masters toward slaves. But who really profited by such a scheme? If we cannot recognize humanity in others, can we ever find it in ourselves?

At times I thought of giving up my position at Magdalene Asylum, of going away, perhaps going West. I had accomplished little toward relieving the suffering of the patients and nothing toward ameliorating their treatment by Matron or their neglect by my employer. I began to pack and, in my mind, played out a scene in which I took leave of Kingston. But while folding one particular shirt, planning to tuck it in my satchel, my fingers stopped over the stitches that closed a rent in the shirt front. And I returned the shirt to the drawer.

As long as Kingston allowed me to stay, as long as Effie Rampling remained at the asylum, I could not go. Had I fallen in love with her? I wasn't sure. But I knew that taking her away with me, even supposing she would go, either openly or surreptitiously, would be in conflict with my solemn oath. I stayed on because I could not leave her. Kingston's will prevailed. No one left the asylum without his permission.

# Chapter 13

Winter came, and with it days of leaden clouds, drizzling rain, and bone-chilling dampness. No wonder the patients were melancholy. And after nights of blackness, split and gashed by lightning, and of bone-rattling thunder, no wonder some patients flew into fits of hysteria.

Only Effie Rampling was always calm. Whenever there was a clear day, or even a few dry hours, I would see her about her work, building a fire under the cauldron, stirring the washing with a long-handled wooden paddle, hanging the clothes on the line. Was it serenity she had found and possessed, I wondered, or had some terrible loss of feeling given her the illusion of peace? I only knew that she was kind.

One day she saw me shivering and led me to warm myself at her laundry fire. I knew the chill running through me was prelude to another bout of fever and only quinine would circumvent it, but the fire brought temporary feeling to my numb hands. Effie held out her own hands to the blaze, turning her wrists first palms down, then palms up; I could see her fingertips were wrinkled by hours spent in water. That momentary closeness I felt to her, our standing side by side before the fire, was only slightly marred when I noticed Kingston at an upper window of the house staring down at us.

Mrs. Glover was not the last patient to sing Effie's praises. Others began to speak to me of her gentleness and consideration. In a lucid moment, Hattie Judice revealed her gratitude that Effie was able to coax her daughter, Jane, to eat again. Lady Ryder believed Effie could make headaches and bad dreams disappear simply by stroking the sufferer's forehead.

Not for the first time, I overheard an elderly patient pouring forth her grief to Effie. "I was the mother of five sons—five—all killed in the war. I was cursed to outlive my children. Five sons dead. My husband sent me here, and he was right to do it. My husband couldn't look at me anymore without weeping, nor I at him." But Effie looked at her, dried her tears, listened to her with an attentiveness that perhaps the old woman had never before known.

Of course, there were patients for whom kindness had little meaning. Their tormented minds rendered them incapable of appreciating Effie's counterpoint to Matron's brusque treatment. And there were those Effie herself avoided, notably the women who attended Kingston's evening parties, which he held more frequently during the winter months.

One night sometime around the New Year, I sat in the rocking chair on my front porch, a woolen lap robe over my knees and a hot whiskey punch in my hands. Gaston had brought me the refreshment, and I had accepted it with thanks, never intending to drink it down but enjoying the warmth of it through my fingers wrapped around the cup. Comfortable from my vantage point, I listened and watched as another of Kingston's soirees played itself out in the front parlor of the big house.

Someone pounded a dance tune on the piano. I could not guess if it was a waltz or a jig, so erratic was the beat. Feminine silhouettes in bell-shaped gowns spun across the drawn curtains. I pictured the women behind the windows, their faces flushed and glistening from their exertions, drinking, feasting, dancing, swirling around Dr. Kingston, like the Bacchae encircling their god.

Months ago I had thought it odd that Kingston could be so exact in his pronouncements and so disorganized in his record keeping. But I had learned that contradiction was a way of life at Magdalene Asylum, not only among the inmates. Sometimes I would hear Kingston dismiss one patient's behavior as simple stupidity or irrational madness. At other times he ascribed to another patient's quite similar bizarre acts and ramblings the most calculated of motives. So, what was lunacy in one was scheming intelligence in another. Kingston appeared quite comfortable having things both ways, having things his way.

Once, after telling me I was showing the strain of being too long confined among madwomen, Kingston suggested I go to town. There was a small establishment there, he explained, that catered to exhausted men. "You might meet an old friend, Robert. Most of the women in the place are former camp followers. Go and enjoy yourself." This bit of advice he offered me not ten minutes after holding forth in censorious tones about the loose behavior of several patients, including Veronique Beaulieu.

Echoing Dr. Hardy's opinion that some female patients invented symptoms to provoke examinations, Kingston contended the women were desperate for a man's touch. "And then, of course, they misinterpret clinical procedures and manipulations. Their aberrant sexual desires, which often brought them here in the first place, must be controlled, even, on occasion, punished. As you must appreciate by now, Matron is invaluable in dealing with the difficult cases."

Yes, I had noted her enthusiasm for driving out other women's demons, had in fact the previous day seen Matron slap Veronique. And after Matron's palm had struck and passed Veronique's cheek, she swung it back, striking the other side of the face with her knuckles. "That was for talking filthy," Matron said in justification of her act. Indeed, Miss Beaulieu had earned a reputation for being foul-mouthed, for telling tales that excited and agitated other patients, a pastime she had indulged more and more in recent months. "Too much idleness," Matron explained. "She refuses to do her needlework."

It occurred to me that what was punished in the women of the asylum, might be rewarded in another sort of house, at least monetarily. And from what little I had overheard of Veronique's tales, she could have been the Scheherazade of a bordello.

Sitting on my porch that sharp midwinter night, I listened to the banging piano and shrieks of laughter that rang out from the big house across the lawn. And I contemplated how the same man who dispensed laudanum and preached pacification allowed selected patients to work themselves into a frenzy.

For those not selected to attend the soirées, I offered an alternative pastime, reading aloud to patients who gathered in the sewing room. In fact, since shortly after Mrs. Glover's departure, the patients had been divided into two camps, one attending Kingston's parties and one congregating for my readings. My group was the less prestigious, no doubt, but met more frequently since participants needed little preparation and no one was asked to look well in a ball gown.

Choosing from Kingston's library a novel suitable for my audience required some care. My employer's collection of French novels and their translations tended toward the sensational. Reading some of them aloud would have embarrassed me, if not my listeners. I had to rule out *Jane Eyre* for its description of a madwoman in a secret apartment was bound to prove upsetting. I settled on *David Copperfield*, its opening lines possessing, at least for me, a certain resonance: "Whether I shall turn out to be the hero of my own life, or whether that station will be held by anybody else, these pages must show."

For the most part, my listeners were a docile group. Even so, some patients occasionally reacted inappropriately, frustrated or angered by their own inability to understand the emotions of the characters, or baffled by a twist in the plot. I soothed and explained as best I could, though some patients simply had to be taken away by attendants.

For one patient, the character of Mr. Dick, the harmless lunatic, was a revelation; she had been brought up by her father to believe that only women were careless enough to lose their minds. Mrs. Cordelay demanded to know where all the characters had been and what they had been up to at the time of Lincoln's assassination. Another patient believed the story I read was my life—that I was reading aloud from my own journal—and nothing I could say would convince her otherwise.

Effie joined the reading circle, sitting very still, looking steadily at me, giving her unwavering attention to the story. When I would glance up from the pages, I would find the expressions of her face mirroring the sentiments of each scene and passage. Sometimes in my own mind I read only for her, and the story became a place where we could meet and exist together. Her silence did not contradict my personal fiction.

One night late in the winter the weather turned mild. During the war, in other parts of the country I had encountered false summer that follows the early chill of autumn, but in Louisiana false spring occurs as well, a sudden spate of balmy days, a respite from the cold rain of winter.

Restlessly, I walked the grounds, a headache and a dull ringing in my ears barring me from sleep. At first I trod the beaten earth of the drive, straight away from the big house and down toward the gate, arching back my neck, inhaling the clean scent of evergreen and the spice of old oak leaves, looking up to view the quarter moon and a bright design of stars. Then I turned from the open path into the shadows of the pecan grove, walking almost blindly, trusting in the wide corridors of grass between the carefully planted rows of tree trunks. I paced out the pattern of the orchard, back and forth among the rows, until reaching the end of the last row I faced the blackness of a thicket.

A breeze stirred the upper branches of sweet gum, sycamore, and live oak, but moved nothing where I stood. The rustling low to the ground in the fallen leaves I thought must be some nocturnal animal, opossum or raccoon, until I heard other sounds beyond the screen of shrubbery, rising above the thrumming in my head: the human sound of moaning, but not in pain, and the repeated sound of slapping of flesh against flesh, but not in anger.

I jerked back, striking my shoulder against the broad trunk of a pecan tree and my temple on a low branch. Within the thicket a dark form rose up and, dropping a white shirt over its head, defined itself as a man. Was he one of a pair of lovers who haunted the grounds, a pair I had once before glimpsed parting at the front gate? And the other, who must still lie on the ground, which servant girl or attendant was she? Should I discover her identity and report her to Kingston? Should I embarrass and humiliate her—and myself—and cause her to lose her employment? All for what? Kingston had demanded I tell him of anything I discovered on my sleepless nights. But if I returned to my cottage now, I would have discovered very little. I had seen a stranger on the grounds, and with that bit of information, Kingston might issue a general warning to the staff. Shouldn't that be sufficient to bring an end to someone's recklessness, or at the least prompt her to choose another trysting place, outside the asylum walls?

Thus, to Kingston I only mentioned seeing a stranger within the walls, but did not elaborate on my suspicion that he was with a woman. Kingston concluded that for himself and assured me he would enlist Matron's help to get to the heart of the matter. The prompt return of inclement weather no doubt put an end, if only temporarily, to the man's visits, and I thought little more about him.

I was occupied instead with the ailments and injuries of my patients. Closely confined in the wards and sewing room, the asylum inmates complained of head colds and chills and were prey to a variety of mishaps. Mrs. Judice's palm was punctured with a tapestry needle; her daughter Jane apparently took a fall and broke her wrist; another patient's cheek was scalded by spilling hot soup, so I was told. Lila Fentroy and her staff shed little light on how these accidents had occurred and offered little sympathy for the lives in their care.

Matron did take an interest, however, in Lady Phillida Ryder's case, as did Kingston and Hardy. For months I had tried to curtail Lady Phillida's dependency on laudanum, a futile endeavor perhaps, since I could not stand guard over her in the ward throughout each night. Then she confessed to me that she needed opiates not only to sleep, but to dull an aching in her breast. I thought at first she spoke metaphorically, as many patients did of their heartache. But then she admitted to me that although Matron had given her sufficient laudanum to forget her discomfort, she now found blood sometimes leaked from her right nipple. Upon examination, I felt the outline of a firm, irregularly shaped mass embedded in her right breast. I told Kingston of my decision to remove the tumor, and he, Matron, and Hardy, rallied around me on the day of Lady Phillida's surgery.

This was quite a different experience for me to perform a surgical operation in a clean, well-lit room, my patient quiet and still, drifting in an ether-induced sleep. Other than for a few minor procedures such as the removal of an old man's toe, I had not taken a knife to a patient's body since the war. I thought then of the frantic rush to be over and done with an amputation before the orderlies lost their grip on the screaming, struggling patient-victim.

But Lady Phillida lay at peace, unconscious of my pressure on the blade incising her breast, or of Matron's repeated dabbing at the blood I drew. Kingston positioned himself at the patient's head, with a vial of ether and a cloth ready to deepen her sleep should she begin to wake too soon. Hardy stood opposite me, leaning on his cane, serving no purpose except to peer at my work and offer criticism.

I knew the operation was going well. The incision was precise, the bleeding controlled, and the tumor I disengaged and removed with little trauma to the surrounding tissue. Never before had I been given this luxury of time. And I was proud of the result, imagining I had proved my competence to Kingston and Matron.

Concentrating on my task, I was even able to ignore most of Hardy's disapproving jabber. Only a few phrases penetrated, but not far enough to shift my focus. "What the devil are you doing, boy? Cut off that damned tit. And I'd lop off the arm, too, if I was you." If my predecessor continued to goad me toward amputation, he had better fear for his tongue.

Earlier, when I had explained to Lady Phillida what I must do to her, she had expressed a fear of being maimed. "Please don't take my femininity," she had said. Now I closed the incision, stitching with meticulous care, confident that one day my patient's scar would fade to a line as narrow as thread. And if another tumor appeared, as Hardy obdurately predicted it would, well, perhaps all I had really done was buy Lady Phillida a little more time in the asylum.

Only after bandaging the patient's breast and assuring myself that her breathing was steady, did I look toward my employer. He had stepped back, still holding the vial and piece of cloth. If he was impressed—and my own pride of accomplishment perhaps deluded me that he was—he refused to praise my work. Instead, he murmured, "Very diverting, Robert," and an odd expression crossed his face, removed, as if what I had done and what he had witnessed bore no relationship to one another.

His next remark was directed to Matron. "I'll be in my treatment room." Then he left us.

I could in some way understand Kingston's detachment from his patients and their various plights. Caring was a complication, perhaps to him a waste of time and energy. I had seen physicians and surgeons adopt similar attitudes. For myself, for the work I did in the war, speed and accuracy were more valuable to my patients than sympathetic phrases or a charming bedside manner. But however one guarded against them, feelings would be stirred, attachments made, losses suffered. These were the burden and the boon of our humanity. Or would Kingston have disagreed?

Matron called in a pair of attendants, one to watch over the drowsy patient and the other, Oralia, to carry out the bloody linen. Oralia had once mentioned to me that, given a choice, she preferred doing the washing alongside Miss Effie to waiting on patients.

Hardy seemed inclined to stay by Phillida Ryder, peering at her with his failing eyes, set to offer his grim opinions as soon as he perceived she was conscious enough to be upset by them. Fortunately, her eyelids flickered open before her mind engaged itself, and I was able to pry Hardy from her bedside, sending him off with the suggestion that noon dinner must be nearly ready.

Later, going out to the yard, I stopped to speak to Effie. She was rubbing a bloodstained towel against the ridges of the washboard, but glanced up at me with a curious lift of her brows. I explained I'd just completed a surgery for Lady Phillida, who was now resting comfortably. Encouraged by the ease and neatness with which the operation had been accomplished, I was hopeful of the patient's full recovery. Effie nodded and continued her work. Oralia joined her with a bucket of fresh water. And I moved away toward my cottage, aware once again of the awkwardness of my relationship to Effie.

She tolerated my attempts at communication, my monologues. When I spoke to her, her face did not register annoyance or contempt; she did not shy away or avoid me. Effie seemed to listen to me, perhaps much as she listened to the old woman who had lost five sons.

# Chapter 14

The mild days of early spring returned, reminding me that I had passed nearly a year at Magdalene Asylum.

In my journal I noted the progress of some patients, the stagnation or deterioration of others. Hattie Judice was calmer than on her arrival, less given to violent outbursts, and remained inseparable from her daughter, Jane. Together, they appeared to have made peace with their surroundings, at times seeming almost to flourish in their state of mutual devotion. Adele Meredith continued to chant "Lord, I am not worthy," etcetera, much of the day, but usually managed to quiet down when I read aloud in the sewing room.

Among those who were just as they had been a year ago was Mrs. Cordelay, who recounted the aftermath of Lincoln's assassination each time I saw her. And Effie was the same, no closer to me, no farther away.

Lady Phillida Ryder had healed nicely after her surgery, but continued her dependence on laudanum. One morning there was nothing I could do to wake her. Her body was not returned to her English lord, but interred in the asylum cemetery. Another burial soon followed. The mother of five dead sons fell prey to a wasting disease that no tonic could cure and died in mid-March.

That spring Veronique Beaulieu grew pale and hollow-eyed, a shadow of the beauty she had been. She was no longer invited to the evening parties and was often absent from the wards, removed to a treatment room, Matron told me when I asked. Then, one morning as I approached the backyard of the big house, I saw Veronique out for the first time in a fortnight. Wearing a ragged shift, she was in the kitchen garden, on hands and knees in the dirt. She was planting a handful of forks and spoons in a garden row, handles upward, mounding and shaping the soil around each piece of silverware. Then, still on all fours, she swung herself round to a patch of collards and began ravenously tearing at greens with her teeth, like a grazing animal gone mad.

I fetched Kingston; he did nothing but watch her feed. Others came to watch also—attendants, patients, Gaston, who swore he'd seen worse. When Veronique had apparently eaten her fill, she lay back between the garden rows and wallowed in the loose soil. Then Kingston instructed two strong attendants to carry her to the water treatment stall, douse her with cold water, and bring her to the third story.

The evening of that same day, I entered Kingston's office unannounced, interrupting him in the midst of his bookkeeping. I was determined to receive an explanation for Veronique's worsening condition.

"Her mental state is not your province. Need I remind you?" Kingston shut his ledger book.

"Miss Beaulieu's physical wellbeing is at risk from her wild behavior," I answered him. "Doubtless you will disagree with me, but I have come to believe no line can be drawn precisely dividing mental and physical health, that one is not necessarily by definition more powerful than the other."

"Then we may add that misconception to the list of your failings, Robert. Besides, what do you really know of Veronique Beaulieu?"

"I know that when I first saw her she appeared to be in vibrant health. Her habits, grooming, and manners met with enough approval from you to earn her a place at your soirees. But in this last month she seems to have forgotten herself."

Kingston looked amused. "How delicately you phrase things, my boy.

How fastidious you are."

"Not as fastidious as some, I'm sure."

"Veronique is a child killer. Smothered her baby. She couldn't bear the crying."

Kingston leaned back in his chair, watching me I assumed for the effect of his words. But I kept my feelings to myself—my memory of my sister's endless weeping and of my own inability to endure it?

"Veronique's adoring husband suppressed the circumstances of the child's death and committed her to me rather than see her sent to jail for murder."

"But if she were already losing her mind," I said, "perhaps she didn't understand what she had done."

"Certainly, Robert. How could anyone hold her responsible? Of course the asylum is the place for her, and always will be. But did you know her husband still writes to me monthly, asking when Veronique will be allowed to come home? I tell you this on the remote chance that someone might appear at our door demanding her release. She will never be fit to enter the world again. Do you understand?"

"Yes, sir, I understand that. What I don't understand is why she has changed so drastically."

"Ah. What you see Veronique going through now is similar to the crisis in a case of fever. If she survives her passage through the valley of the shadow, she may reach the other side to find a more peaceful existence and a proper sense of remorse for her past."

"And what precipitated this crisis? Is it something you do in your treatment room, Dr. Kingston, leading patients into the valley?"

"A journey we must all make, Robert. Patients are fortunate when I choose to guide them."

A sudden image crossed my mind of Kingston casting a woman into a ravine.

One day, after finishing a round of the wards, I stepped out the front door, nearly bumping into Oralia, who was sweeping the yellow-green dust of pollen off the veranda.

"You going into town today, sir?" she asked, looking at me sideways around the broom handle.

"I thought I might."

"You mind me coming along, sir?"

"Of course not. Reverend Jonas was asking after you last time I saw him. Said he and Asa were missing you."

She leaned the broom against the porch rail. "Matron don't like us going to town. She say we always toting things to our kinfolk. But take a look for yourself, Dr. Mallory, my hands is empty." She spread the fingers of her open palms. "I just wanta go to town."

I suspected she wanted to use me as a safe escort, a way around Matron and her edicts. I suspected the "sir" and "Dr. Mallory" and deferential tone would disappear outside the gates. But even so, I said, "Come on, then."

Her face brightened and she fell in step beside me going down the drive. A few other attendants watched over patients on the veranda or strolled the lawn with their charges, but apparently the only duty Oralia abandoned was her sweeping. If Matron should scold her for going to Lorraine, I told her, she was welcome to say I had given her permission.

"That's mighty nice. Kinda like when Mrs. Glover took off. Matron laid every bit of that at your door and never said nothing 'bout my part."

There had been a recent rain shower, but I found the grayer the day, the brighter the glow of the trees' new green. And the powdery rain of yellow pollen, floating on the surface of puddles of rainwater and dusting the tops of fence rails, shone luminescent as sulfur.

"Spring makes a body restless," Oralia commented as we started down the river road.

"Are you thinking of leaving here?"

"I'm considering. You been all over, traipsing after the war. Ain't there someplace better outside this here parish?"

"That depends on what you want, on who you want to be with."

Briefly, we stopped by Jonas's cabin. He asked Oralia if she were coming to prayer meeting that evening, but she made an excuse.

On the path again to town, she confessed to me she was off to see Velmina.

"You're not ill, are you?" I asked.

"Oh, no." She smiled. "Not with nothing you can cure."

Lovesick. Oralia was lovesick for a married man. I pieced this together during the day and night that followed our walk to town.

While I had been off tending to a baby's colic and an old man's sour stomach, Oralia had visited Velmina for an elixir of love. This much Velmina hinted at when I stopped by her cabin later in the afternoon to pay my respects. Then, with a little prompting from me, she bragged on the specificity of her many potions, which included mixtures called "bad memories be gone," "man-power to get woman with child," and "leave wife and go with another."

I remembered how one day Oralia had stopped on the road from town and looked at a man, while he was chopping wood in his yard, a man with a wife and children. I remembered how he had looked at her, how their eyes had met with knowledge of one another. Before the dawn that followed my conversation with Velmina, I learned the man's name was Wheeler, and it was he who met with Oralia on the grounds of Magdalene Asylum.

Oralia did not accompany me back to the asylum. She had gone on ahead and was once again sweeping the porch when I returned, sweeping with a passion.

The long walk on that humid afternoon had wearied me, and I retired early to the cool darkness of my shuttered cottage. I dozed off, slept for hours, in fact into the night, lying fully dressed on the counterpane. Bad dreams came: I was working again in the surgery tent, focusing only on the operations I must perform, one amputation after another after another. Everything outside the circle of my work was darkness and noise, distant rifle-fire and nearby screaming. Then, when the surgery table, an old door laid across a couple of sawhorses, was empty at last, I stepped outside the tent and viewed a quivering pile of severed limbs, legs and feet, arms and hands. We all give ourselves piecemeal, I thought, and if we live, we learn to live without.

The crack of a pistol shot woke me. I might have incorporated some outside noise into my nightmare. I must have done so, for an actual shot could not have been close by, yet I had experienced it in my first waking moment as a bullet meant for me, an explosion against my skull. I leapt to consciousness as if to dodge my own death and tripped over a supper tray Gaston must have left by my bed. Dishes clattered, and a plate broke under my heel as I ran for the door.

On the porch I hesitated, looking toward the asylum, which was in darkness, except for a single lighted lamp in the window of Kingston's study. All was quiet. The shot must have been illusory, like the intermittent ringing in my ears, the humming I sometimes imagined I heard. Unarmed, for I'd dismissed a fleeting notion of going back for my gun, I crossed the lawn, stopping halfway to the big house. The shade of the study was raised; no one was visible inside the room.

I turned where I stood, revolving in the confusion that follows deep sleep and sudden waking. I must have spun twice around before realizing that the light that flickered between a pair of tree trunks was more than my memory of light at the study window, smeared across the darkness as I turned.

Advancing toward the orchard, I perceived voices, both low and shrill, tangled in argument. Perhaps I thought of the lovers in the thicket, of potions and illicit meetings, of secret plans unraveling in the dark. Perhaps I thought of our trespasses and those who trespass against us. Perhaps I thought of nothing—heart pounding, mouth dry—except drawing closer to the source of my unease. In retrospect, I cannot be sure.

What I confronted was not a pair of lovers, but a whole cluster of human figures, their shadows made huge by the lantern set on the ground. From that cluster a woman struggled, broke free and ran. Kingston's voice rang out after her, calling her by name, commanding Oralia to stop, even as I saw him raise his arm and fire his pistol after her, into the dark. Lunging forward, becoming part of the aggregation, I caught at Kingston's wrist, forced the revolver to his side. Matron shrieked and slapped at me with her hands broad as paddles. I lost my grip on Kingston. Hardy struck me hard across the back of my head with his cane, and my legs gave way.

Gasping in pain, I sucked in the odors of unwashed flesh and newly spilt blood, sucked them in as if I'd swallowed the things themselves and gagged on them. I was not alone on the ground. Near where I reeled on my knees and tumbled forward, a man lay on his back, shirtless, his broad black chest collapsing with the escape of a last breath. One side of his skull had been shattered, blown away, I surmised, by a bullet fired at close range. My own cheek was dampened by a rivulet of his blood.

Above me, Kingston made pronouncements, gave orders, that familiar voice droning in my aching head. "I hit her. Look there. She's fallen up ahead. Gaston, get after her!"

I rolled onto one side, raising a protective arm over my ear to fend off further blows. No more came in my direction. But Gaston, shuffling from the dark periphery into the circle of lamplight, was driven out again by a thrust of Hardy's cane. "That way, she's down that way, you fool nigger!" Gaston lurched away among the trees.

Kingston cut a glance at me as he proclaimed the man beside me dead, not after feeling for a pulse, but after prodding the man's ribcage with the toe of one boot. Then, pocketing his revolver, Kingston pulled me to my feet, admonishing me. "Fools rush in, Robert."

Gaston soon returned like an old Judas goat, it occurred to me, pulling Oralia after him. Nearing the lamplight, she ceased to struggle against the direction of their course. Instead she broke free of him and threw herself forward, howling in grief, over her lover's body. Her skirt was torn and bloodied down one side; perhaps the bullet had clipped the flesh of her thigh. But I was not to examine her possible wound. Kingston had other plans.

He instructed Gaston to stand guard over Oralia. The sight of my employer handing his revolver to a former slave, entrusting him with it, gave me a queer turn inside. Until that night, I had thought of Gaston as a benign, befuddled old retainer, nothing more. Would he fire on her, shoot to kill if she bolted?

The rest of us were to accompany Kingston to the riverbank. Yes, after being assaulted by Hardy and Matron for my interference, I was to be included on their excursion. Taking up the lantern, Kingston led us away.

My employer was fully, if not immaculately, dressed, as was I, although I had fallen asleep without undressing, while Kingston might not have been to bed. Matron billowed after him in a flannel dressing gown, and Hardy, unwaxed whiskers drooping, stumped along behind, spearing the ground with his cane and looking ridiculous in ill-fitting long gray underwear. Gaston, whom we left muttering in the dark beside the corpse and the sobbing girl, wore the loose trousers and shirt that served him day and night.

I maneuvered myself past Matron and Hardy, to one side of Kingston, but angled to watch over my shoulder for any sudden movement of Hardy's cane. "What's happened?" I asked. "Did you shoot that man? Why?"

Kingston, answering none of my questions, said he had me to thank for the night's events, for bringing to his attention the possible presence of a trespasser.

"But he was only here to meet the girl."

"You make assumptions," Kingston reminded me.

"But why shoot at her? Why kill the man?"

Hardy chimed in with the answer. "He was a trespassing nigger. Don't need more reason than that to blow his brains out."

"But I *have* more reason," said Kingston with the voice of rectitude.

He brought us to the path that led in one direction to Hardy's cottage and in the other to the river bank, near to the stockade fence. Holding the lantern high, Kingston shone it toward a great cypress tree that rose from the water's edge. From its branches hung a swath of Spanish moss, like the tangled gray-blue hair of an ancient witch. And sprawled over the rough gray-brown knees, as if it had been a rag doll—a tattered poppet tossed into the witch's lap—was the body of Veronique Beaulieu.

I knew she was dead, even before I waded into the mud and touched her. She was limp, not yet quite cold, but lifeless. There was blood on her mouth and blood streaked across her bare arms, her torn gown, her pale, exposed legs that straddled a cypress knee. One bare foot dangled in the water.

"I saw them standing over her body," said Kingston. "They killed her. Wheeler and Oralia."

"The devil and his whore," Hardy added.

"Veronique was locked in the padded cell," said Matron. "I locked her in myself."

"Oralia was supposed to be on duty," said Kingston.

As on the night Rachel Poncet wandered into the creek, I thought. Had it not occurred to Kingston that former slaves, apathetic or hostile to the women in their care, might provide negligible security?

"But Oralia was taking her pleasures out of doors," said Hardy.

Standing in the mud by the cypress tree, I looked toward the three of them. Kingston held the lantern at arm's length, just above waist high. The light played back and up on the three faces.

I focused on Matron's heavy features. "Are you saying Veronique found a way out when she was left unsupervised?"

"She must have." Matron sounded defensive. "She was always sly."

"Got out and came upon that pair rutting in the woods," put in Hardy. "So they shut her up."

Kingston lowered the lantern as he spoke, his clear voice disembodied in the darkness. "I think not, Dr. Hardy. I propose that Oralia took Veronique with her tonight, into the woods, to offer her buck a little variety. And I propose this was not the first time she played the procuress. I might even go so far as to speculate that Veronique was not her first victim. I know, Robert, you've not forgotten about Rachel Poncet."

"I don't believe it," I said. And yet, I felt sick with doubt.

"Believe what you will. I saw them, the three of them, together."

"You said you saw them standing over her body."

"Yes. Look at her, Robert." He shone the light again on the body. The head lolled to one side, the full lips caked with blood, the white legs splayed. "Look at her, all of you. This was more than deadly rape. This was some dark ritual, some piece of voodoo. Mark my words."

Oh, I marked them. I had seen the way Oralia had looked at her man. I knew of her visit to the *traiteuse*. I had sensed her restlessness, guessed at her hopes. In her way, that girl begot in a breeding shed loved Wheeler, or so I had believed. That love might include superstition and faith in a worthless potion. It might include tempting him to leave his wife and children. But could it also include the mutilation and murder of another woman?

To Kingston the question was more evidence of my credulity and my inexperience with perversion and madness. How true. My own work for years had been to saw off limbs that men might return home, unfit for service but alive, or pronounce men well that they might return to battle, fit for a second chance to be maimed or killed. What on earth did I know of insanity?

# Chapter 15

I argued with Kingston. Belatedly, I argued with him. This was after he and I had carried Veronique's body between us to the asylum, laid it in his consulting room, covered it with a sheet. This was after he and Gaston had hauled Oralia, clinging to Wheeler's corpse, into town and left them both, the living and the dead, in the custody of Captain Purvis and his federal peace keepers. This was after I'd had time to question Matron and Hardy and think over the night's events, and after I'd made a trip into town, unauthorized by Kingston.

Matron told me her story in the asylum's warming kitchen, while she stoked the fire in the stove and started a pot of coffee brewing. Hardy joined me at the kitchen table. It was early morning, none of us were going back to bed, and soon the household would be stirring.

According to Matron, a slight indisposition had disturbed her rest— not the sort of phrasing she used when referring to patient's digestive complaints. While up and about, she decided to look in on Oralia, make sure the "lazy slut" was on duty. Discovering Oralia and Veronique missing, Matron hurried to report to Dr. Kingston, but he too was missing from the house, although a lamp burned in his study. Then Matron thought she heard a scream, not from upstairs, where she was used to hearing screams, but from somewhere outside. The noise sent her off, lantern in hand, to wake Hardy at his cottage. I didn't bother to ask her why she went to him, not to me, for help.

"Dr. Hardy and I found Dr. Kingston in the orchard," said Matron. "The doctor was trying to hold his gun on Wheeler and tussling with Oralia at the same time. It was that girl's doing that the gun went off."

"Damn it to hell, Lila," Hardy piped up, "give credit where credit's due. Kingston executed that murdering nigger, as well he should."

"And what about Gaston?" I asked. "When did he join the fray?"

"Oh, I took him with me to Dr. Hardy's cottage. Didn't I say?" Matron poured herself a cup of coffee and set the pot on the table. No, she hadn't said. It was so easy to forget servants, forget they were in a room or watching from a window, forget they had ears and eyes, forget they had feelings and desires.

Fortified with a cup of coffee, mostly chicory, I set off on foot for town. I passed Kingston and Gaston returning in the wagon, a circumstance of which they were unaware, since I dove back in the shrubbery as they rolled past.

The Federals—few enough for an unimportant little town—struck me as largely indifferent to their duty, just ordinary men who would rather be back home. Only their earnest-faced, hollow-chested, young commanding officer, Captain Purvis might have been the exception. He seemed not indifferent, but ill at ease in his well-furnished office, issuing orders with nervous gravity.

He expressed some surprise at my request to see Oralia, saying he and my employer had already settled the matter of her arrest and the charges against her.

"I realize she's in custody, accused of murder, sir. But Dr. Kingston fired on her, and I suspect the girl may have a bullet wound in her leg."

"Is this true, Buford?" The captain glanced toward a squat, pockmarked man leaning in the doorway. The man was not in military uniform, but wore a sweat-stained chambray shirt and butternut trousers. A heavy ring of keys hung from his cracked leather belt. I had heard of Buford from the townsfolk. He had been jailer at the courthouse long before the war or the Federal occupation. Some said he'd had no trouble switching loyalties, since he only really served himself.

"Is the prisoner wounded?" Purvis again addressed Buford.

The jailer shrugged and with his tongue slowly repositioned the slug of tobacco in his cheek. "Might be."

"Captain Purvis, I request your permission to examine the girl and treat her, if necessary."

The young officer looked at me strangely. Perhaps at his current post he was unaccustomed to tones of deference from those outside the military. "You would treat anyone," he murmured, "anyone who was wounded?"

"Yes, sir."

He told the jailer to escort me to Oralia's cell.

Buford took his time. "So, you come all the way to town to lift her filthy skirts and take a peek? Or did you come to saw off a leg? Your specialty, I hear tell." I let him ramble as we climbed the back stairs of the three-story courthouse. The cellar jail was full of thieves and vagrants, white men separated from black. But something out of the ordinary, he told me, like a "colored murderess," warranted the attic.

There were two cells in the attic, the stairwell and a passageway between them, and a cupola above the passage. One door stood open, revealing an empty cell about eight feet square, with a bare planked floor, plastered walls, and a single high barred window. Through it the afternoon sun shone in shafts of dust motes that spun despite the stillness of the air and barred the floor with light and shadow. The other door, across the way, was shut and padlocked.

Buford fumbled and cursed his set of keys and at last opened Oralia's cell.

It was a closet compared with the other cell. The girl was shackled by her wrists to a beam nailed across supporting lumber in the unplastered wall. Filthy straw was littered under her feet. Above her head, a single window, mostly boarded over and leaving its opening so narrow it required no bars, admitted a slice of daylight.

I told Oralia why I had come, that I thought she might be hurt and wanted to dress her wound as Kingston had not allowed me to do before he brought her to town. She shut her eyes and turned her face away from me, as far as her bonds would permit.

Buford straddled a cane chair in the passage outside the cell and watched me open my black bag. He chewed and spat.

Placing myself between his line of vision and the girl, I raised her skirt above her thigh. There was a gash in the flesh, crusted over with dried blood, but on examination I could find no sign a bullet had entered. I applied a cleansing salve, bandaged the wound and lowered her skirt. But as I had bunched the skirt above her thigh and again as I let the cotton fabric fall, I was a aware of the contour of the girl's body, the drape of worn-out cotton over a swollen belly no longer hidden beneath a starched apron. Oralia must have been many months with child.

"That it?" asked Buford. "That the whole show?"

I ignored him, but whispered to Oralia. "Shall I ask the Reverend Jonas to come to you?"

Slowly, she turned her face toward me, slid open her dark eyes. "What for?" Her voice was a dry rasp. "He say one sin be as bad as another."

"Was it the man acting alone?" I asked. "You didn't kill Miss Beaulieu?"

"And you didn't carry no tales to Doctor." Her words were laced with scorn. Again, she shut her eyes and averted her face.

The jailer shoved aside his chair and came forward, ending my attempt to interview Oralia. He locked the door of her cell and sent me on my way.

As I left the courthouse, I saw men milling in the street, gathering along the boardwalks, all talking of the murder of a white woman.

Late that afternoon, Kingston told me his version of events. Oh, he was not pleased that I had gone to town and seen Oralia, but seemed willing, for the time being, to let that particular matter rest. It was the circumstances of Veronique's death that we disputed.

He and I stood on opposite sides of the table in the consulting room, Veronique's sheet-covered body between us. "What I found at the riverside was a horror," he said, in that tone of his that implied only a fool would disagree with him. "My response, my choice of action, Robert, was quite natural. I pursued the beasts and I fired on them."

"You saw them in the act of mutilation?"

"I saw them by the river, beside the body."

"And they saw you."

"Are you as thick as you pretend to be? Of course they saw me, why else would they have high-tailed off, forcing me to chase them?"

"Oralia and Wheeler were lovers meeting in secret," I said. "She wanted him to leave his family and run away with her. She went to the *traiteuse* for a potion, not a lesson in butchery."

Kingston's face tightened. "You think you know a great deal, yet you know nothing, Robert."

"Lately, Veronique Beaulieu's madness had taken a wilder, more violent turn. You've said as much yourself. And I have seen her wandering the grounds. Isn't it possible she attacked them first?"

"You want me to believe the pair of them couldn't have fended her off without killing her?"

"With Hardy, Matron, and Gaston there to help you, you still killed

Wheeler. You didn't hold him at gun point to turn him over to the authorities."

"I *am* the authority here."

"Then you have a duty to consider all the possibilities." I folded back the sheet and revealed the distorted features of Veronique's once beautiful face. "Isn't it possible she hurt herself, even mortally hurt herself. Perhaps what you saw last night was simply two persons pulling a body from the creek."

"Is that what the girl would have you believe?"

"She's told me nothing."

"Ha!"

"I have pulled a body from that water, of a woman I didn't kill. And since coming here, I've lost count of how many inmates' minor injuries Matron tells me were self-inflicted. Why discount suicide?" I asked, drawing the sheet away from the corpse. "Didn't you first imply that was how Rachel Poncet met her death, before this new theory of ritual murder?"

Kingston's breath quickened, became audibly impatient. I had made him angry before now, but never before now had I experienced the sensation of playing out his anger, uncoiling it with my own words and deeds, heedless of its venom.

"You said I lacked experience with madness, but I'm learning. You said what you saw at the riverside was a horror, that your reaction to it was natural. Sir, I have seen every manner of human mutilation—flesh and bone hacked or shot away, wounds as ragged as the edges of sleeves and trouser legs ripped away with the limbs. And I've been the one to mutilate, sawing through rotted flesh and shattered bone, dismembering men by the cartload. I wish I could feel the horror of it all before I feel the overwhelming sense of familiarity."

My hand shook as I reached down for my black bag, then steadied as it gripped the worn leather handle. I set the bag on the edge of the table, opened it, and drew out a pair of surgical scissors. Kingston said nothing, but I felt him watching me as I cut away Veronique's tattered, bloodstained shift. Her body was scratched and bruised, but her head, throat, and upper torso bore no obviously mortal wounds. The blood caked on her lips was drawn, I surmised, when she bit her own tongue, which was still clenched between her teeth.

"If it was murder, Wheeler might have done it alone," I said. "But, if so, how did he do it? Her skull is not crushed, her neck is not broken. She has not been shot or stabbed. Perhaps he drowned her. But he can't confess now. Did you ask Oralia her side of the story?"

"Oh, you are the self-appointed champion of females in distress, are you not, Robert? And yet your sister…"

"Lucinda has nothing to do with this, sir."

"Of course not."

"Why did you go to the riverbank last night?"

Kingston's eyes shifted focus beyond me as if he had suddenly discovered an imperfection in the wallpaper across the room. "Why did you come under my roof, Robert? Lord knows you are not worthy." His right hand hovered for a moment over Veronique's body, over the part of it I had left covered by a blood-darkened remnant of her shift. Then he let the hand fall to his side. "You haven't finished your examination," he said.

I lifted the cloth.

I don't know how many minutes ticked by before I heard Kingston speaking again. "A woman is born wounded. For all her secrecy and coverings, she may still be violated without our knowing, penetrated, robbed of her soul without one outward sign upon her flesh."

But Veronique bore one outward sign. Between the blood-smeared legs

I found the tip of the hilt of a silver dinner knife, and slowly I withdrew the handle and the blade that had been hidden from sight.

"A piece of the good silver. That suggests planning on someone's part," said Kingston. "Oralia must have got hold of it, given it to Wheeler. The rituals these folks practice go far beyond a little sprinkling of hot pepper. I think your mother may have warned you of that."

Indeed, my mother had warned me that we must live in fear of savagery and counter it at every turn with our refinement and exclusivity.

"Women have done such things to themselves," I said. "Attempted such things—in desperation."

"Are you suggesting…?"

"She might have believed she was. She was out of her mind."

"Ah, you're remembering what brought her here, that Veronique killed her infant. Born or unborn, it's all the same, isn't it?"

I made no comment.

"Well, was she carrying Wheeler's bastard or wasn't she? Cut her open, Robert. Satisfy your curiosity."

I found her womb as I had expected to find it, lacerated and empty.

"You don't look well, my boy. Time for a dose of quinine?"

I nodded agreement, though I felt neither chilled nor feverish, only numb. And I doubted Kingston had any sincere interest in my health. Reminding me of my infirmity, and by implication, his superior fitness, was just his way of ending our conversation.

I went to my cottage, washed up at the basin and changed clothes. Gaston carried off my soiled garments. Then, near twilight, I walked the grounds and spotted Effie, bending over her wash tub. I approached and saw that my shirt and Kingston's had turned the water a dark red. Effie rubbed the shirts against the washboard, scoured them with a cake of lye soup, twisted and wrung them. Her face was puckered and as close to tears as I had ever seen it. But she didn't cry.

Sensing her agitation, I tried to reassure her. Miss Beaulieu had met with an accident, I told her, at night by the river. Effie must stay close to the big house, always stay in her room at night, come to me if she ever felt anxious or afraid. There was something about the way she turned her head, narrowed her eyes as if she were measuring me, measuring the distance between us. I thought Effie seemed mistrustful of me, as she had not seemed before, and I had no remedy for that.

Impulsively, I promised to look after her, a promise I had no idea how to keep, and, for want of another way to show my sincerity, I hauled fresh water and helped her finish the washing.

Night fell, but I did not retire to bed. I sat in the rocking chair on my porch, a rug spread over my knees, staring at the big house and pondering over what to do when the sun came up again. Should I talk with Jonas? Question Velmina? Would Oralia receive some legal counsel? Would I be called to testify, to describe aloud the cause of Veronique's death? God knew what passions such a description would inflame.

Whatever had happened the previous night, I could predict the likely outcome. Oralia and, posthumously, Wheeler would be blamed and condemned for the murder of Veronique Beaulieu. If they were guilty, there would be an end to it. If they were not, Wheeler was already lost, and innocence was not likely to save Oralia. And if they were not, and Veronique's death were not self-inflicted, would her murderer kill again?

Had he killed before?

I resolved to go into Lorraine the following morning, to discover what I could from whoever would speak to me, to offer whatever I knew of my own knowledge to Captain Purvis. But for all my good intentions, I might just as well have been paving the road to hell.

# Chapter 16

After little sleep and no breakfast, I was summoned to the asylum. Adele Meredith had fallen on the stairs, descending from the day room, and broken her ankle. All the while I worked to set the bones, and it was a complicated break, she made no resistance, but chanted ceaselessly: "Lord, I am not worthy... Speak but the word... My soul shall be healed... Lord, I am not..." It seemed to me her singsong calmed her as well as a draught of laudanum might have done, but Matron told me that Mrs. Meredith enjoyed her sufferings, believed her misery was a gift from God.

A succession of patients with minor complaints followed, requiring my cursory attention. Many of the ailments I thought Matron might have dismissed without treatment on any other day, when I was not anxious to leave for town.

The last patient Matron brought me was Effie Rampling, who had received a slight burn from the laundry fire on the back of one hand. As I bathed and salved and bandaged her blistered hand, she never once looked at me. But Matron watched us both. I tried always to be diligent. I treated Effie with no more care than I had the other patients, but I felt more.

At midday, I left the treatment room and met Gaston in the hallway.

"You be having yo' dinner in the big house, sir?" he asked.

"I didn't plan to."

"Dr. Kingston, he just come back from town. Said you be joining him."

"Not today, Gaston."

I left through the kitchen, grabbing up a handful of dewberries for a meal, and set off toward Lorraine, though not with the vigor and determination I might have brought to the journey earlier in the day. The air was unseasonably hot and dry, the sun glaring as if midsummer were somehow misplaced in early spring. I thought of the river road, cool, shaded, dark, as I walked between crusty wheel ruts on the bleached road to town.

If Oralia would confess, if I could know for certain that she and Wheeler were guilty of murder and that now they would do no more harm... I squinted in the dazzling sunlight, looking ahead toward the respite of a giant cottonwood. Though the leaves of its upper branches shone silver in the glare, the leaves of its lower branches were dappled lush green and dark ash, color and shadow overlapping. The vast shadow of the tree itself sprawled across the road. And beyond it knelt Asa, Oralia's young brother, rocking on his heels.

Nearing the boy, I heard his keening moans, saw the pale dust of the road caked on his face and streaked with his tears. His eyes were lifted, fixed, staring. I followed their direction, turning back toward the tree, gazing upwards at its leaf-shrouded branches. Then I saw the pair of bare feet, the ragged hem of a blue dress, the limp hands crossed and bound, the face fallen forward over a circle of rope. Oralia's body dangled from a broad cottonwood bough.

I turned back to Asa, gripped his shoulders, pulled him to his feet. Brokenly he told me what had happened. White men had burst into the jail—or were let in by Buford, I suspected—had taken Oralia from her cell, dragged her to the outskirts of town, and lynched her.

"None of it never would've happened," he said, "if she hadn't been working at the madhouse."

I sent Asa up the tree with my pocket knife to cut his sister down. As he leaned out on the branch above me and slowly worked the small blade through the thick braided hemp, I held her legs steady. Then, as the last strand of rope snapped, her body pitched forward and downward, causing me to stagger under the sudden weight. I caught her to me, regained my balance, held her draped over my shoulder, then gently lowered her to the ground. This was the completion of an act I had begun countless times in my mind and never finished—still had not finished, for the body before me belonged to Asa's sister, not mine. The face before me was burgundy, not crimson.

My father had told me that Lucinda's death was nothing like the efficient work of a benevolent executioner. She had had a good drop from the upper balcony, but the noose she had fashioned from an old hemp cord did not snap her neck and bring a quick end. Instead, it had slipped upward, catching under her jaw, and while the rest of the household slept, Lucinda, alone in the night, had slowly suffocated.

Oralia's neck had not been broken, either. Then again, like Lucinda she had not received the help of a benevolent executioner. No, she had been strung up in a hurry, yanked off her feet, hoisted. Only afterward had the rope been tied to the bough. Her blood-engorged eyes bore blind witness to her suffering. If only the boy had not seen it, too.

"I gonna kill somebody," said Asa. "I got to."

"You can't kill them all. You'll get yourself killed if you try."

"Don't matter. Someday I gonna kill somebody for my sister."

The Reverend Jonas would have to talk to the boy, make him see reason.

I lifted Oralia's body and, with Asa walking beside me, headed toward town.

When I had carried the cold, decaying remains of Rachel Poncet, Asa had straggled along behind me, reluctantly bringing my luggage. I remembered the river-soaked wool of my suit and of the minister's robe, clammy, scratchy against my skin. Now my sweat-soaked cotton shirt clung to me, smooth, slick as a second skin. Oralia's body was warm and soft in my arms, her life having been only recently extinguished. Every few steps we took, Asa reached out and patted her tangled hair.

The men who had lynched her were nowhere in sight, but I feared they might be returning, for I heard a murmur rising, rolling toward us from the road to town, a sound more complex, more human, than the humming that droned only for my hearing. The boy and I stopped in our tracks, and he placed a hand protectively over his sister's face. We waited.

The road shimmered in the heat, and out of the distant wavering air a crowd appeared, not a rowdy lynch mob nor an orderly line of soldiers, but a congregation coming to reclaim its own. The Reverend Mr. Jonas led his people forward to meet us. Without a word to me, he took Oralia's body from my arms and brought her into the midst of parishioners that closed around her. And Asa joined the throng, of which I was not a part, as it moved away from me. Their backs turned to me, two women put their arms around the boy's shoulders, which had begun to quive. He must be sobbing, I thought, and another woman nearby reached out and stroked his bowed head. I watched Asa go until he and all the others were out of sight.

What use is it now, looking back, to say I might have done something differently? Hindsight never resurrected the dead.

Excluded by those who mourned for Oralia and comforted her brother, I still managed to share the common feeling I had seen in the faces of those who bore away her body. Resignation. Why could it not have been outrage?

Hunger, thirst, fatigue, all reminders of my continued existence, wore at me on my return to the asylum. The blazing whiteness of the hot afternoon receding behind me, I moved toward evening, the shade of live oaks, the carpet of grass, the fragrance of Magdalene's garden. In the failing light, patients and attendants crossed the lawn or rounded the broad veranda, returning to the big house, drawing in for the coming night.

I started for my cottage but found myself straying instead to an arbor of wisteria, sinking there upon a stone bench. Then, with my second breath of sweet air, I caught a whiff of expensive cigar smoke. Kingston approached me from the garden path.

Before he spoke, his mouth tightened, twitched for a moment, then relaxed and allowed his words to flow. "While you've been away, Robert, on some pressing business, I assume, we have buried Veronique Beaulieu."

"With all the others," I thought, but lacked the energy to say.

"This morning I spoke with Captain Purvis and offered him my professional opinion as to how she met her end."

Kingston waited, and I muttered the requisite, "How's that, sir?"

"Veronique suffered from delusions, was sometimes hostile, even violent. And as we both know, she had a penchant for the silverplate and cutlery. After great deliberation—soul-searching, if you will—I must pronounce her death a suicide." Kingston pulled on his cigar and exhaled a blue-gray cloud. "Tomorrow I will write to inform her family."

"And what about Wheeler's family?" I said. "He's left a wife and children."

"He should have thought about them before he trespassed on my property. I acted well within my rights."

"And Oralia? Did you tell Captain Purvis this morning that you were mistaken, that you really never saw her mutilating a white woman?"

"I did see her and the man beside the river, by the body. That's God's truth. Naturally, in the heat of the moment, the horror…"

"And you said I made assumptions."

"Robert," he said with the scolding tone of a schoolmaster. "The girl will be released. But she can't come back here. She must move on."

"She has moved on. Passed over. This afternoon Oralia was lynched. The townsfolk didn't wait on your deliberations, sir."

"I see." Kingston dropped the butt of his cigar on the gravel path and ground it under his heel. "And you believe this event is somehow my fault?"

"I want her exonerated."

"What?"

"For the sake of her brother and the Reverend Jonas and all the others. I want her memory cleared of blame."

"Oralia was not blameless, my boy. Why was she out that night? She had abandoned her duties and was carrying on like the slut she was, that's why."

"If she was so worthless, why did you employ her?" The words were out of me before I could give a thought to what he would make of them.

"If exemplary character were a prerequisite," he replied, "I might find myself without a staff."

"I'll speak for her, even if you don't, sir."

"Robert, you're obviously exhausted, perhaps ill. Go to your cottage and rest. I'll send Gaston along with some supper and a fresh bottle of quinine. Then, come to my study tonight. There is a matter of importance that I must share with you."

That night Kingston circled his broad mahogany desk, which was heaped and strewn with papers and letters. He had talked for several minutes about nothing of consequence, but at last began a sideways approach to the reason for my summons.

"I had planned to break this… this piece of news I must relate to you, when I found you in the garden. But I was unable to find my way to the subject. You were upset, Robert, understandably, by recent misadventures. In your distressed state, you would have been unreceptive, I think, to my concerns for you."

Kingston ceased his pacing of the Turkish carpet, leaned against the edge of his desk, and swirled the bourbon in his crystal shot glass. He had given me a cup of coffee, and I sat drinking it, baffled by his strange show of solicitation, wondering when he would finally wind his way to the point.

"This morning, while I was in town, I not only had a chat with Captain Purvis." Here, Kingston stopped to refill my cup, and a pulling at the corner of his mouth, a sort of spasm of the cheek muscle, played on his face. Perhaps the effort of being kind to me was taking a toll.

"I collected the mail," he continued, returning to his desk. "And I'm afraid, my boy, that I have some bad news for you." He touched a folded page of cream-colored paper that lay on the blotter.

I set my cup aside and stared at him. Foreboding and regret swept over me with painful suddenness. "My mother," I said.

"Your mother has written to me, Robert, asking me to tell you that your father has passed away."

My father, and not my mother.

"You understand my hesitation, forgive my delay in telling you?"

"Yes, sir."

"Baton Rouge has lost a fine physician."

"Was it his heart?" I asked. With the thrumming starting in my ears, my voice sounded as if it were echoing from some corner of the room. The ache in my bones began, despite that evening's dose of quinine, filling me with the dread of another bout of fever.

"Yes, his heart," said Kingston. "You must go home, Robert."

"For the funeral?"

"No, my boy. That's done with by now. You must go to comfort your mother."

"Has she asked for me, in her letter?"

At no time in our conversation did Kingston question why my mother had written to him and not to me. If she had given him any explanation, he did not share it.

Kingston talked on of how kind my family had been to him while his wife was dying, of how he had appreciated my mother's hospitality and enjoyed my sister's diverting sweetness.

"Has she asked for me?" I repeated the question he had ignored. "I want to see the words in her own handwriting."

"You must go to your mother." But Kingston had hesitated long enough before he spoke to convince me that she had not requested my return. She had only written to him to request that I be informed. However much I might hope that Mother could put aside Father's banishment of me now that he was dead, she had not.

"There's an old saying, Robert: 'A man doesn't become a man until his father dies.' Now it's time for you to be a man, to be a consolation to your mother."

"How long ago did my father die?"

"Three months ago. Go to your mother."

"Perhaps I will. In another week or a month."

"You must go tomorrow, Robert."

"No, sir. Tomorrow I have business in town."

"I will take care of that."

"As you took care of it this morning?"

"That's enough."

"A woman has been lynched. The men who did it must be held accountable. I intend to see Captain Purvis."

"Our conquering hero, who will put everything to rights. I will speak to him, Robert, and you will listen to me."

Kingston's demeanor underwent one of its abrupt shifts. Earlier in the evening he had been patronizing, moments ago avuncular, now he was imperious, his most frequently practiced self. "You will leave at daybreak tomorrow, and you will visit your mother. But first there is a service you must perform for me and for one of our patients." Lifting a piece of gilt-edged stationery from among his scattered letters, he perused it briefly before speaking again. "We have an unusual situation on our hands, Robert. I am releasing Miss Rampling."

"Sir?"

"You heard me. I am releasing Effie. And I am making it your duty to escort her safely to New Orleans."

"Her family has asked for her return?" My voice rebounded back to me from the far wall.

"No. Her family has not asked for her." Kingston seated himself behind the desk, tossed aside the letter. "Her family refuses to pay."

"But her family will take her back?"

"They have made no such offer. Her brother-in-law has asked me to dispose of her, find her some suitable employment. A lady I know in New Orleans, a widow who owns a boarding house, Mrs. Fabre, has agreed to give her a roof over her head in exchange for a little light housekeeping."

"Are you saying Effie's cured?"

Kingston shrugged. "She's compliant, docile, quite the domesticated creature."

"If she may go now, why couldn't she have gone before? What's changed, except a financial arrangement?"

Why was I raising an objection, provoking him? Merely habit. Wasn't this what I had wanted, to take Effie away from Magdalene Asylum, to be her protector?

"I don't run a charity, Robert. Would you have me turn her out tonight?"

"No, sir. I'll take her away in the morning."

"That's settled then. Leave your gate key on my desk. You won't be needing it for a while."

# Chapter 17

Effie Rampling and I began our journey in a mule-drawn open buckboard, lightly equipped with a few cooking utensils and food stuffs, a tarpaulin, and a couple of moth-eaten quilts. My patient and I were not expected to fend for ourselves for long. Kingston had sketched a map for me, describing landmarks and the inns and houses that would provide meals and shelter. He estimated a brief trip to New Orleans and a speedy return for me to the asylum. Even so, I asked him for a full bottle of quinine to pack in my black bag, and I gathered most of my few personal possessions, including my notes and sickbed journal into my satchel. Effie's two bulging carpetbags surprised me, for I had reckoned her wardrobe and personal effects to be as simple as my own.

As we headed off that morning, Effie sat very straight on the wagon seat beside me. She wore her butternut brown dress, starched and ironed. But her primness was softened by the loose braiding of her hair, which lay over one shoulder. A passing breeze lifted and blew an escaping strand against my cheek. Taking up the reins, I glanced sideways at her. Her eyes were vivid blue, even in the shadow of the wide, woven brim of her straw hat.

As we drove toward town, where we picked up the main road leading south from Lorraine, I spoke to her about the arrangements made for her in New Orleans and tried to ascertain how much she understood about her future. If I interpreted her nods correctly, she had visited New Orleans before the War and had no particular objection to going there again.

We met other travelers coming and going, as if the spring weather had stirred us all to be on the move. A band of former slaves of various ages and conditions walked with us for a couple of miles, before turning west, traveling barefoot through the stubble of a fallow cornfield. A stoop-shouldered old farmer, his widowed daughter, and her baby boy crossed our path in the early afternoon and shared our meal of wheat bread and smoked ham. Later, when we were on the road again, a pair of Union soldiers on horseback stopped to ask our business and confiscate the remaining ham.

All the day, Effie was silent as always, barely seeming to notice my attempts to fill the quiet or make conversation with the various other travelers. Only when the soldiers had ridden up to us, and I reined in the mule, did I sense a sudden change in her. Sitting beside me in the buckboard, she pressed herself into the side of my arm and bowed her head against my shoulder as if she would disappear into me.

The men were abrupt, still smug in their status as victors. They demanded to see the papers Kingston had given me which explained that I had custody of a patient. Apparently Kingston's name was not unfamiliar to them. Perhaps they had met him on one of his trips to collect new patients. Perhaps they had met him more than once, since they had hesitated— waiting for me to offer them something?—before helping themselves to the ham.

As we continued on, the road cut through a forest, and I saw the dogwood was in bloom. The trunks and branches of the small dogwoods merged with the surrounding dark trees and became indistinguishable from them. The white petals of the dogwood flowers appeared suspended in space, flecks of light scattered across the shadows, caught in mid-air.

Toward evening we still had not come to the settlement Kingston had recommended. There he said I would find a farmhouse that served as an inn. From its porch, as he described it, was an outside staircase leading to a guest room, so family would not be disturbed by strangers spending the night. I anticipated settling Effie in the room and taking my own rest in the bed of the wagon.

After some confusion at a crossroads where a weathered sign had fallen over, I turned down the broader of my two choices, a red dirt road deeply rutted by wagon wheels. Out of the blue dusk a man proceeded toward us, swinging himself along on one good leg, a peg leg, and a crutch. Since the war, the sight of a man missing a limb was commonplace. Amputation had been our best defense against gangrene and other morbid conditions. But the man's movement, lurching simultaneously forward and diagonally to the right or left, was made a sight somehow as whimsical as it was pitiful by his eager companion, a three-legged mongrel dog, hobbling gamely beside him, crooked tail wagging, tongue lolling from one side of its mouth. They were a pair.

The mule was ready enough to stop as the man swung his way toward us—would gladly have stopped all night where it stood if there had been fodder within a neck's stretch. When the man reached the wagon, he steadied himself by catching hold of the wheel rim, and the dog plopped itself down on the hip of its single hind leg, bracing itself with its front paws in an attempt to sit straight. Both peered up at me, the man with bloodshot eyes from under his slouch hat. His skin was creased and tanned a deep yellow-brown, and a scar drew back his upper lip, exposing blackened teeth. He wore a homespun shirt, hanging loose like a smock over mud-caked trousers. The leather of his one boot was cracked over the toe. One pant leg was rolled up and tied just above the knee, where the pegleg was strapped to his thigh.

I greeted the man and asked him if we were headed in the right direction. He looked us over and told us to keep on going as we were. Then, when we reach a fork, don't go for the uphill road, he said, but take the tow path along the bayou. Could we reach the farmhouse before nightfall? Maybe. Not too likely.

While the man and I conversed, Effie found a fatty scrap of ham, missed by the soldiers, and tossed it to the dog, which caught it and downed it in one gulp.

I thanked the man, regretting that he was traveling the opposite way and could not accept a ride. Then he and the dog set off with their awkward gaits, and I slapped the reins on the mule's rump, inspiring it to reluctant action.

Despite the warmth of the evening and my doing no more than riding in a wagon most of the day, I was feeling weary and slightly chilled. The ringing had started in my ears. After handing the reins to Effie, I reached under the seat for my black bag and rummaged inside it for the bottle of quinine. Finding it, I pulled the cork and took a swallow directly from the bottle. I said something to Effie, no more than murmured it, about the inconvenience of malarial fever. She continued driving the mule down the road to the fork and off along the tow path, while I waited for the quinine to bring me back to myself.

Near nightfall we still followed the course of the bayou without sighting farm or settlement. I had grown up in a town, was college educated, bookish, thought my learning could always be traded for goods and services. I had known little of surviving on the land, away from town, until the war. Then what I learned was requisitioning, foraging, and doing without. For myself, it would have been nothing to spend a night on the ground, but I was sorry to fail in my duty to Effie and told her as much. She, however, simply accepted our predicament with a nod.

The disused tow path gradually faded until we lost it in a tangle of grapevine and creeper that draped the cypress and water oaks, covering trees, path, and bank like a gray-green shroud. I climbed down from the wagon and walked at the head of the mule, leading it away from the bayou and up to a grove of live oaks. Quickly, before I would be forced to light the lantern and burn what little oil we had, I unharnessed the mule, rubbed it down with a piece of sack cloth, offered it corn fodder and a pail of water, and staked it to graze. Meanwhile, Effie took our bags and food box from the wagon and set them under a spreading oak. When she began gathering kindling, I hollered a warning to her to watch for water moccasins. In this warm weather they might be active even after sundown.

Later, after Effie had attended to her private ablutions, I went down to the bayou to attend to my own and to fetch the cooking water. Returning from the water's edge in near darkness, climbing back up the bank with a full bucket, my cleated boots digging deep into the wet clay, I looked up the rise to the grove and saw Effie finishing the task she had begun in my absence. Yards and yards of mosquito netting were draped over the low branches of the live oak, creating a diaphanous tent. Carrying a stump of burning candle, Effie moved about behind the netting like a moth caught in a web. No, more like a diligent little spider examining her handiwork for rents or gaps.

She was humming—she must have been, there was no one else—an old tune, "Greensleeves" I think it was. But as I approached her, the sound grew not louder but fainter, until it died away as I entered the tent, lifting and ducking under the netting.

"Where did all this come from?" I asked, looking round me. "Is this what you had stashed in those carpetbags? You didn't take it from the wards, did you?" Effie shook her head "no." "From Matron's room, then?" I guessed. She shrugged her confession.

I set down the bucket, and she dipped a tin cup into the water, offering me a drink, which I declined. "The water's brackish," I said. "We'll boil it first and flavor it with some chicory." Then I added with careful nonchalance, "I heard you humming."

I couldn't read her eyes. Evening had become night, and under the oak branches the single candle created more shadow than illumination. I couldn't know if I'd embarrassed her, but she did move away from me and set about arranging and lighting the kindling in a circle of stones.

When my back was to her as I rummaged in the supply box for the kettle and the packet of chicory, I thought I heard the rustle her skirt and petticoat make when she walks. I was in my shirtsleeves, and I felt a light pressure on my shoulder, just her fingertips through a single layer of sweat-dampened cotton.

"Don't turn round." The voice was close behind me. Startled at the sound of it, my first impulse was naturally to turn, but I stopped myself. "I can speak to you," she whispered, her voice sounding weak and thin with disuse. "But not if you look at me."

I felt I'd caught a wild bird in my hand, and if I moved too fast I'd lose it. "Then I won't look at you," I whispered back.

"You promise?"

"I promise. Speak to me again. Tell me why you've kept silent."

"I was asked to say no more."

"Asked by whom?"

"He didn't want to hear another word from me as long as he lived. But he must be dead by now. Otherwise, I would not have been let go in the world."

"Then can it matter if I look at you when you speak?"

"It matters to me." Her voice was tremulous. "You must know, Dr.

Mallory. Is he dead?"

Looking through Kingston's records, I had learned that Effie's father had committed her to Magdalene Asylum and for years must have paid a handsome fee for her keep. Because Kingston told me the money was now no longer forthcoming and Effie must be placed elsewhere, should I assume Mr. Rampling was dead? Kingston had not exactly said he was, but the order to remove her from the asylum had come from another male relative. And if I expressed some doubt whether Mr. Rampling were alive or dead, would Effie fall silent again? Was her father the "he" who didn't want to hear another word? Or was "he" this other man, her sister's husband, who had ordered her release, but would not take her in, instead allowing her to be sent to New Orleans to take up menial employment in a boarding house? Instead of answering her question, I simply said, "Dr. Kingston no longer receives payments."

"Ah."

She moved into my line of vision and said no more, as we prepared a meal of corn pudding and dried peaches. The night was mild, but still as we ate we sat close to the low-burning fire. I apologized for losing the way, missing the inn I had expected us to reach before nightfall. Effie seemed unconcerned. I told her I was sorry the food was so meager and tasteless, sorry she would have to sleep in the open. She only sighed and set aside her empty tin plate. I asked if she would like me to add more wood to the fire, but she shook her head "no." I turned my back to her, hoping she would speak again.

"Then we'll let it die down," I said, and waited. Waited for her to tell me that each night while suffocating in the crowded wards, tormented by the moans and cries of patients, she had ached to lie in the open, lulled to sleep by the song of peepers and crickets. But that had been my old longing, not hers, not as far as I knew. And the campfire we had hardly needed once the cooking was done. That too was my longing. A circle of fire on any night, warm or cold, signified the gathering of human beings, eating and talking and bedding down together, done for the day with the killing.

In silence we spread quilts on the ground, several feet apart, and I gave her my folded jacket for a pillow. The buckboard stood outside the tent of net she had arranged. I thought of making a more comfortable resting place for her there, folding the quilts in the wagon bed, with a length of mosquito netting laid over her supported by the plank sides of the wagon. But then I pictured it, the wagon bed resembling a coffin draped with lace. No, I couldn't suggest that.

Lying on my back, I looked up through the fine netting and beyond it, through the gaps between the tree branches, at a half moon and a smattering of stars.

I cleared my throat, preparing to tell Effie Rampling "good night." But I hadn't formed the words when she began to speak to me.

"That last year of the war, we were always hungry, and the food was bad. Just now and then something delicious would appear—a sprig of mint, a patch of dewberries, a fresh egg laid and forgotten by a careless hen. But such delicacies hardly lasted a moment. Sometimes I imagined I could have lived in my thoughts, in my dreams if it were not for that ever-returning hunger. That slow starving. I eat enough now. Enough and no more. But I never want to care about food again. Have you ever felt that way, Robert Mallory? That you don't want to care about something 'cause sure as you do, somebody will snatch it away from you?"

I murmured my agreement, hoping my answer would not stop her flow of words. And she went on, offering little bits of information, stray thoughts, glimpses of her past, sad, bleak images interspersed with flashes of bright memories. Confirming what I had read about her among the papers in Kingston's office, she described growing up on Woodbine, a cotton and sugar plantation near New Orleans. Her father, Charles Edmund Rampling, was a rich old man, a widower with a nearly grown daughter and three rowdy sons, when he married the very young, very beautiful Euphemia Charlevoix. She gave him Effie and died not long afterward.

As Effie continued to speak, her voice lost its wavering and broken rhythms, becoming stronger and sweeter, as if with practice she were discovering the music of her words.

"One by one, as each of my brothers turned fifteen, he left the big house and moved across the lawn to live in the *garconniere*—gentlemen's quarters, indeed! —where each one would learn to take up drinking and gambling and smoking cigars and whatever else gentlemen do.

"I didn't much like the changes. Our slave children were growing up, too, and put to hard work. They had been our play friends. We spent our childhood with them and loved them. But then, as we grew older, we were told to turn away from them, told that they were childish, simple, unworthy of us in our new found sophistication. 'When I was a child, I spake as a child, I understood as a child, I thought as a child…'"

Involuntarily, I finished for her, "'But when I became a man, I put away childish things.'"

She didn't speak again for several minutes, and I was afraid I'd spoiled things. Then she began again. "Why did growing up mean learning to stop loving? How was that a step toward maturity and wisdom? To turn away from our best feelings and take up the worst feelings of our elders?"

She drew a deep breath. "First, Charles Edmund III, after Papa, and big as Papa, left for the *garconniere*, then Parker, then handsome Bliss. Of course, I stayed in the big house, chaperoned by Aunt Mina and my sister,

Jeanetta, waiting for some other planter's gentleman son to call and ask for my hand. That's what I was supposed to be waiting for, and Jeanetta, who was far older than I, was still waiting, too. But no gentlemen came, not even the one with whom Jeanetta had an understanding. They all went away... they went to war."

Effie paused, and when she spoke again her voice was lower and softer.

"One Sunday, the summer before my brothers rode off with the cavalry, while everyone but me was at dinner, I planned a surprise for my big brothers. I would lure them back to the big house and make them boys again. I gathered a clothesline cord and fishing line and ropes and yarn and colored string. Up in the attic, I tied all the different pieces together and fixed one end to a beam. Then I uncoiled my great length of twine, winding all through the house, down hallways and stairways, in and out the summer parlor and balcony, under beds, around sofas and chairs, out the front door. On the steps, I weighted down the end of the rope with a brick and attached a note for my brothers. 'Follow the twine. Find the treasure.' Then I waited and waited in that stuffy attic most of the afternoon, wondering if they'd ever find my note and come on. Finally, I climbed out a window onto the roof and lay slantwise on the shingles to feel the evening breeze. And then I heard it, the clomp of their boots running through the house.

"Oh, what a ruckus! They were shouting my name, laughing their deep barrel laughs, turning over furniture, crashing through the rooms, and thundering up and up the stairs. Aunt Mina was hollering at them to get outside, and Jeanetta was shrieking. But they made it to the attic, all three of them.

"They claimed the treasure: a basket of ripe peaches, a jug of cider, and a beautiful deck of gilt-edged playing cards that one of our house guests had forgotten and left behind months ago. They devoured the fruit, peach juice running down their chins and over their shirt fronts. Charles Edmund was in such a swivet to eat the most, he chipped a tooth on a peach pit. Oh, when I hugged my brothers to me, they smelled like an orchard in August. And when I kissed them, their whiskers were sticky and sweet.

"That was when we had plenty. Later on, there was so little of anything to go round. Things were sold off. Maybe some things were buried, and then unearthed by who knows who. Things were requisitioned. Stolen. Other girls' brothers stormed through houses, breaking furniture, searching for treasure."

Effie said no more, and soon the steady rhythm of her breathing convinced me she had fallen asleep. I turned toward her. By moonlight, I could see the outline of her lying on her side, the downward slope from her shoulder to her waist, the rising curve of her hip, her dark skirt tapering toward her feet and spreading over the quilt. I closed my eyes, knowing her cheek rested against my folded jacket.

# Chapter 18

Though I had slept most of the night as deeply as an opium slave, my last hour of rest was marked by fitful dreaminess, and I was awakened by the feeling of being watched. Sure enough, I was. Effie sat upon her quilt, hugging her knees and staring at me. I asked her if she had slept well. She shrugged and turned her gaze to the spot where I had staked the mule. The animal and the wagon were gone.

I pulled on my boots and scrambled out from under the mosquito netting. An unobscured view of the scene changed nothing. Mule and wagon were still gone. The mule's water bucket lay on its side, the spilt contents having soaked the ground. And in that muddy patch I saw the mule's churned hoof prints, a dog's pawprints, and a single boot print accompanied by a round hole about the circumference of a peg leg I'd seen the day before. It crossed my mind that the man of whom I'd asked directions had sent us off to get lost, the easier for him to rob us in the night.

There was little we could do, except go on with what we had left. I was charged with delivering Effie to New Orleans. Later I could write to Kingston and explain the loss of his property if I decided not to return to the asylum myself. Not going back seemed more and more possible with each mile I had traveled away. What lasting good had I done anyone there, save Mrs. Glover, whom I had let go? My interference had done nothing for Oralia and Wheeler, nor would my posturing after the fact of their deaths. A war had been fought, killing thousands, ravaging an economic way of life, but changing little more than the surface of the social hierarchy. I knew well enough who cared that a pair of former slaves had been killed, and I knew who did not. The thought appealed to me of walking on in a line, not in a circle.

I made a breakfast of chicory coffee and fried corn cakes, just enough to get us started for the day. Then I set to work gathering the belongings removed from the wagon the night before. There was my black bag and satchel, Effie's two carpetbags, and the wooden food box, an awkward thing to carry any distance. I bunched the quilts and as much of the mosquito netting as I could into one carpetbag, stuffing it in with Effie's few clothes. The other bag I filled with our cooking supplies and little remaining food and left the wooden box empty.

Effie took no interest in my preparations, going down to the bayou to wash and ambling back, while I was still at work. She had unbraided her hair, the corrugated pattern of the braiding still running the length of it to her waist, and had tied it back at the nape of her neck with a supple twisted pendent twig of black willow. I knew the tree; its fine-grained wood was sought after by makers of artificial legs.

The one piece of netting I had discarded for lack of space in the carpetbags, Effie gathered up, draping it over her skirt, winding it at her waist, tossing a length of it over one shoulder, and still the excess trailed on the ground behind her.

We set off then, she carrying my light-weight satchel and I insisting on carrying the other three bags. After having consulted Kingston's written instructions once more and the position of the sun, I felt some small confidence that we were headed in the right direction.

I attempted conversation, taking a chance on mentioning that I had enjoyed Effie's reminiscences and hoped to hear more. She paid me little or no mind, just toyed with a loose string in her netting overshirt and kept walking. We continued that way for hours, trudging in silence.

By midday my confidence flagged. I had expected we would soon be winding our way along another bayou, not still cutting across sun-dried fields and through stands of trees and underbrush. By late afternoon the fever was creeping up on me, and when Effie took my black bag from me to add to her own burden, I made little protest. The quinine I had taken earlier, when we had paused for a meal of leftover corn cakes, had brought me scant relief. In fact, all the past year I had been troubled and frustrated by the medicine's decreasing effectiveness on my symptoms. How was I to fulfill my duty to Effie, I wondered, if I were lost and ill?

But there were times that afternoon when I hardly spared a thought for Effie or her welfare, times when I was conscious only of the clamminess that inched across my shoulders, the sweat of exertion competing with the sweat of fever to bring me down. Lady Phillida Ryder came briefly to my mind, as I had seen her pacing an upper room in the asylum. Would my illness, like hers, become that last, only companion? Would the ache in my bones become the ache in my heart that would stop its beating? Oh, some lived with malarial fever for years, for full lifetimes, but I doubted I would be one of those.

Then I paused, caught my breath, and truly thought of Effie, who might be near me for such a short while. The sun was too bright, the fever seared my eyes. I longed for nightfall, the healing dark, the coolness, the chance that Effie would speak to me again.

As the sun lowered, we started across a meadow of high, golden grass. I faltered and stubbed the toe of one boot against a firm mound hidden beneath the tall grass. Then the cleats of my other boot dug into the incline of a second ridge, and I realized the field had been plowed in rows before having been abandoned and overgrown with weeds. Effie passed me by. Advancing before me, she balanced from ridge to ridge, the bags she carried held at arm's length on either side of her, the trailing white, gauzy net skimming over the pale yellow sheen of the grass bent down by her steps. She reminded me of the girl on the tightrope I had seen at a circus so many years ago, when Lucinda and I were children.

The girl on the rope. I cannot cut her down.

At last the earth evened out, and the grass thinned away to reveal the remnant of a path. Effie flitted ahead of me, down that path toward a line of live oaks and disappeared. I called after her, but the familiar ringing had begun in my ears, deafening me to the sound I made of her name, and I couldn't know if I was shouting or whispering.

I dropped the carpetbags as if my arms could fall away with them and thereby rid me of the aching in my shoulders. I staggered backward until my spine slammed against a tree trunk, then let myself slide downward to sprawl among the roots.

Moments or hours later—I would never be sure—I came round to the bitter taste of quinine. Effie was tipping the bottle to my lips, forcing the liquid against my tongue as I spat it out again. I flailed my arms, I must have done, as if drowning, then perceived a sudden shattering sound, heard it clearly as I realized the ringing in my ears had ceased. I sat up, opened my eyes, saw nothing. It was night, cool darkness under the live oaks.

"Now you've done it, haven't you?"

Effie's voice was close, just behind me.

"What?" I asked, shaking my head in an attempt to clear it.

"You've thrown the bottle away, smashed it up against a tree."

"You ran ahead. Effie, where did you go? How long have you been gone?"

"Shhh. There's nothing we can do now. Lie back."

Uncertainly, I eased down to my elbows, then felt her hands cradle my head and bring it to rest on the lap of her skirt. The air moved and settled again as Effie pulled a length of netting over us. Then her fingertips brushed my forehead and closed the lids of my eyes.

"Rest now," she said. "There's nothing more we can do, not until morning."

"But where did you go? Where have you been?" Did I sound as petulant to her as I did to myself?

"Not far. I only ran ahead a little ways. I thought if I followed the path between the trees... Oh, I thought I was home."

"At Woodbine?"

"But I was mistaken."

Keeping my eyes shut, I shifted slightly, turning one cheek to the woolen fabric of her skirt. Effie spoke again, and in the dark, before I slept, she told me stories of the sun and moon.

"The parlor of our house was on the west side, you understand, and it turned golden in the late afternoon. Papa was King Midas. And when the sunlight angled through the row of long parlor windows, he would touch each thing in the room. The gilt-framed mirrors, the brocade-covered divans, the waxed parquet tiles, the embossed wallpaper, the glazed china bric-a-brac and porcelain figurines—everything Papa touched was made gold. I was dazzled by the riches surrounding me, even as I danced around the room, escaping Papa's touch. I was a summer bee, beating my wings inside a sun-drenched honeycomb.

"But at last, I would cease my spinning and come to stand still before King Midas and bow my head for his blessing. Touching my chin with his forefinger, he would lift my face and turn it just slightly until I looked toward the west sun at the window. Then I would shut my eyes against the glare and become a golden statue. Even so, I could feel the heat of the sun on my closed eyes and see shooting stars behind my eyelids.

"Then one evening, in the midst of our game, Papa was called away and left me standing there in the parlor. I stayed, unmoving, till past nightfall, waiting for him to come back and break the spell of his golden touch. Without opening my eyes, I knew the room had darkened. The shooting stars had faded away. The air cooled. I heard the others calling me, from somewhere in the house, calling me to supper. 'Effie Louise! Get yourself down here 'fore your supper's stone cold.' But I couldn't move. I was a golden statue. My big sister Jeanetta found me and shamed me for my foolishness."

Effie touched my forehead with the back of her hand. "You're cooling down, Dr. Mallory, little by little, despite this warm night. Walking in the heat of the day, I didn't think much of it, but now, well, we must be getting close to New Orleans, the air's so heavy. Don't you reckon?"

I murmured agreement, hoping she were right.

"At home, on summer nights, when upstairs I was too hot to sleep, I'd come down after midnight to the front hall. That hall was grand as a ballroom, with double cypress doors opening at one end to the front drive and at the other end to the back lawn and the lake view. The floor was Italian marble, frosty white and cold as ice. I'd crisscross it barefoot and open both sets of doors to let the breeze from over the lake run through the house and stir the front garden. And then I'd lie down on that smooth marble, in a pool of moonlight, and let its coolness chill me right through my muslin gown.

"Oh, but my brothers like to a' ruined that floor! In the spring, just before they left for the fighting, none of them could hold still. Parker got the idea first. He always had ideas. And those boys took to galloping their horses straight through the hall, from garden to lake and back again. Like a storm whipping through. Horses all lathered, blowing hot breath, hooves cutting and scarring that beautiful white marble floor."

# Chapter 19

We stayed another day where we were, I in hopes of recovering my health to travel again and Effie for reasons of her own. At night when she had spoken to me, she had made few references to our current predicament, offering instead glimpses of her past. By day, although she might nod or shrug in response to my words, she did not pantomime her thoughts. Effie simply did things.

At sunrise she led me to the high bank of a bayou I'd not known existed the day before, though it was not far from where we had spent the night. She spread a quilt for me and brought my black bag. There were no more bottles of quinine, I told her. I dared not begin taking laudanum for the aching. Laudanum was seductive, and the aching was always with me. Perhaps by the next day the fever would abate, and I would be stronger. If not, I'd walk with Effie as far as I could, then send her on. Surely we would come across a settlement, find someone who would help us.

Our food supply was as meager as my appetite. Effie served us the last of the cornmeal mixed with water and molasses—and a few spring midges that happened by. Dutifully, I ate my portion, even as it clung like paste to the roof of my mouth. Then she redeemed the meal by bringing me a tin cup of water, cool, flavored with crushed mint leaves.

What I remember of that morning, more than anything, was the sensation of drifting, lying back, listening to the droning of insects or the intermittent humming of old songs whenever Effie moved out of my sight. In my indolence, I recalled the old feeling I'd had during the war, that when I ceased to work, I ceased to exist.

Of that day I also remember Effie's relentless occupation. The laundry.

Turning on my side, looking through a haze of fever down the steep bank to the bayou below, I watched Effie at her work. She had found a gap in the growth of water lilies and leaned out from her perch on a cypress root to dangle a length of cotton netting into the slow, drifting current. That day she washed everything: the netting, the quilts, all the clothing we had worn. She took away the quilt I had been lying on and left me on the spring grass. She brought me my single change of clothes and a dampened wash cloth, retreated, and returned for my sweat-stained suit, her butternut dress now exchanged for one of indigo. Then down she went again among the cypress knees, where she continued her work, rubbing lye soap into each garment. She would scrub at a spot, hold it up to the sunlight to inspect it, and scrub it again. She rinsed and wrung out and spread every item over a bush or a low bough to dry. I wondered when Effie finished if she might simply start all over again.

As afternoon wore on, I slipped in and out of consciousness, shuddering with chills, then racked with fever. At intervals, I called for Effie, but she didn't come. I was desperate for water, my throat so dry that the sound of all my shouting might have been illusory. Still, she should have come because I wished her there. I turned my face toward the edge of the bank, expecting to see her climbing up, but saw instead, quite close to me, the tin cup. It rattled against my teeth as I drank down the hot, metallic water. Had it been cool and fresh when she had left it for me?

The laundry was all gathered up and gone. Effie was gone. I pulled myself up to standing, forced myself to walk, though for my first several steps the ground pitched under me like a raft over rapids. I staggered away from the bank and on among the trees, which gradually, eerily, evened themselves out into two long rows of live oaks, branches laden with resurrection fern arching over a broad red-earthen drive, weeds encroaching along its borders. Was I again on the grounds of Magdalene Asylum? Had Kingston capriciously fired all the hired help and let the place run down? Was I returning after some indeterminate absence of mind, not of body? And would the big house lie just ahead, Effie sitting on the top step of the veranda, braiding her hair?

The unkempt drive was a portent of the sight beyond. A gutted mansion lay ahead, crumbling chimneys, fallen columns, charred timbers. Yet in the softening light of evening, the ruin entranced me, for over every remaining supporting beam and up every vestige of wall, trumpet vine, honeysuckle, and wisteria twisted as through a labyrinthine trelliswork of ingenious design.

A quilt, still warm from the sun, was laid folded across my shoulders, and there was Effie at my side bringing me forward through the wide arch that had been a doorway and into a shadowy hall. A flock of doves ranged over the stone floor, an eddying mass startled by our arrival. The birds fluttered past us and upward in unison to branches entwined with the rafters. The beating of departing wings breathed like life exhaled, sighed like a soul escaping a body.

On the few remaining stairs that now curved toward empty space, carpet bags, satchel, and black bag had been placed, and below them was a well-stocked reed basket. Effie had somehow found provisions. I spoke my gratitude that she had come back, speculating on where she had gone, whom she had met, wishing night would fall and she would tell me everything.

We sat on the floor, the basket between us. It was filled with the sort of merchandise a sutler or a traveling patent medicine salesman might provide: waxed packages of crackers and raisins, a tin of hard butterscotch candies, a packet of salted jerky, canned milk and a brown glass medicine bottle with a smeared label that claimed some miraculous results as a "system renovator." Effie uncorked and handed me the bottle, which may have contained a little quinine but was mostly extract of boneset, a remedy equally vile tasting and some believed almost as potent against malaria. I drank a hearty dose. Then with my pocket knife I cut two slits in the top of the milk can and offered it to Effie, and we dined on the contents of the basket. All we lacked to finish off the meal was a sutler's bad whiskey and rum-soaked cigars, but I'd lost my taste for such delicacies. During the war cigar smoke had been a welcome distraction from the stench of decay, but later I could rarely get a whiff of one odor without remembering too clearly the other.

The moon shone between the rafters. Without lighting a candle, Effie spread out the quilts and drew the mosquito netting from a carpet bag. I lay on a quilt, turning my back to her, hoping she would speak.

"Effie, where did you go this afternoon? Whom did you meet? Did you find the money in my black bag? I wanted you to use it. Is there a town nearby, a store?" Were we near Thibodaux, I wondered, or had we passed it? I tried to think of other place names that might mean anything, or nothing, to Effie. Bayou Lafourche? Des Allemands?

My fever was lowering, my aches diminishing. I felt the stir of air as Effie shook out a length of the netting and settled it over me, up to my shoulders. She knelt down beside me. I wanted to hear her voice, listen to her answers if they would come. But suddenly, even more, I wanted to look at her, and selfishly wanted her to look at me, to read my face by moonlight and understand what I could never say to her—not in the dark, not with my back turned, never—and so burden her with the knowledge of my burden. But when I turned to her, she was bending over me, her shadow and not moonlight lay on my face. Effie's hair, washed that day perhaps when she had done with the laundry, hung loose over one shoulder shading her features, and for a moment fell across my cheek, fragrant, soothing as balm. She lifted the edge of the gauzy cotton net and covered my face.

Effie fell asleep quickly, wrapped in her own chrysalis, no doubt exhausted by her day's labor. And I regretted my impatience in turning to her, when she might have spoken had I given her more time. Orpheus, ascending from the Underworld, had turned too soon to look on Eurydice, and so lost her forever.

I lay awake for hours, having slept too much of the day, and listened to the nearby whine of thwarted mosquitoes and the distant scuttling, perhaps of raccoons, in the upper reaches of the ruined house.

At last feeling some relief from my malady, I was clearheaded enough to wonder why a patent medicine of questionable ingredients and quality had proved more effective for me than the quinine upon which I usually relied. Then I considered my source of quinine for the past year. Was the extract of poor quality, for the sake of economy? Was it haphazardly prepared? Diluted? Was Kingston providing me with inferior medicine, another example of his random carelessness or of his deliberate cruelty?

Sleep must have come to me, I have no other explanation for the sensations that followed. The waxing moon, like a bowl, turned in the sky and spilt light over the stone floor, a white marble floor. Netting and quilts blew away, vanished. Effie stood before me, her unbraided hair swept back by a breeze, the breeze that came from over Lake Pontchartrain and rippled her muslin gown and seemed to set her in motion, even before we began to dance. Someone was humming "Somebody's Darling." Not Effie, for the sound drifted toward us from another room as we skimmed over the tiles. She rested one hand in mine, the other lightly on my shoulder, and my other hand I pressed against the curve of the small of her back.

And I held on to her, held on as we spun, as she dissolved in my hands, as my cheek grew cold where it was pressed against the stone floor and my fingers stiffened as they dug into the chinks in the marble.

I became conscious of the sound of a voice, droning, unintelligible. Opening my eyes and drawing away the netting, I saw in the archway the shape of a man standing face to face with Effie. He was speaking to her. Moonlight delineated Effie as an indigo shadow against the door frame, but the man was prominent in a light-colored suit and hat with a flat crown. He was tall, bulky, and stood with his weight slung over to one leg, his head inclined toward Effie, the wide brim of his hat bearing down toward her.

His already muffled voice dropped to a murmur, and other sounds reached me from beyond where he stood, familiar sounds attributable to a horse or mule restless in its traces, the clinking of snaps and pole chains, the creaking of shafts, the animal's own whickering. Then the man's voice rose again. The words, at first sounding like gibberish, gradually began to signify. But what they signified remained for me beyond reason, that there was some intimate connection between this stranger and Effie. In his thick drawl, he was presuming that she was in some way obligated to him, holding forth the unbelievable notion that she had agreed to an assignation.

"We made a bargain," he said to her, laying his hands on her shoulders. "You know damn well how that works."

He closed the space between them.

I'd hardly risen from the floor before lunging at him. I grabbed his shoulders, tore him off her, slammed my fist against his jaw. That was my supreme effort, before he boxed my ears and sent me staggering back from him to a good striking distance for his pummeling of my belly with his fists. I doubled over, dropped, rolled to one side, but did not draw up my legs fast enough. The toe of his boot shot under my ribs and kicked the wind out of me. I was suffocating, drowning, strangling.

Through half-closed eyes, I saw the blurry outline of that boot, aiming for another kick, saw it well, for this time its target was my face. I had no strength to move. My body had deserted me, and only a vestige of consciousness remained. I watched the booted foot pull back, start forward, and suddenly drop and stomp down on the stone floor. The man staggered, regaining the balance lost in his swift change of direction. I sucked air into my throat, forcing it past the blood pooling in my mouth.

I squinted up at the man, whose hands were raised, palms open, fingers splayed. Slowly, he shook his head from side to side, staring above me, past me, and shuffled backward through the archway. I had been numb, but now I felt the hem of Effie's skirt brush my hands, which were clenched against my chest, as she stepped over me.

She swept forward to the archway through which the man had disappeared. I heard his voice again, this time raised in a curse. The snorting of a horse, the creaking and rattling of a wagon gave me hope the man was leaving us. I saw the outline of Effie, her back to me, arms raised above her head, hands clasped together around an object. While I had struggled with the man, she must have taken the army revolver from my black bag. Into the night sky she fired a solitary shot. The sound of it rang in my ears long after it should have died away.

When I had recovered my breath and pulled myself to my feet, I went to Effie, who leaned against the lintel, still gripping the revolver in her two hands now lowered to her waist. Night was fading, and I could see Effie's face, her eyes staring away down the empty drive.

I asked her if the man was the source of the food and medicine she had brought us. She didn't answer. How had she asked him for his goods? I wanted to know. How had she paid for them, or planned to pay? Had she struck a bargain with the man? Agreed to his terms? He said she had.

"Did you speak to him?" I demanded. "Speak to him face to face? The way you don't speak to me. What would you have done if I hadn't wakened when I did?"

Effie had saved my life twice over, and yet I heard myself railing at her like a jealous lover, for I had seen her, seen her standing motionless, unresisting as that man laid hands on her. The more ashamed I felt of my jealousy, the more I vented it, as if I could not destroy myself fast enough in her estimation.

When I finally shut my mouth, Effie turned her eyes toward me. She looked directly at me. And the expression on her face was just as I imagined mine had been when I had looked at my father in the old days, while he lectured me for roughhousing or making poor marks in school or wasting time. Effie held herself aloof, gave nothing away. She stared at me, but she was somewhere else.

I took the revolver from her, returned it to my black bag where I noted the packet of money remained unopened. I salved my cuts and bruises, drank a dose of boneset, straightened my clothes, and gathered our belongings.

Meanwhile, Effie had left me to make her own preparations for the day's journey. When she returned, her hair was center-parted, plaited, coiled and pinned at the nape of her neck with unprecedented severity. Every strand was locked in place, not one would be lifted by the breeze. And as if to make doubly sure, she placed her straw hat upon her smooth crown.

# Chapter 20

We followed a bayou, then the Mississippi, found a ferryman to take us across the water, and traveled on, arriving in New Orleans in the late afternoon. This day there was no danger of our becoming lost. My head was clear, and I was galvanized by a sense of duty and self-reproach. But even if I had faltered on the path, we would have reached our destination with equal certainty—inevitability—for all day we seemed to have been hurtling toward the city, only the weight of our baggage slowing our fall. Gulls circling in the sky, ibises perching in the cypress trees, blue herons standing in the shallows marked our descent toward the delta. The air itself submerged us and swept us down into the current of the *Vieux Carre.*

Briefly, I had sojourned there in pre-war days, before leaving for medical school, and glimpsed the Quarter's conspicuous opulence, built on a bustling river commerce and slave auctioning. I knew my way around New Orleans far better in post-war days, having lingered there for some time after my duties as an army surgeon came to an end, gathering my courage for the trip home. By then opulence had gone underground, and Federals imagined they controlled the city, whose convolutions were well-designed to keep its secrets.

Effie and I wandered through the market square. She couldn't have been much more than a child the last time she had visited the city. And for the past six years, her life had been the monotony and the seclusion of Magdalene Asylum. I watched Effie, tried to interpret the myriad emotions flickering in her eyes—wonder, curiosity, amusement, pity—as she took in her new surroundings. Heedless of me, she dropped her satchel, tossed aside her straw hat, and hurried forward among the stalls.

Effie skimmed over the uneven cobblestones as lightly as she might have glided over a marble floor and wound her way among carts of cabbages, lettuce, red peppers, and purple grapes, past fish stands displaying baskets of pearl-gray shrimp and silver mackerel. At a stall offering caged finches and canaries and parrots chained to their perches, Effie stroked the big birds' feathers and offered the little ones her fingers to peck at through the bars.

Sounds everywhere competed for Effie's attention, and she tilted her head first one way, then another. Around her, wagon wheels creaked and hooves clattered. Peddlers and merchants shouted the virtues of their wares and haggled with customers in a confusion of French, English, Spanish, African and Caribbean patois.

I lost sight of Effie in the crowd, for I could hardly keep up carrying our four bags. Stopping and turning where I was, I scanned groupings of customers, mostly women of every age and complexion, baskets over their arms, gathered around each stall and wagon. Then I saw that Effie had moved apart from them and stood on the banquette, not far from where a legless man in a gray forage cap slouched against the wall of a shop. He was playing a quick, lively tune on a harmonica, and an old Negro accompanied him on a fiddle. But when the pair of them saw Effie, they nodded to one another and slowed their tune to something sentimental.

Effie shut her eyes, stood still, poised as a statue in a patch of afternoon sunlight, and the shadow of a wrought iron balcony railing fell over her skirt like a mantle of lace.

Though the market was hardly the vast confusion it had been before Federal occupation, and many citizens were not so finely dressed or grandly conveyed about the town, one thing had changed little in New Orleans—the way it smelled. Sewage running in an open drain, refuse moldering in an alleyway, fish and potatoes and onions frying, peppery soup boiling, breads and cakes baking in a row of boarding house kitchens, perfume wafting from a flower seller's baskets or from the warm hollow of a woman's throat. New Orleans was always a concoction of the unsavory and the delectable, and as I inhaled the city, I realized how much I had missed it. One could be anyone there and not be out of place.

I didn't know if Effie was still angry with me, of if she had ever been more than indifferent to me and occasionally kind because that was her habit, her nature. Even so, I was loath to part with her. After buying quinine for myself and fruit and bread for us both, I walked with her to Jackson Square, where she fed the pigeons nearly as much bread as we ourselves ate. The evening sky clouded over, threatened rain, and it was time for me to complete my duty.

"I would be most grateful, Miss Rampling, if you would write to me now and again. I want to know that you're all right, that you're well."

Then I wondered if the man who had prohibited her speaking had forbidden her writing, too. Perhaps that was why at the asylum she had refused my offer of pencil and paper. Or she might have been obeying Kingston's orders, for he had certainly discouraged any of the patients from keeping diaries or sending letters home. At least this time Effie did not obviously reject my suggestion.

We left the park, walking up St. Ann's and along Royal Street, past the shops of carpenters, candle makers, confectioners and dressmakers until we found a stationer, who was fastening his shutters, preparing to close shop for the day. But he allowed me to purchase a thin sheaf of paper, pen, and ink, which I gave to Effie.

I also wrote down for her my mother's address in Baton Rouge, saying Effie might prefer to write to me there, in care of Mrs. Mallory. Before returning to Magdalene Asylum, if I returned, I planned to call on my mother and attempt to explain the arrangement to her then.

The boarding house where Effie was to be employed had not always provided a roof for unattached businessmen and rootless travelers. It had been a private residence before the war, like others along the same banquette, whose changes in status were announced on painted placards hanging from balconies: Furnished rooms for rent.

And like the other houses, this one was fronted by a high gate that sealed the passage to its hidden courtyard, a space enclosed by walls, higher still, of brick and peeling plaster and tenacious vines. The lady of the house, now the landlady, Mrs. Fabre admitted Effie and me.

"I expected you days ago, Dr. Mallory. Delayed, were you?" Mrs. Fabre took the envelope from Kingston that I offered her, hardly glancing at it. But arching her blackened brows, she cast an appraising look at Effie. "Not much to her. Work hard, does she?"

Mrs. Fabre was tall and gaunt of face, not so well-fed as Matron. But her manner impressed me as hardly more charming than Lila Fentroy's, and I wondered at Kingston's affinity for such women. I also speculated that Mrs. Fabre's heavily looped and twisted black hair was of something other than human origin. A piece of miscalculated vanity, perhaps, but then I suppose most of us have affected some form of deception in appearance or in character.

"Well, I promised Douglas," said Mrs. Fabre. "I suppose I must take her. This way."

Rustling before us in lavender taffeta, a ring of keys jangling at her waist, she led us through the narrow flagstone passageway to an interior jungle of hanging wisteria and potted palms and banana trees, their leaves fanning out, catching the last of evening's light that filtered from above, turning it dusky green and faded purple. Night had already come to the courtyard.

Across the way a fountain trickled, nothing more than a small, dark circle of water surrounded by blanched figurines, the chipped remains of angelic statuary. Past the fountain, on a wrought iron table, a lamp burned low, and near it a man in a pale linen suit squinted at a newspaper. Behind him a narrow flight of stairs rose and connected the three stories of the house, the upper floors each with their own landing and railed gallery extending around three sides and overlooking the courtyard.

Mrs. Fabre sent Effie ahead, instructing her to take her bags, go to the top of the stairs, and wait. The man's proximity to the stairway necessitated Effie's passing quite close to him. His newspaper made a crumpling sound as he lowered it to squint at her as she went by and started up the stairs. I was torn between watching her go, not knowing if I would see her again, speak to her again, and watching that man staring after her.

"May I speak to you in private?" I asked Mrs. Fabre.

"I suppose." She led me through a pair of French doors into a parlor, occupied by other gentleman boarders, and then on to her small office.

"Want a room for the night?" she asked. "The best I can do is put you in with one of the regulars."

"All right. But that isn't why—"

"Douglas said the girl doesn't speak. That true? Not a single word? Of course I haven't taken her in to make conversation."

I was perplexed. "Mrs. Fabre, how long ago did Dr. Kingston arrange to send Miss Rampling here?"

"A few weeks, maybe a month."

On the occasion of Kingston's telling me of my father's death and of asking me to escort Effie to New Orleans, he had intimated that the change in her situation was recent news to him. Now I realized he had, in fact, saved it up, perhaps saved my mother's news as well, to use when it suited him, when he wished to have me gone. And if filial duty would not move me, Kingston gauged rightly that my fondness for Effie would.

"Is that all you wanted to know? I hope you're not expecting supper."

"No, ma'am. I wanted to tell you something about Effie Rampling."

"Well?"

"She's very young. A woman in years, maybe, but I want you to understand that she is a stranger to the world. She grew up on her family's plantation and has spent the last six years at the asylum."

"But she's nobody's darling now, Dr. Mallory, and nobody's patient, either. Oh, I'll look after her. I look after all the servants. But don't expect me to puddle up over her reduced circumstances. I've seen more than my own share of changes."

In a corner of the cluttered room I was to share for the night with not one boarder but three, I made myself presentable for the evening. Afterwards, stepping out on the second floor gallery, pacing the length of it several times, I hoped to see Effie again and at last met her as she came up the stairs with an armload of bed linen. Passing me by without a glance, she entered the room I had vacated, leaving the door open behind her. From the doorway I watched her make up the cot on which I was to sleep.

Effie unfurled a sheet. It billowed and settled over the mattress tic. She smoothed the cotton cloth, and I noted and memorized each place touched by her hands. How could this be enough? Could I never ask for anything more? Was she my patient, or wasn't she? Had that relationship ended, as

Mrs. Fabre so bluntly stated it had? No, I didn't believe so. Money changing hands, or not changing hands, was not the measure of my duty. Still, even if it was madness that kept Effie silent, there were times such as this one when I would willingly have entered the silence with her.

As she crossed the threshold onto the gallery, I caught at her sleeve.

"Effie."

She looked up, but not at me, and heaved a sigh that I took for impatience, for at that same moment she pulled her arm free and hurried for the upper staircase. I was no different from a man who would send her to an asylum, or a man who would cast her out of one, or a man who would abandon her. Why should she look at me, listen to me, speak to me? I was no one.

# Chapter 21

That night I returned by a long, narrow lane to a tall, narrow house that I had visited years ago, not exactly an old haunt of mine, but entered more than once, though never before in so sober a state of mind. Perhaps my clear head allowed me to see for the first time the establishment's architectural peculiarities. In the courtyard of pitted flagstones, behind the high gate, labyrinthine staircases spiraled and interconnected rooms and galleries at various levels though none were level to a plane. The balustrades and railings were bowed and rickety, the stairs dangerously uneven. Upper floors were warped and tilted. Not a painting nor a gilt-framed mirror hung straight. It seemed as if the house had been designed and built by the drunken revelers who filled it.

Entering a lushly carpeted drawing room, I recalled an image in the convex mirror of the asylum parlor, though the colors of the women's gowns—mauve, pale blue, primrose—had darkened now to purple, midnight blue, blood red. And the cut of the silks and velvets exposed more than white shoulders. Rouged and scented, the women swirled, not around one aloof man, but among many desirous ones, who leered and fondled and panted after them to private rooms. We excuse our use of such women, saying we merely pay for services that they willingly provide. A convex mirror would be unnecessary in this house, its distortion superfluous.

The proprietress approached me with the same speculative look she had given me years ago. What were my tastes, and what would I pay to indulge them? And years ago I had paid for a girl with a sweet face, though her manner was already well practiced.

"It's all the same," the girl had said, shrugging out of her dressing gown. "Every day of my life before I came here my father told me what to do and how to do it. When I left him, I fooled myself that I was getting away from all that. But look at me now. Every day Madame tells me what to do, how to do it, and what to charge for it."

She had laughed then, good-naturedly, and gently made light of my efforts to please her as well as myself.

"I don't know what you're doing here, sir, a man like you. Why, you could make somebody fall in love with you and give it away."

Her remark had come easily, as if she might have said it more than once in a night. Still, she smiled when I replied, "Make somebody fall in love? I'd say that's more likely true of you than of me."

"Well, here's your chance."

Tonight I told the proprietress my taste was for a girl who wouldn't make conversation, and I paid for her company with part of the salary Kingston had paid me.

The girl who joined me in a private room seemed comfortable enough with our mutual silence. She was cold-eyed, not sweet-faced, yet she was beautiful. She saw the purple bruising over my ribs, from the battering my body had endured the night before, but expressed neither curiosity nor revulsion. She offered no flattery and no tricks of the trade, only her beauty, which was enough.

For what we were about to do, it was not necessary that I kiss her. Still, I wanted to. I kissed her shoulders and her throat, but not her quiet mouth. For a moment I rested my cheek against the curve of her neck. She was tolerant and allowed me my pretense that there existed some affection between us. As for the other, well, having seen a few soldiers crippled with syphilis, I took the precaution of a sheath. I suppose the girl was relieved that I did not belabor my performance. But when I was finished, she went so far as to lace her fingers through my hair, a gesture I had not expected and for which I felt grateful.

I left the house knowing I had performed more nearly an act of isolation than of intimacy. Even so, sleep on the boarding house cot came a little more easily than it might have otherwise. And I dreamed—candles burning, a lace fan and a pattern of lace laid across a lady's cheek, a gentleman holding up a crystal flute of champagne and offering a toast, murmuring something about a bank of violets.

At the river's edge, that was where I had found the remains of Rachel Poncet, and I had descended the muddy bank to retrieve her body.

Rachel had come to Magdalene Asylum from New Orleans. I leafed through my sickbed journal, in which I had jotted down various bits of information purloined from Kingston's files, and noted her husband's address. I decided to call on him that morning, to offer my belated condolences, before leaving the city.

Arriving early enough to find Mr. Poncet still at breakfast, I was shown to the dining room by a maid servant. Mr. Poncet, like his house in the Garden District, breathed old money and sighed with recent petty economies. I was served a poor substitute for coffee in a Limoge cup and offered a seat on a rosewood chair with a brocade cushion patched with burlap.

"Dr. Mallory of the Magdalene Asylum." Mr. Poncet repeated the information I had given as introduction. Peering at me over the tops of his spectacles, he appeared eager, almost hopeful, as he asked a strange question. "Am I to understand my wife is much improved, sir? Please tell me that Rachel may come home."

"I beg your pardon, sir."

"Surely that's what you've come about. You don't dare tell me Dr. Kingston is increasing his fees again. And I've never been remiss in my payments."

"Oh, Good Lord, sir. Have you not received Kingston's letter regarding your wife?"

"I have received many letters from him about my wife. She worsens, she improves, she worsens again, she improves again, but she never comes home. How much longer must this go on?"

"Mr. Poncet, don't you know that your wife has passed away?"

A look of horrified disbelief froze on the man's face, his eyes fixed wide, his mouth agape.

"I am in town on business and came here today to offer you my condolences, belated as they are."

The chair legs scraped the floor as Mr. Poncet pushed himself away from the table. He rose, shuffled across the room to a curio shelf, took up a silver-framed daguerreotype, brought the picture to me, all as if he were in a trance. Had the madness run both ways? I wondered. Had he denied his wife's death long past the first moments of grieving?

"Is this the woman you tell me is dead?"

I saw in the frame the image of a lady of aristocratic bearing, with strong features and abundant fair hair.

"I never saw Mrs. Poncet in life, sir. But Dr. Kingston himself verified her death a year ago. I'm very sorry for your loss."

"My loss! My wife!" His mouth trembled, and he caught the picture to his breast. I led him back to his chair, where he sank and swayed, rocking the silver frame.

"If this is a lie, young man," he whispered, "oh, beware, if this is a lie."

"Sir, it is not a lie. Your wife died more than a year ago. She met with an accident by the river. Apparently she had wandered away, and before anyone knew it, she had fallen in the water and drowned. I found her body. And I know that she had beautiful yellow hair."

"My God! Was that all about her that was recognizable? Why, before melancholia took her, Rachel was perfection."

"Another patient told me that your wife had been a very lovely lady."

I didn't know what else to say that would be of any comfort, or of any use. But when Mr. Poncet spoke again, he voiced a thought that was forming in my mind as well.

"I have been swindled, Dr. Mallory. Were you aware of this? But how could you have been, coming here and offering me condolences? I have paid—and paid—Dr. Kingston. For years I have paid and continue to pay. He has written nothing to me of her death. He wrote me a month ago as if she were alive, as if there was hope. I have the very letter still on my desk. But you were not aware."

"I am now, sir."

Voices echoed in my mind, Gaston's as well as Kingston's. "I never seen one of them leave here…" "Without my permission, no one leaves Magdalene Asylum."

If Kingston would enrich himself by lying to Mr. Poncet, would he not lie to Hannah's family and Phillida Ryder's British lord and Veronique Beaulieu's young husband? Kingston need only take care that he did not pretend a patient lived beyond excessive old age.

All those files, all those names of patients I had never met. All those fees collected and spent. All those graves.

When I left Mr. Poncet, he was drafting a letter to his lawyer.

# Chapter 22

I returned to Mrs. Fabre's boarding house to collect my luggage, and Effie. I did not know what sort of bargain had been struck between the landlady and my employer, but I'd had little faith from the outset that it had been made with Effie's best interests at heart. Now I had none. Dr. Kingston was a confidence trickster. He was no better than a blackmailer, preying on families ashamed of mad wives, mothers, and daughters. He charged exorbitant fees to keep dead women in his graveyard. I owed him nothing. Effie owed him nothing. And I would not allow her to be sold away as a laundress, or worse.

No one sat in the courtyard. Through the French doors I glimpsed Mrs. Fabre in the parlor, moving among her guests, offering them refreshments and smiles of cordiality that she had not offered me.

I headed straight to the back of the house, through the kitchen, passed the startled cook, and entered the alley. There the air was heavy with steamy wash water and greasy soap, thick with alleyway effluvium of rotting garbage and raw sewage. Over the cauldron, through the cloud of steam, I saw the turbaned head, broad, black face, and bulky arms of a washer woman, wringing out a shirt with a force that could snap a neck. She no more than shrugged when I asked for Effie. I asked again, and she briefly, grudgingly lifted her chin and glanced toward the upper reaches of the house, before resuming her throttling of the boarders' clothes.

I returned to the courtyard and looked up to see Effie leaning over the third floor gallery railing, pinning a nightshirt to a clothesline. The line ran around on a pulley system, attaching to the gallery eaves and across the way to the far wall, where a hook was embedded in the mortar. As Effie tugged on the line, sending the nightshirt on its way, a few droplets the woman in the alley had not squeezed from the garment fell on my face.

"You still here?" Mrs. Fabre called to me from the open doorway of the parlor.

"Just came back for my bags, ma'am. I'll be gone in a minute."

I started up the stairs. Effie was leaning out above me, stretching to attach a clothespin to the line. I reached the first gallery, the second story. She was trying to hang out a blanket, but hadn't lapped it over the cord far enough, and the weight of the damp wool caused it to slip from the pins. Effie climbed up and stood on the railing, one hand grasping the clothesline, the other snatching at the blanket, reaching for it, leaning far out over the courtyard. I began to run up the stairs. And as I ran, from the corner of my eye I saw a shape tumble from above, though I did not hear a scream. Not then.

An instant passed, and I heard a crashing of something falling through the branches of palms and banana trees. Mrs. Fabre began the screaming. I kept running, as if I could outrun gravity, to reach the second gallery, the third story, and still catch Effie in mid-flight.

But Effie was crumpled in a heap, though not on the flagstones. She had fallen on the gallery side and now hugged her knees, bowed her head, and shuddered against the rail. Even so, I caught her in my arms and held her, while Mrs. Fabre bellowed about a dropped blanket that would have to be washed again and about broken palm fronds and a shattered terra cotta pot.

When Effie's breathing had steadied and her shuddering had ceased, I raised her to her feet. "Get your things together," I told her. "Then go to the gate and wait for me. You won't be staying here after all."

Taking my own bags down with me, I faced Mrs. Fabre in the courtyard.

I would have thought the incident would make it easier for her to part with Effie, but the woman opposed me.

"The girl stays. She can work off the damages." Mrs. Fabre had snatched back the veil of reserve, momentarily discarded during her outcry over the pottery shards.

"Miss Rampling will go with me."

"Your employer gave her to me."

"She wasn't his to give."

"Yours then? You were quick enough to leave her here yesterday."

A few boarders entered the discussion. Clustering in the parlor doorway, they shouted at me to be gone, accusing me of disturbing their peace. But they made no move to enforce their words or to prevent me from taking Effie with me.

Mrs. Fabre followed me to the gate, threatening me under her breath with notifying Kingston posthaste of my insolence, but she did not bar my way. Only for an instant, I saw her hands stretch forward, toward Effie, then pull back and knot themselves together. If she had not had an audience of boarders, perhaps Mrs. Fabre might have done more to prevent our going. At that moment I was grateful for whatever pretense of decorum restrained her.

Outside, on the banquette, Effie and I took up our bags and started off. She came with me willingly, nearly matching my rapid pace. Before I could think of what to do next, I simply wanted some distance between ourselves and the boarding house. And I used the luggage I carried to cut us a path as we were jostled among pedestrians, horses, wagons, and carriages. Effie in her wrinkled butternut dress, no hat nor shawl, and I in my threadbare suit, once black, now faded to charcoal, were a pair, though no more disreputable looking than many others we passed.

When I spotted a cafe, we stopped for a meal of gumbo and salad. I had little money left and spent too much of it, finishing our midday dinner with café au lait and a caramel custard for Effie. I felt reckless. For the space of half an hour, I sat opposite Effie at a corner table, and we shared a meal together. Yes, I believe she savored it as much as I. And I talked too much, telling her that I had called on Mr. Poncet and discovered how Dr. Kingston had deceived him, telling her that we could not trust in the arrangement Kingston had made for her at the boarding house and must find another way to provide for her future.

Effie set down her coffee cup and looked at me.

"We have only Kingston's word that your family is unable to take you back." I rummaged in my black bag, found my notebook, and thumbed the pages. "Here it is. I have an address for your sister and brother-in-law. We can go to them."

Effie's eyes narrowed with doubt, suspicion, I wasn't sure.

"We can at least try," I added. "They might direct us to your brothers or your mother's family. Someone."

Effie reached across the table and touched my forehead with her fingertips, a gesture that took me by surprise. I fell silent a moment. Was the look in her eyes concern? I took a breath, began again. "I will make certain there is someone to take care of you, a safe place for you to go. I'll think of something, I promise you."

She withdrew her hand, opened my black bag herself, and extracted the new bottle of quinine. I started to protest that I had no need of the medicine. Then I touched my own brow, the cold sweat that beaded there. Effie had recognized the onset of my illness before I had sensed it myself, and I took the remedy she offered.

Walking more slowly now than when we had set out from Mrs. Fabre's, we headed for the Garden District, which I had already visited once that day. Along St. Charles Avenue we asked directions of a fruit peddler, who pointed us to a quiet side street. There we found the address I had noted from Kingston's files and faced a white clapboard house, not as fine to begin with as Mr. Poncet's, but better kept.

"Have you been here before?" I asked Effie.

She indicated not with a shake of her head.

A young mulatta servant would not admit us to the house. Although I gave my name and Effie's, the girl insisted we wait on the porch, saying she'd hear what Mrs. Howard had to say, and shut the door behind her.

Jeanetta Rampling Howard had little to say at first, at least to Effie and me. But she did allow us into the front hallway, ushered us in, in fact, casting a quick glance past us to the street, perhaps anxious that her disheveled callers not be seen by the neighbors. Then she dispatched her servant to find the yard boy and send him to the Cotton Exchange to fetch Major Howard home at once. "And when you've done that," she called after the girl, "get yourself upstairs and stay with the children. Don't let them come down, you hear?"

When the maid was gone, Mrs. Howard still offered no greeting to Effie, expressed no concern for her. Far taller than Effie, her height made it easy enough for the older sister to affect an attitude that the young sister was beneath her notice.

She turned to me and spoke under her breath. "Dr. Mallory, this is not the agreed upon arrangement."

"I know, ma'am. But circumstances have changed."

I glanced at Effie, who stood no more than an arm's length from me and from Jeanetta Howard, but she could have been anywhere. While Jeanetta avoided directly addressing Effie, Effie behaved as if Jeanetta and I had become completely invisible. I recalled the expression that had come over her when I had vented my jealousy: removed, irretrievable.

It was a mistake bringing Effie to her sister's house. I knew it in that moment, but could not turn back. There was a rift in her family as surely as there was one in my own. Perhaps the Ramplings' estrangement had begun by a misunderstanding. Surely not by some sinful action. Then one or another's explanations went unheard or were ignored. Family members argued and pleaded at cross purposes. And at last, the silence fell, proud and unforgiving. But, no. I was confusing families.

Effie had not protested coming to her sister's house with me, but then I'd never seen her protest anything. What in the world did she want? What on earth could I do for her?

She stared past me, and I turned and followed her line of vision through an open double doorway into the drawing room. There, the broad leaves of potted palms by a bay window filtered the afternoon sunlight. But even without them, I thought, the room would always be dark, for it was crowded with heavy pieces of fine furniture—cabinets, desks, armchairs, card tables, glass-fronted bookshelves—all designed for a house constructed on a far grander scale than the one that now contained them, a plantation mansion. Woodbine, I supposed.

Jeanetta waved Effie away to a stool by the hat stand and admonished her to "stay put." Then she summoned me to the over-furnished drawing room. Passing through the doorway, I noticed a leather-bound and embossed copy of *Pardue's Illustrated Mythology*, my childhood favorite, lay atop a pedestal bookstand. And I wondered if the Howards had acquired it since the war, or if it had once belonged in Mr. Rampling's library, and there had once fascinated Effie.

"What do you mean by bringing her here? Major Howard made his wishes quite clear to Dr. Kingston. We are not to be bothered." Her tone was hushed, as if she did not want her voice to carry to the hall, but neither did she want to close the doors and closet herself with a stranger. "My husband will be here soon, and then you'll have some explaining to do, sir."

"Mrs. Howard, I apologize for causing you distress. For reasons I will explain to you and your husband, the arrangement at Mrs. Fabre's boarding house has proved unsuitable. Even if you are unable to take in Miss Rampling yourself, I hope that you can guide me to another relative, perhaps someone from her mother's side, who can help her."

"From her mother's side!" This time Jeanetta was heedless of Effie's overhearing. "Don't you know anything? Those people were all Creoles. They disowned Miss Euphemia Louise when she married my father. And if any of them had survived the war, they wouldn't be likely to take on Effie."

Jeanetta continued on a theme of the social and political animosities between Creoles and Anglos, a bitter choice of topic for drawing room conversation. But it was a safer choice, perhaps to her, than what she had chosen not to say. As she spoke, she stood very straight, the muted light at the bay window behind her. Her hands were clasped over the crisp ruffles of her skirt. The metallic sheen of the fabric, the dark russet color of it, the taut, unyielding line of the bodice gave me an impression that she was not merely dressed in the restrictive clothing of a lady, but encased. How could she breathe? And yet she must, for she rattled on, snipping her words between tightly controlled lips, keeping her eyes fixed on me, immovable as the narrow ridges of copper-brown curls that bore down on her brow and appeared pasted onto her forehead. Property, I thought. Her hatred of Effie had something to with property—possessions and jealousy and something more I had yet to understand.

Whether Jeanetta could hear it in her own voice or not, a more personal story flowed in the undercurrent of her words. I pictured a young woman, perhaps only appealing by virtue of her youth, whose claims on the attention of her widower father were usurped first by a beautiful new wife, then by a new daughter. The young woman, Jeanetta Rampling, watched her little half sister become the petted daring of father and three brothers. But Jeanetta was consoled by her fiancé. She anticipated a wedding day, one that was suddenly canceled by war. Then years of waiting and uncertainty followed, years locked away at Woodbine in the company of a girl she resented and, at last, despised.

But why? Jeanetta now had the husband she had waited for, the children, the servants, the house, the family heirlooms, while her half sister had none of these things.

Major Elijah Howard arrived, by cab I judged from his promptness. Though a businessman, he had kept his title of rank and a military bearing, which provided a ready explanation for what he had lost, his left ear and two fingers of his left hand. I could imagine the moment when he had raised the fingers to the side of his head, perhaps to adjust his cap or brush away a mosquito, and suddenly a minié ball had torn a path betwixt hand and face. The thick wheel of a scar marked the left side of his head, which was devoid of hair. He wore a mustache, but no sidewhiskers on the right where he might have grown them, and his graying hair was clipped short as if he had chosen to maintain what symmetry of feature he could, despite his maiming injury.

Howard, unlike his wife, made a dash through the ritual of greetings. Then he offered me a seat and made himself comfortable in an armchair, taking with him a glass of whiskey. Jeanetta did not exactly sit with us, but she joined us, more or less angling herself along a settee and proving the rigidity of her garments.

"What's all this about?" Howard addressed the question to me, although his wife answered it, leaning in toward his right side, his existing ear.

"This man has gone against Dr. Kingston's instructions and against our wishes. He won't leave Effie at the boarding house."

"And why not?"

To this question Jeanetta allowed me a chance to reply. But I found myself hesitant to speak of Kingston's deceptive business practices. The Howards might counter that those practices had nothing to do with their situation, their desire to be rid of responsibility for Effie. Besides, though Kingston may have overcharged Mr. Rampling in the past, he was no longer receiving payments. Though earlier I had spoken precipitously of Kingston's confidence game, I checked myself now. I had no right to offer the Howards details of other patients' cases and their families' circumstances. Nor did I yet wish to risk slandering my employer, until I had accumulated more evidence of my suspicions. How many times had Kingston already exonerated himself to his own and others' satisfaction, if not to mine?

To the Howards I chose to emphasize the unsuitability of the boarding house as a refuge for Effie. "Mrs. Fabre caters to a bachelor clientele," I said. "And the heavy work demanded, the harsh living arrangements... Miss Effie's upbringing and her years of seclusion have not prepared her to take such a position. Surely your sister should have a guardian, Mrs. Howard, not a taskmistress. Didn't your father make any other provision for her in the event of his death?"

"My father is not dead, sir, except perhaps to reason."

"Oh. I see. And you, Major Howard, now act on his behalf?"

"That I do, sir. And I don't see you having any right to meddle. Kingston assured us the girl's interested in nothing but laundry. An obsession, if you will. But if that's her particular madness, let it pay her way in the world. If her mania had been prayer, I'd have sent her to a convent."

Jeanetta spoke up. "Father used up everything, every cent he had saved and hidden and hoarded after the war. He spent it all on Effie, keeping her in style at that private asylum. There's nothing left, nothing for us, nothing for his grandchildren. Not a blessed thing!"

My glance flickered over the lavish furnishings, the clutter of porcelains, the gold clock on the mantel.

"And now that addled old man is on my hands, too. My husband and I support him. But not her. No, sir. She's an ablebodied girl, and she can work for her living."

"What of her brothers, Mrs. Howard?"

"My brothers, her half brothers."

"Would any of them be able to help her?"

"Hardly. Charles Edmund and Parker are dead—Charles Edmund at First Manassas and brother Parker at Natchez-under-the-hill."

"And your youngest brother?"

Jeanetta turned to her husband. "The man's asking what happened to Bliss."

"Wouldn't we all like to know the answer to that?" said Howard. "The boy was wounded at least twice. Lost most of an arm and all of his memory. Didn't know any of us when he was brought home. Then he took up with some woman. We're guessing they went to Texas."

"We haven't seen Bliss or our silver candlesticks since," said Jeanetta.

I was finding Major and Mrs. Howard no more suitable than Mrs. Fabre as possible custodians of Effie's welfare, but I wanted more information from them.

"Miss Effie doesn't speak. I understand Mr. Rampling asked her to say no more about—what? And why?"

"Oh, that nonsense!" Jeanetta patted at her pomaded curls, as if her brief outburst could possibly have disturbed their arrangement.

"You mean to say the child's still silent?" asked Howard.

"Yes, sir."

"Well, that's the one thing we're blessed with," said Jeanetta. "When Effie lost her mind, we didn't want to hear her babbling dreadful things, things that couldn't possibly be true. Of course Father told her to hush up. I told her myself that I never wanted to hear her ugly lies."

"You still believe your sister is mad, yet you refuse to help her?"

"We can't afford to help, not the way Father did," Jeanetta replied.

"We're hardly destitute, my dear," her husband reminded her, perhaps concerned that his wife's poor-mouthing cast him in a bad light as an insufficient provider. Still, like his wife he showed no inclination to help Effie, adding, "We must look to the future of our own children, Dr. Mallory."

"Exactly," said Jeanetta. "Besides, Effie's settled down, hasn't she? That's what Dr. Kingston said in his letters. She can take orders and work."

"Dr. Kingston told me your family home was raided, and that was when Miss Effie's troubles began." I watched Jeanetta Howard's face, the darting of her glance from me to her husband and back to me.

"There was some little unpleasantness at Woodbine. Raiders, foragers, whatever you want to call them, might have come once or twice. But we always managed. And what Effie said, well, it couldn't have happened. She was with me. Remember, Elijah, how I told you she was with me in the house the whole time?"

"What happened, Mrs. Howard?" I asked.

"Nothing. Like I told you, Effie made the whole thing up."

"What did she make up? And why?"

"Oh, the usual thing, to give herself importance. I won't repeat her lies. I won't."

"I thought she never spoke."

Howard inclined his head toward me. "Where is the girl now, Dr. Mallory?"

"In the front hall," his wife chimed in. "You must've seen her. That's where I told her to wait."

"She wasn't there when I came in."

"What?" In a single movement, Jeanetta pushed her hands back against the settee and thrust herself forward to stand bolt upright. "Don't tell me she's gone up to the children. What if she decides to start jabbering again? Elijah?"

Major Howard, who had also risen, pointed toward the bay window. "Now, now, my dear. Isn't that the girl outside, there, in the garden?"

It was. The three of us watched Effie walk slowly along a flower-bordered brick path, turn back, retrace her steps, turn again, and continue. The garden was on the east side of the house, catching the afternoon shadows, not the sunlight, and the old man Effie approached was barely visible, shrunken down and sunk deep into a sagging wicker armchair.

"She's going to Father," Jeanetta breathed.

"He won't even know her," Howard said, placing an arm across his wife's shoulders.

I left them standing there at the window, left the house, and went out to the garden.

Effie had reached Mr. Rampling and knelt before him. She placed a hand on one of his, the one that dangled over the arm of the chair. I watched their faces in profile, hers with chin up-tilted, lips closed, eyes wide, the old man's with eyelids drooping, mouth and jaw hanging slack. Effie bowed her head and turned her cheek to rest it against his knee. Then she brought his limp hand down and laid it on her hair, lifted the hand, laid it again on her loose braid, repeating the motions as if her father were caressing her.

I stepped closer, but both of them were heedless of me. I surmised the old man that Jeanetta called addled had, in fact, suffered a stroke and was partially paralyzed, a diagnosis further supported by his attempt at speech. Half his face remained motionless as words slurred from one corner of his mouth.

"Effie?... That you, Effie?"

She looked up at him, and he searched her face with his cloudy eyes.

"Little girl," he whispered, "come to life."

I think I gave her time. I looked away from her and waited. But she didn't speak to him, to her father with the Midas touch.

Major Howard entered the garden, and I stepped aside with him, not knowing what he might say in Effie's hearing. "My wife wants her gone, Dr. Mallory. Take her on back to the boarding house and be done with it."

"No, sir. I won't take her there."

"We're not paying your employer another penny."

"I'm not bargaining for him."

"What then? You get this straight. Mrs. Howard won't have that girl under our roof. And I won't have Mrs. Howard aggravated."

"I realize that, sir."

"Then between you and me," he said with a confidentiality I did not wish to share, "you can do what you like with her. Just so we don't set eyes on her again, you understand. You get her out of here, and you do whatever you like."

A part of me wanted him to face up to what he meant by that. Suppose "whatever I liked" included seduction? Rape? Even murder? He didn't know me, he didn't know what I was capable of, and he didn't give a damn. I could swear to him that I had the best intentions of good conduct. But then, why should I comfort him, ease what conscience he had, with any assurances whatsoever?

I carried our luggage out to the gate then went back for Effie. Her gentleness toward the old man, who had silenced her and shut her away, was something I could not share. I wanted to curse him, if he could have understood me, and the Howards with him, for their selfishness and cruelty.

Standing behind Effie, I covered her shoulders with my hands and raised her to her feet. "We must go," I said.

Her father's head dropped back and his bleary eyes rolled up with a look of sudden panic. What if she were moved by that look? What if she refused to leave him, clung to him for some reason from the past that I did not understand? What then? He ground out her name in the twisted corner of his mouth, ground it out until the sound was like gravel under the heel of a boot. And she withdrew from him. I felt her shoulders press back against my breast, and she turned in the circle of my arms and allowed me to take her away.

# Chapter 23

I didn't know where to go with Effie, what to do with her. I resisted the impulse to spend what little money I had left on lodgings in New Orleans, as the night before I had not resisted the impulse to squander money on a woman in the Quarter. I told myself I must conserve our resources for some directed purpose and briefly contemplated what the Howards' legal obligation might be to Effie. But the law couldn't force anyone to be charitable, to be kind. What I really hoped to do was to take Effie away from the city, buy her a passage to sanctuary. But where?

Without a direction of my own, I found myself following Effie as she wound us through the narrow streets and by nightfall brought us out somewhere along the levee.

I smelled the damp grass and the deep Mississippi, felt a river of air, cooled as it traveled over the river of water. Effie and I set down our bags and stood, side by side, staring at the black water that rolled and lapped against the levee. For a moment Effie was so close to me, her arm at her side, that the back of her hand brushed my trouser leg. And I caught myself wanting what I had wanted the night before. Not what I had paid for and received, but what I had wanted.

Effie turned away from me, opened her carpetbag and drew out a length of mosquito netting. Wrapping it around her shoulders, draping it over her skirt like a little girl playing dress-up, then she defined herself in the darkness as the pale shape of a woman, moving away from me, under the moon and stars.

Following her, searching for something to say, I called, "Effie, I'm sorry about your father." She slowed her pace, and I continued, "He's ill, as you saw, and can't afford to keep you at Magdalene Asylum. That's why your brother-in-law told Dr. Kingston to send you out to work. But you know I can't leave you with Mrs. Fabre."

Effie stopped.

"I'll find someplace else for you, someplace better. Tomorrow."

She turned slowly, walked toward me, languorously, I would like to have thought, the gauze net flowing along the ground after her, and pooling around her hem when she stopped before me. I perceived a change in her expression, a softness, an unguardedness, perhaps. Had she come to trust me more than I trusted myself? I never wanted to cease looking at her. But I made my offer anyway.

"If I turn my back, Effie, will you stay close to me? Will you tell me something, anything? Will you tell me what you want?"

She knelt then at the top of the levee, facing its grassy incline, and I sat near her, facing the river.

As the silence lengthened between us, I tried to bridge it. "You were kind to your father, but you didn't speak to him." I don't know why I brought up her father again, surely there were other things we could have talked about. But I went on, as if saying things I didn't care to say could keep me from thinking of the things I cared too much to say. "He wanted you to speak to him."

"No," she whispered behind me. "No, he didn't."

"He asked you to. He asked you to come to life."

"He's old and facing death. He wants to be forgiven."

"And have you forgiven him?"

"I have obeyed him. That'll have to do for him." Her voice was low and deliberate. "What I have done, and what I will do in this world, is forgiveness enough. I can do no more. And I ask for nothing more. You understand, Robert. You *will* understand."

"I want to, Effie." I spoke her name so soon after she had spoken mine, as if I could link us together with the sound of our names. She had said my given name.

Was there some way, I wondered, that I could deny she had ever been my patient? Wasn't she really Dr. Kingston's charge? But he had entrusted her to me. Medical ethics, honorable intentions—neither one offered me a solution. If only permission could somehow come from her, consent… and then I could take that consent from a girl whom others had labeled as mad and let her share the blame for my transgressions. Would that be so very different from previous compromises I had made, fooling myself, giving what was asked for, not giving what was needed?

I had asked Effie to speak to me, but I wasn't listening to her. I was imagining knowing her, not as a patient released from an asylum, but in some other circumstance. I imagined forgetting myself as I should never forget myself. And I'd had a dose of quinine and had no fever to blame for my thoughts.

"At Woodbine there was a swing hanging from a live oak tree," she said, "down the hill from the big house. I would swing there when I was a little girl. Higher and higher. Knees bent, straight, bent and straight. Even after I was older and Papa discouraged me from such pastimes, I would go without his blessing and swing alone, after dark."

"Effie, don't tell me childhood stories," I protested. "Don't give me glimpses. Let me see. You said I would understand something. Tell me what it is."

"Tell you what you want to hear. Tell you what you want to understand. Tell you what you think you understand already." The sound of her voice was rhythmic as a chant, but devoid of the lyricism I had heard in her reminiscences.

"No. I'm sorry, I didn't that mean that. I want you to tell me the truth. You were so very young when—"

"When I was locked away," she said.

"If the war hadn't come along and changed us all, what do you think your life would have been like? What would you have done?" Then I thought, but didn't ask, Whom would you have married? Would you have had children?

"When I was locked away," she repeated the phrase, "I was unfinished. You want the truth about a future I never had?"

"But you had hopes, didn't you?"

"I had the moment."

"And now?"

"Now I have questions for you, about you. You must talk to me."

Effie's words startled me, for in my reveries of her I had hoped but not allowed myself to presume she might have a personal interest in me. I told myself that she was kind-hearted when she had washed and mended my clothes and shared with me the warmth of the laundry fire, that she was compassionate when she had cared for me through my bout of fever, and that she was resigned, in her vulnerability, to the necessity of trusting someone when she had trusted me.

But with her persistent questioning, Effie led me through the winding path of my becoming a physician and surgeon, to my unlooked for specialty of amputation, to my confession of the absurdity of my career, that I had followed an army marching to its own destruction and thereby followed my calling to save shattered men and boys by further maiming them.

"For a little while," I told her, "as the men lay in the hospital tent, I would try to be the thing that they had lost—the hand to write a letter home, the eyes to read a loved one's words. And, in that way, for a little while I eased my conscience."

"Of what?" she asked.

"Of not being able to take someone's place, someone with a sweetheart or a wife waiting for him to come home. But now… well, I wish that I could be something for you, Effie. Something you've lost, anything. Anything I'm capable of being for you."

I heard a rustling behind me. Effie moved about, shifted position, knotted herself up close beside me, drawing her knees to her chest and covering her head with her arms. I didn't understand why, but she was weeping inside that tight, quivering coil she had made of her body, and I placed my arms around her shoulders, as if together we could construct a shelter in the dark.

Sleep overcame her, unwound her in my embrace. And I held her until morning.

# Chapter 24

I would take Effie to my mother's house. That was my waking resolve. If Father had still been alive, I would have been forced to decide differently, for he had vowed never to admit me there again. But I trusted that Mother would not extend her disaffection for me toward all others associated with me.

After buying a little food at a waterfront market, we set off on foot, following the convolutions of the river upstream. On the long, quiet stretches of our journey, I pictured myself taking Effie somewhere other than Baton Rouge, anywhere, going west, maybe, as I had dreamed of before now, where no one knew either one of us. We could begin our lives again in a new place. Except that I carried more with me than a black bag and a satchel. And Effie, well, I had only an inkling of what she carried. So we walked on together on a course neither one of us had designed.

The trip took a little more than two days. Fever set me back the first night, and I dosed myself with the quinine bought in New Orleans, full strength, I hoped, unlike the solution from Kingston's dispensary. Yet, I found my relief was only a slow reduction, not elimination, of fever and a slight dulling of muscle aches, which persisted throughout the following day. Perhaps quinine of all sorts was losing its power to restore me.

On the second day of our journey, Effie and I veered off from a bend in the Mississippi and traveled part way on a flat boat along a canal. We didn't have to pay for our passage or for the meal the bargeman and his son shared with us. I traded my services as physician and removed a skin tumor from a fold in the bargeman's swarthy neck.

Effie and I spent that night on the deck, leaning against our bags, moving over the black water by no effort of our own. And when I slept, I dreamed of floating on the river with no barge underneath me, the current swirling my body into the waiting arms of the Reverend Mr. Jonas's parishioners.

In the morning Effie and I resumed walking, leaving the canal, crossing a fallow field to rejoin the river, which we followed to Baton Rouge, arriving in late afternoon. I felt myself in strong need of a hot meal and a hot bath, wishing I could have managed at least one of them before facing my mother. Effie seemed indifferent to her own hunger. Only a certain listlessness betrayed her there. And I think she had managed to do some washing and rinsing out of things while we were on the barge, her fresh appearance now belying the rough conditions she had endured throughout our journey.

Mother's house, like all the others along the street, was a tall clapboard construction in need of whitewashing. A few boards of the front porch were warped, a few balusters from the porch railing were absent. The scrolling woodwork under the eaves was here and there chipped or broken. Nothing about the exterior of the house had been repaired or replaced since I last saw it. Apparently, Mother, like Mr. Poncet and so many others, had resigned herself to live in what was called genteel poverty.

I entered the yard, the patch of garden, where a few purple irises bloomed. Effie waited by the gate. Standing on the flagstone path, I arched my neck and stared upward at the balcony railing, which still bore a mark where a rope had cut into the wood and worn away the white paint, the rope Lucinda had tied to the rail. I cannot cut her down.

The way my father told it, my mother had nearly followed Lucinda to the grave. That morning when all the neighbors had seen what Lucinda had done in the night, the shame of it had just about killed Mother. But that was Father's version, and I suspected she understood more about shame and surviving it than he gave her credit for.

At the front door, my mother received me in her way as coldly as Jeanetta had Effie, but I believe it cost her more. And when I explained to her that the arrangements in New Orleans which Dr. Kingston had made for Miss Rampling had proved unsuitable, she allowed us to cross her threshold, expressing a sincere interest in Effie's plight. Mother was a lifelong member of the sisterhood of civility. On that I would bet my life.

Until Effie was comfortably situated in the guest room and I had washed and changed and returned to the confines of the parlor, not an unpleasant word crossed between my mother and myself. Even then, when she spoke, it was not her carefully chosen words but her demeanor that disturbed me. When Father had sent me packing, Mother, however obedient she was to his will, had appeared regretful. Now, on my return, she skirted around me, avoiding the slightest possibility that I might touch her, as if something about me appalled her.

"Dr. Kingston wrote me that you might stop in on your way back from New Orleans," she began, her voice flat, as if she were opening conversation at a tea party with a guest she had not wished to invite.

"You wrote to him, not to me, of Father's death." I suppose my words sounded like an accusation. I suppose they were.

"It seemed the right thing to ask him to break the news," she said.

Inadvertently, I smiled. Had she expected me to be shocked by the news? Overcome with grief? Leaving Baton Rouge over a year ago, I had hardly expected to see my father alive again. He had made it quite clear to me that the only way I would ever again cross his threshold was "over his dead body." The house had been too small for us then, but even now, with Father gone, I felt stifled in it. The tight dimensions of the rooms, the narrowness of the stairs reminded me of how much space he had occupied, how much air he had consumed, as if his spirit still inhaled and puffed itself from wall to wall and floor to ceiling.

"Dr. Kingston has been very good to us," Mother was saying. "All of us. He's been a mentor to you, even if you didn't always appreciate that."

"Oh, he's taught me something."

"After the nice recommendation he gave you, and the post at Magdalene Asylum… well, I have never understood your animosity toward him."

"And I have never understood your blind regard."

Weary as I was, I would not sit in her presence, not while she stood and wrung her hands. I thought of how Kingston had made use of the news in my mother's letter to distract me from his part in Oralia's arrest and subsequent lynching.

"Before Dr. Mallory…" Mother referred in that formal way not to me but to her husband of over thirty years, "…before he passed over, we were in difficulties, as you should know. Who wasn't? The money worthless, the stores empty. But Dr. Kingston advised us and helped us to preserve a little something, on which I now exist, and I am grateful for it."

"Father took financial advice from Kingston?" I shook my head in dismay. "Mother, at the very least, Kingston is unscrupulous. And for all I know—"

"If you don't know it for a fact, don't repeat it." Years of reprimanding me throughout my youth had made her pronouncement of aphorisms a habit.

"Mother, I do know some things about the man for a fact. I have proof of his dishonest business practices at the asylum. I saw for myself how he threw out Miss Effie Rampling to work as a menial in a boarding house, not because his diagnosis of her delicate mental state had changed, but only because her family's willingness to pay his exorbitant fees had changed. As for Kingston's medical ethics—" Immediately, I regretted my choice of words.

Mother stared at me. Then her question, whispered, yet thunderingly clear, struck me as sharply as my father's belt ever had. "Who are you to cast such a stone?"

Father must have told her what he had sworn to me he would never tell her, told her in such detail and in such terms as only his censorious mind could devise. Had he decided to drive the last nail of shame into her coffin? Told her on his deathbed, perhaps, hoping she would follow him that much more quickly to the next world, preferably bringing him a covered supper tray and his pipe and slippers.

Suddenly, quite as suddenly as our heated exchange had begun, it ended. For a moment, my mother's look softened. Did I read nostalgia there in her eyes? Sorrow? Once more, regret? When she spoke again to me, her voice held a kindly concern I had not heard in it for a long while. "You're ill, Robert. Is it the old trouble? The fever?"

"Yes."

"There's quinine in the medicine chest. You know where to find it, son." She was gazing past me then, and I turned to follow her line of vision toward the open doorway, where Effie stood.

Over a plain supper, which Mother cooked and served, I led our stilted conversation toward an inquiry into her household arrangements. Fortunately, Father had not left her with a mortgage, but neither had he left her with much money for upkeep or repairs. She still retained a maid, who came in once a week or when Mother was down in her back. But she contemplated letting the girl go or else letting rooms, leaving me to infer that she must do so in order to afford hired help. Knowing the value my mother had always placed on her privacy and recalling her aversion to most strangers, I could hardly visualize her as a Mrs. Fabre, ruling a boarding house parlor.

Mother understood from me that, although Effie would not speak, she heard and comprehended what was said around her. So, perhaps Effie's presence inhibited Mother's admission of reduced circumstances. I wanted to believe that was the reason, and not that my mother doubted my interest and my desire to help her, or that she wished to reject my offers of support. With my father dead, the natural thing might have been for me to take over his medical practice in Baton Rouge. Might have been, but was not. I would have to find some other way.

While mother and I conversed, I noticed Effie looking toward a small watercolor landscape which hung over the sideboard. How many times as a boy I had escaped into that picture, imagining myself hidden among the tall grass and wildflowers or high in the branches of the live oak, during Father's interminable harangues at the table. Mother also noticed the rapt attention Effie gave the picture and briefly smiled toward the girl. The painting was one of Mother's own efforts, accomplished before she had married.

Mother, Effie, and I cleared the table together and washed and dried and put away the bone china and silver, that had been carefully hidden and preserved all through the war years. Strange how for some, particularly for ladies who shared my mother's sensibilities, the implements for serving and eating a meal were more significant than was the food itself. I remember my mother once claimed that blindfolded she could taste the difference in a cup of coffee if it had been stirred with anything other than a real silver spoon.

My mild feverishness and perhaps the supposed limitations of my gender caused Mother some doubt that I was up to taking part in domestic tasks. I would surely drop the plates, she predicted. But I managed to do no particular harm, and for a brief interval appreciated an easing of the tension between us. It pleased me to watch Effie moving about the kitchen and pantry, putting things away with an intuitive understanding of Mother's sense of order. I was sorry when the chores were done and Effie went upstairs and Mother and I were again faced with only each other.

Carrying a lamp, I followed Mother from room to room, from the kitchen to the dining room to the parlor to the front of the house, where Father's examining and consulting rooms were located, as she made sure each window and outside door was locked for the night. We stopped in the consulting room office, which was much as I remembered it, walls lined with shelves lined with leather-bound medical texts and, in one corner, the towering desk, every cranny of which was stuffed with notes and memoranda, the writing surface covered with stacks of letters and files. All was just as if Father had moments ago stepped into the adjoining room to conduct an examination. The sickly sweet odor of his brand of pipe tobacco still hung heavily in the air.

I thought of how I had found my old room, when earlier I had gone upstairs to change clothes. The bed was stripped, the mattress tic rolled up and bound, and all my personal items—books, journals, pictures, mementos—were crated in a corner. Was this in preparation, I wondered, for a boarder who would want to know the room had been thoroughly cleaned? Or was it in preparation for locking a door against the past?

Mother was smoothing the curtain, after having inspected the window casement behind it, when I spoke to her bluntly. "What do you know now that you didn't know when I left here?"

She hesitated before answering with an evasion. "Why do you ask me that?"

"You accepted that Father and I were no longer on terms, if we ever were. Well, I suppose he told you that you had to accept it. But I sense it's your choice now. He told you something, after I was gone, didn't he? He would want you to know before he died."

"Dr. Mallory was not expecting to die."

"You knew he blamed me for Lucinda's death?"

"Yes. He said you had hurt her, and finally she couldn't bear it anymore. I didn't understand him then. You and Lucinda had always been so fond of one another. I had lost my daughter, I wanted my son with me, but he told me 'no, never.'"

"And now you know why." She nodded. "Yet you let me back in the house."

"The house is not my heart, Robert."

"I see."

"If no one had ever found out, that would still not excuse what you did." She went on aligning each pleat of the curtain, running her forefinger and her thumb along each fold, restoring order.

My grip on the lamp had become unsteady, and I set the low-burning light on the desk top. "Lucinda was in such misery," I said. "All she wanted was that no one, most of all you, would ever know."

Mother spun from the window, her shadow spinning with her. "Lucinda couldn't live with what you did to her." Catching at the back of the settee, she steadied herself, as if her own outburst had unbalanced her. She edged around the narrow piece of furniture and sank upon its cushion. But her back stiffed when I joined her there.

"Is that what you think?" I asked her. "Or is that what Father told you?"

"You violated your oath. You violated your sister."

Her second sentence I had heard before in this same room, spoken just as low, but through my father's clinched teeth. Oh, he had made reference to my violation of the Hippocratic oath, too. But dwelling on that subject might have left him open to question and debate, or, worse still, have allowed that he and I were colleagues, fellow medical men. Far better for him, more certain, to assume the position of an outraged father disowning his son. Although, on that rare occasion, Father had refrained from bellowing his condemnation of me throughout the house for all to hear, giving me hope that my mother might not have to know the entire story of my disgrace.

And his condemnation had run a twisted course. When I could not produce on his demand the name of Lucinda's seducer, he had concluded that I was covering up for a friend, that I had irresponsibly introduced my sister to a cad. Then, in labeling my own relationship with Lucinda "unnatural," Father had barely stopped short of accusing me of possessing incestuous desires.

"Mother, I admit the violation of my oath, but as to more than that, I hope you have not accepted Father's own perverse ideas as the truth about what happened."

If my mother could have looked more distressed than she had in the moment before, I suppose she did then. "You misunderstand me," she said, fumbling for her pocket handkerchief as tears spotted the lap of her skirt. "I am a Christian woman, and I have no perverse ideas."

"Forgive me. But the last time Father spoke to me—"

"Remember that your father is not here to answer your assertions."

"But it's important to me that you understand."

"How can I? How could you do such a thing to your sister?"

I shook my head. I couldn't answer that question, but I asked one of my own. "Why did Father believe that what I did for Lucinda was a greater sin than what some other man did to her?"

"Your father made a distinction between a sin of passion and a sin of premeditation."

"Oh, yes." In my mind's eye, Father stood before me, loomed before the fortress of his consulting room desk, the lamplight leaping up behind him like an intimation of hellfire. I heard again the echo of his voice, intoning the litany of my sins. The liberties that some bounder had taken with Lucinda, the secret knowledge he had possessed of her, his seduction and betrayal of a young woman— none of that compared to the enormity of my transgression, to the secret knowledge I had possessed of Old Dr. Mallory's precious daughter.

Mother stated it more delicately. "Brothers and sisters should not be so intimate with one another that they could even discuss such a personal situation as... as that in which Lucinda found herself. She should have come to me."

Old Dr. Mallory had said she should have come to him, that it was his right, not mine, to decide Lucinda's fate. But my little sister whom I loved, had come to me, not to him. On her knees, she had begged me, not him. "Robert, make it as if it never happened... rid me of what this man has done... make me as I was before I met him."

But she—none of us—was ever as we were before.

I had not decided her fate, but I had given in to her demand. I had been too fond of her, making it so easy not to notice how her admiration of me had been distorted into mere flattery. Excusing her faults, indulging her remained a habit for me, even after I saw the awful change in her. I had entered her body with my instruments to undo the consequences of the entering of another man though I could never enter her mind and undo the damage he had wrought there.

The weeping began again, this time my mother's weeping. My head ached as it had on the nights I had listened to Lucinda's inconsolable sobs.

"You aborted her baby, my grandchild. There will never be another."

Aborted. I think that was the only time I had ever heard my mother say that word aloud.

"You feel the loss now, Mother." My impulse was to pat her shoulder, take her hand, but I didn't want to feel her pull away from me, recoil from what she must perceive as my murderous touch. "Imagine what Lucinda felt then," I said, "how she dreaded your disappointment in her, how she feared Father's anger. That doesn't excuse what I did, what I regret with all my heart. But what if she had presented you with a child, you and Father, when she had no ring on her finger and no husband at her side?"

"Lucinda was engaged to be married. Of course I disapproved of her giving in to the young man's impatience. But things could have come right in the end."

A sudden ringing in my ears nearly drowned out the sound of her words, the sense of them. I clamped one hand over my forehead and felt the sweat starting on my brow. "Did you take your quinine? Did you take enough," she was asking me, and I was muttering, "Yes, yes, I think so," all the while wracking my brain for some reason behind her distortion of events.

My mouth went dry as I formed the question. "Mother, when do you think I performed that… that procedure?"

"Oh, Robert, must we go on speaking of it?"

"Yes. When?"

"After her engagement party. I don't know why—why she would have imagined that was the thing to do—why you persuaded her to take such a course of action. There was hardly any time at all till her wedding day. She could always have said—"

"No, Mother," and my heart pounded with every word I spoke, "Lucinda could not have said the baby was premature. I aborted it months before she even met Kingston's nephew, well before they commenced their whirlwind courtship. And I'll swear she never loved him or wanted him. There was someone else, even then, after the engagement, someone for whom she had feelings. But Lucinda wouldn't give him away."

Mother looked stunned, confused.

"Father told me Lucinda had left a written record of what I'd done, a letter to him. I don't know what else was in the letter. He said he would destroy it. But then he must have changed his mind about your knowing."

Mother shook her bowed head. "No. I never saw any letter. Your father told me what you had done was unspeakable. He died leaving me in the dark with that thought. But among his personal things, I found Lucinda's diary."

"You read it?"

"Some of it. Enough."

"And that's what she wrote in her diary? That the abortion had taken place after her engagement?"

"Yes. She'd have no reason to lie in her private journal."

"She had no reason to take own life," I said.

"She must have lost her mind."

"Exactly. But did she lose it before or after she wrote that story you read in her diary?"

Mother's mouth trembled, but she didn't answer.

"I want you to listen to me," I said. "My intention is not to shock you or to hurt you or to try to excuse myself in any way in your eyes. But you must understand that I did not choose my actions lightly."

She murmured into her handkerchief, "I'm listening, Robert."

"Remember I had been following the army for more than three years before I came home for a rest. For more than three years, I'd been in the camps, waging war on dysentery, measles, and syphilis. I'd been in the surgery tents, letting blood and practicing medically sanctioned carnage. When I came home, I was sick with malarial fever and, more than that, I was sick of death. But we didn't discuss the war, you, Father, and I. You told me then that Lucinda was taking things hard, distressing herself over the losses of others, of family and friends."

"I thought it best," Mother said, "not to raise a painful subject, when she was so poorly and nervous."

"Lucinda was sick to her stomach and weeping day and night. I assure you, she had more than a case of nerves, Mother. And her endless sobbing was not for others, but for her own predicament. She had given herself away to a man who couldn't marry her because he was married already. That's what she told me. But she wouldn't give him away, wouldn't tell me his name. Long before Lucinda's so-called fiancé ever darkened our doorway, she had come to me in black despair."

I stopped myself then. If I recounted how Lucinda had pleaded with me and clung to me, how she had threatened to harm herself if I failed her, how she had sworn her life was in my hands and there was only one sure way I could save her, well, Mother could rightly say that my sister was not here to answer those assertions.

"Some physicians, and philosophers, make a distinction," I said, "permitting abortion if it is performed to save the woman's life. At the time,

I believed I was acting to save Lucinda's life. But I was wrong."

"I don't understand you." Mother's voice broke with her sobbing. "At every turn, you contradict her diary, her written record, her own words."

"I am telling you the truth as I know it." Following the impulse I had earlier repressed, I reached for my mother's hand, which she withdrew from me.

Abruptly, she rose from the settee and crossed to Father's desk. And I sprang up after, the ingrained response to a lady's rising, dizzy with the quickness of motion. Had I really taken enough quinine? Had I forgotten it entirely? Had I purposely failed to take it, purposely let the fever come on as a kind of self-inflicted punishment, a form of penance?

A shudder passed across Mother's shoulders as she bent over the desk drawers. Her hands shook as she extracted a leather-bound volume and thrust it toward me.

"Take it," she said. "Read it. Read your sister's words. And then you dare to tell me what you know to be the truth."

There was only the one lamp in the room. Neither of us would take it and leave the other in the darkness and so we went upstairs together, Mother carrying the light and I behind her, like a ghost haunting her steps, invisible to her.

# Chapter 25

Alone in my old room, I found a lamp burning brightly on the otherwise bare surface of the desk, saw the bed had been made, bed linens smoothed and blanket folded back, saw the bottle of quinine and a glass tumbler on a table beside the bed. Effie had been seeing to my comfort, I was sure.

I laid Lucinda's diary on the desk, then crossed to the table and poured and drank a bitter draught of quinine. The room was devoid of rug and curtains, and despite the few pieces of furniture and the crates in the corner, every noise I made—the sound of my footsteps, the clink of the bottle against the rim of the glass—echoed around me as if I were in an unfurnished cell.

Returning to the diary, I didn't lift it from the desk, in fact, felt a passing, inexplicable aversion to touching it again at all, but opened its cover, which fell crookedly aside. The binding was loose, in places coming unstitched, and I soon discovered the reason as I leafed through the volume. Here and there pages had been torn out, only jagged edges in the margin left to mark where they had been. Who had torn them out? Lucinda, Father, someone else? The true answer to that question mattered if Mother expected me to find any truth in the pages that remained.

Turning back to the first few entries, I read of my sister's annoyance with the outbreak of the war, how she feared there would be a scarcity of silk and ribbons for new dresses, a lack of delicacies for the table, a dearth of gentlemen in the parlor. Her distress over the losses of others, as Mother had expressed it, had come later. But if Lucinda's early perceptions of the nation's tragedy were shallow, well, I hoped they spoke more of her upbringing than of her character. Through the years, the more Mother had devoted herself to charity and austere religion, the more Father had indulged Lucinda's interest in fashion and frivolous society. He could be dour about anything except Lucinda. I, too, had been charmed by her, all who had met her were, and that had been her accomplishment.

"Last evening a group of medical men gathered in Father's study," she had written, "and Father called me in to meet them. There was Dr. Desselle, who treats only the best and richest people in New Orleans. And a distinguished specialist from France, an associate of Dr. Kingston, who was also in attendance. Oh, and some young buck of a surgeon in the new army, who wouldn't stop talking to Robert about enlistment. Well, it wasn't long before most of us moved off to the parlor, and Father persuaded me to sing..."

Lucinda might not have thought we had taken proper notice of her, but I recalled the army surgeon stumbling in his discourse to me, turning to stare at her as she swirled into the study. And I remembered the old specialist stubbing out his cigar, the better to breathe in the fragrance of the gardenias pinned in her hair. What I could not remember was Lucinda's singing.

What lingered in my mind was Effie's humming, and for a moment, I thought I heard it again, perhaps a refrain of the tune I had heard after falling ill at Magdalene Asylum. But I did not see Effie passing in the hall outside my open door, nor on the staircase.

The end of the hallway, opposite the landing, was closed off by a pair of French doors, and beyond them was the balcony with the scarred railing. Approaching the doors, whose frames outlined two narrow rectangles of night sky, I perceived in one frame a blue-white shape beside a pillar, near the rail—Effie, in one of the white shifts the women of the asylum sometimes wore, her hair loose down her back. Through the glass pane,

I stared at her, my hand on the door latch. She could not have known what had happened on that balcony, yet there she leaned over the railing, dangling one pale arm far over the edge, playing her fingers back and forth in the night breeze.

Slowly, not wishing to startle her, I opened the door. But Effie spun immediately to face me.

"You'd better come in now," I said.

She shook her head.

"Please, Effie. Come away from the rail." I stepped toward her, offering my hand. Again she shook her head and backed away from me until she leaned against the rail, all the while swaying her hands back and forth at her sides. "Don't do that," I said, suddenly advancing and gripping her wrists. I had to stop that swinging motion.

Effie dropped to her knees, pulling me down with her, for I would not let her go. And though her face was hidden in shadow and by the veil of her hair as she tossed her head side to side, I felt her expression of protest, her fierce energy, as her arms twisted free of my grasp. I could have held on and taken her anger as the only form of passion we could share, but that would have undone everything between us. Everything I imagined between us.

"I'm sorry, Effie. I was afraid for you." That was part of the truth. For an instant, my mind's eye had seen a young woman tumbling over the edge, as I had feared Effie might have done at the boarding house, with no rope to stop her fall. The rest I could not explain to Effie. Whether or not her dangling of her arm over the railing was a random gesture or some perverse manifestation of her intuition, the movement had filled me with dread.

When I ceased to hold her, Effie ceased to pull away from me. Both of us still kneeling by the rail, she turned her back to the house, and I turned toward it, my back against hers. Back to back, as we had sat on the levee nights ago. "Does this mean you'll talk to me now?" I asked.

"It might. Are you listening."

"I am."

She began with familiar words. I had heard them before and had interrupted their singsong rhythm, but not this time. "At Woodbine there was a swing hanging from a live oak tree, down the hill from the big house. I would swing there when I was a little girl. Higher and higher. Knees bent, straight, bent and straight. Even after I was older and Papa discouraged me from such pastimes, I would go without his blessing and swing alone, after dark."

So, the swaying movement of her fingers had traced her memory, not mine.

"One night in early autumn," said Effie, "I was sailing back and forth on that swing, my hair blowing free, my skirts aflutter. Barefoot and without stockings. Jeanetta would have called me a hoyden. She did call me that sometimes, and gypsy, and worse. But I adored the feel of the breeze on my skin, on my bare legs when the breeze ruffled and lifted my petticoats.

"Cicadas were chirping, frogs croaking, and there I was humming to myself, humming that dance tune 'Hop up, pretty girls, don't be afraid.' So at first I didn't pay any mind to other sounds—a sharp crackling that could've been a branch breaking off somewhere in the woods, or could've been rifle fire. And then the rustling among the trees at the edge of the woods. It was the voices of the men that scared me.

"I clambered up the live oak tree, scrapping my shins on the bark, and hid among the foliage. Men—soldiers—were coming out of the forest, into the full moonlight. And there I was, clinging to a branch and looking down at the empty swing, that was still swaying back and forth.

"That swing must've caught their attention, 'cause the men headed straight for it. And I thought right then they would find me and kill me for sure. But they were carrying the carcass of a whitetail deer with them, and that was their concern. They cut the swing down and used its ropes to string up the doe from a low branch. The men, five of them, set to work skinning and butchering that deer and stoking up a campfire to cook it over, throwing in the seat of the swing to feed the flames, all of this happening just under me, everything so close.

"I smelt the men's sweat, and the doe's blood, and then the meat's aroma as it roasted over the fire, drippings sizzling in the fire. My stomach turned in on itself I was so hungry. But I didn't dare come down.

"Time went by. The fire died down to a smolder, and the smoke rose up, nearly choking me. But I stuffed a fist in my mouth and stayed quiet up there in the live oak tree and watched those men, circled around their camp fire, eating with their hands, drinking out of jugs, all of them talking and laughing together. And under me hung what was left of the deer, bones exposed. Entrails and strips of hide littered the ground. I reckon those men made a mess of things everywhere they went."

"They were soldiers foraging?"

"I thought they were soldiers, but from whose army I couldn't guess. They wore bits and pieces of uniforms and some civilian garb, too. In shadows and moonlight and with enough dirt on them, blue, gray, and butternut look pretty much the same. I'd heard about men deserting their regiments and banding together, even men from opposing sides, living in the woods or back in the hills, trying to wait out the war. But wherever these men came from, they were men nobody else would want to claim." Her voice had risen with those last words, then dropped again, almost to a whisper. "And yet, even so, watching them from above, for a little while I thought they had a kind of beauty about them…"

Effie went on speaking, but I was momentarily deafened by a sudden thrumming of my own jealous thoughts. I dreaded what she might be saying next, dreaded that any one of those men had ever come to mean something to her. And then I forced myself to listen as penance for my suspicions.

"Each man was different from the others, particular in some way of his own. One, who wore a dark jacket with gold braid on it, was tall as a column, and he tried to order the others about. But the biggest of them, big as Hercules, just laughed. That man was the one who had done most of the work butchering the deer and had stripped to the waist and wiped his bloody hands on his trousers. I could see by the firelight that his face and chest were swarthy and all shiny with sweat, and his hair was curly and rusty-colored. Another man, fair-haired and pale as a poet, his unbuttoned shirt hanging loose on him, was so thin his ribs showed above the bandage that bound his waist.

"Watching them all that time, I imagined what might have brought them to where they were, under that live oak. Maybe the tall one had turned tail in a battle and let down his men, and now he was trying to take command again, in secret. And the big one wasn't going to have any of it. He'd do as he pleased. The wounded one had tried to be a good soldier, but he was so tired he'd lost his faith."

"You said there were five men. What of the other two? What did you think of them?" I could dread her answers, but I must have them.

"The older one, who had straight black hair and coal black eyes, kept close to the fire, staring into it. His hands were cupped around a mouth harp, and he was playing the same tune over and over, one I'd never heard before, maybe something popular in the North. But it was a sad kind of song, and the boy leaning against the tree, who didn't look much older than

I was at the time, asked him to play something else or stop entirely."

"And what did you imagine brought that pair to Woodbine?"

"I don't know. Maybe the black-eyed one got himself run out of his regiment for playing that infernal song over and over. As for the boy—"

Her voice broke.

"Effie, are you all right?" I felt the pressure of her straight back against mine, felt her lungs fill with air and exhale her response.

"'Course I am. It's just words now, Robert. Just words."

"Effie?"

She went on. "I don't think the men had realized they were so close to a house. The big house and outbuildings were over the rise, just out of sight of somebody by the live oak tree. And that live oak was out of sight of someone up at the house, which had made it nice for me when I wanted to go there and swing and not be seen by Papa.

"But that night Papa must've noticed something, maybe when he was going his rounds of the outbuildings, locking up. Maybe he saw the glow of that campfire, or smelt the wood smoke and venison, or heard the rusty-haired man laughing at his own filthy jokes. Maybe he heard that wailing mouth harp. Whatever brought Papa down the hill, I wish he'd stayed at the house."

"Why is that, Effie? What happened after he came down the hill?"

"Oh, Papa, with his house slave Lemuel hiding behind him—Lemuel wasn't but twelve or thirteen—blustered up to the men, demanding to know what they were doing on his property. There they were, five of them, and every one of them armed with something—rifles, pistols, knives—even their fists were better for their purpose than Papa's old shotgun was for his. But he stood his ground. *His ground*, he told them.

"The men argued back at him and ridiculed him and made him so mad that Papa took aim at them. Then his shotgun misfired, and the soldiers all set on him at once. They bound him with the bit of rope they'd had left over after stringing up the deer. And all the while Lemuel stood there looking back and forth from his master to the men. He wouldn't leave Papa, but he wasn't about to take on those men either. He just stood there. They all stood there under the tree, the soldiers talking about what to do. Should they get on back to the woods? Should they go up to the house with their hostage and see what they could steal?

"Papa was past angry. He was sputtering so. And then Lord knows what possessed him, he looked up. He looked over the heads of the men, up at the branches of the live oak, and straight into my eyes.

"Papa fell silent, that fierce, red anger in his face turning to a kind of sickly horror. The big rusty-haired man saw it first, that change. He whipped himself around, and before I could even think of climbing higher, he'd jumped up and grabbed me by my ankles.

"I don't remember screaming, not after that first shock of being yanked down from the tree by the big man. I tumbled forward, caught for a moment by one of the others, the youngest one, who then fell backward with me on top of him, the wind knock out of us both. The other men laughed, said I was too eager for the boy and they'd make him wait till they were finished."

"Effie..."

"Do you want to stop listening now, Robert? Are you going to tell me to say no more?"

"No. No, I'm not. Go on, if you will. I'll listen."

She no longer leaned her back against mine. We were no longer touching.

"With his arms bound to his sides," she said, "Papa charged at the rusty-haired man, head lowered, and butted the man in the belly. The man didn't budge, but Papa stumbled and dropped to his knees. And Lemuel sort of huddled down by him. I guess one or another of the men made them stay where they were after that. I caught a glimpse of the tall man gagging Papa with a kerchief, while the big man was picking me up off the boy.

"But he no sooner had me in his arms than he was throwing me down again. I lay in the dead leaves, barefooted, without stockings, and felt his big, coarse hands shoving my petticoats out of his way. Maybe I did scream when he had first caught me, but I know I didn't scream again. All the while he and the others were taking turns, I know I didn't scream. All I could do was try to catch my breath, try to breathe again to keep from dying."

I realized my own breath had stopped some moments ago, and her words reminded me then to make the effort, to keep from dying.

"If they had been much the same," she said softly, and I strained to catch her words. "If they had blurred together in my senses, the way the separate strokes of a beating blur together... But they didn't. Each was different. Brutal in a different way.

"The first man tore me apart with the pain he brought me. And his sweat poured down from his forehead and stung my eyes. The tall one took his time—privilege of rank—and with a pocket knife he cut away all the buttons of my shirtwaist and the ribbons on my camisole. The black-eyed one was quick and frantic. The wounded man only pretended, putting on a show to convince the others he was as manly as they. He finished off by slapping me across the face and calling me a whore. Then the big man came back again.

"And the last one, the young one, when I was exhausted beyond pain, he was gentle. He lifted me up and carried me somewhere a little distance from the others, who had lost interest and gone back to their drinking. He laid me down on the long grass that was cool and wet, on ground that was not yet churned into mud by men's boots and knees and hands. He kissed my mouth. Imagine that. And I think in his fevered effort, he fancied that he was making love to me. But I know he wasn't."

In his fevered effort, in his fevered imagination, was he so far removed from me? I was repelled by Effie's story. I wanted to believe she had invented it out of nothing. But that would have made me not so far removed from Jeanetta Howard, and from her husband. Even if I could have gone back in time and killed the men who had raped Effie, I could not enter her mind and kill the memory of the rape. If ever there was an obstacle between Effie and me, it was this wall of memories, hers and mine.

"Finally, the men moved off, into the woods," she said, "and disappeared. I was cold and shaking so badly that I could hardly walk. Papa and Lemuel were just a few yards from me, still huddled together. Why he hadn't untied Papa, I don't know. I struggled with the knots and at last they gave way. Papa was sick to his stomach, but when he recovered himself, he readied his shotgun.

"I cried to Papa, 'Don't you go after those men. They're not worth your life.' I didn't know he wasn't going for them. No. My papa stood up and turned around and aimed the barrel straight between Lemuel's eyes. The boy tried to jerk away. But the blast caught him on the side of his head, and he took his time dying."

"Your father killed his slave? But why?" Or why not? A man who owned others was already conversant with cruelty.

"At the time, I was too stunned to understand. But I figured it out later. Lemuel was a witness, and Papa couldn't abide that. No one must know that he could not protect me."

"And then he silenced you to protect himself."

"He was ashamed."

"And you forgave him."

"It was never my place to forgive him for Lemuel. But for myself… We are what we are."

"Kingston knows what happened to you. Surely he knows." And I was sickened by the thought of how Kingston must have worked Effie's experience into his grand scheme of things. If Effie had obeyed her Father, she would not have gone to the swing, not have been there, hiding in the tree when the men came, not have been found, yanked down from the branches and raped. What a homily Kingston could make on the error of Effie's ways.

"Jeanetta is the one who knows," said Effie. "When Papa and I came back up toward the house, she saw the state I was in. She wouldn't let me through the door till she'd taken away all the clothes I had on me. Out in the yard, in the dark, she drenched me with buckets of cold rain water and rubbed me raw with burlap sacking. And out in the yard, she lit a fire and burned up my clothes, where the washerwoman built the laundry fire on wash day. That was the hardest work I'd ever seen her do. Papa was hunched up on the back step, sobbing into his hands. I was shaking as if the whole mess was happening all over again, crying to Jeanetta to cover me, afraid those men might come back, crying till my voice gave way. And she kept on working away, taking care of everything, making everything the way it was before."

"She couldn't bring the boy back to life."

"Oh, Lemuel was nothing to her. Papa just told her the raiders shot him."

"She wouldn't listen to you?"

"I couldn't speak. For I don't know how many days, I couldn't make a sound in my throat. Then Papa came to me, where I was holed up in my room, and told me I was a good girl, who never had and never would contradict him. He told me that my being quiet was the right thing for me to do. And he put his hands on my head and made me promise with a nod that I would say no more, ever."

"You obeyed him, and yet he still sent you to the asylum. Why?"

As Effie explained, I sensed her rising and moving a little away from me. I stood, also, still facing the house. "Turned out my silence wasn't enough," she said. "Much as he said he loved me, before long he could hardly bear to look at me. To other people he made excuses about my affliction. Maybe he started believing the stories he told about how I'd lost my wits in terror while watching him fight off a band of raiders. Then one day Dr. Kingston called on him, and things were settled between them."

"Effie, have you ever broken your silence with anyone other than me?" To my own ears the question sounded like the whine of a jealous lover, seeking reassurance. I was remembering Effie beside the peddler, silhouetted in the doorway of the ruined house where we had sheltered for a night. I was imagining Effie alone with Kingston in his consulting room.

Then Effie replied to my question, though in a paradox. "Perhaps I have not broken my silence, Robert, but you have heard me anyway."

Quickly I turned to her, thinking to protest her answer, but stared instead at her face, half in starlight, half in shadow, at the closing of her parted lips. How could anyone live for long with the madwomen of Magdalene Asylum and not be affected by their madness, not speak madness now and again as well? Or think it? A coldness came over me. Supposing Effie had heard what I had not said?

# Chapter 26

After seeing Effie to the door of her room, I returned to my own and to Lucinda's diary, but could not yet focus on my sister's words. I was shaken by Effie's story. And I was struck by how much Effie and Lucinda had in common.

Like so many other girls, they had been brought up from earliest childhood to be pleasing and obedient, particularly obedient to those in authority. And who were they, the authorities, if not a host of men, both relatives and professionals— fathers, grandfathers, uncles, brothers, brothers-in-law, tutors, ministers, lawyers, judges, doctors, soldiers. And what if one of them was corrupt? More than one. More than one man had betrayed Effie. If I cared to make the distinction my father had made between sins of passion and sins of premeditation, Mr. Rampling might rank above any in the band of Effie's assailants as her chief tormentor, silencing her, locking her away, denying the truth of her experience and the existence of her memory. As for Lucinda, according to Father, I, myself, had abused her, in league with her seducer.

Effie and Lucinda had both obeyed men unworthy of their trust. That was what they had in common. But I also believed there were awful differences between them.

I pulled a chair up to the desk and began to read my sister's diary, every word that remained in it, that had not been crossed out or ripped from the binding. Lucinda had created a strange retelling, reordering, of events. She had left a few vague references to her indisposition, which I understood to be the nausea of early pregnancy. If she had ever written of her lover or of the actual time of her abortion, those passages were gone now, and where they should have been, in the chronology, I found a narrow margin of rough edged paper. Lucinda had devoted several pages to her courtship, writing in a detached, passionless style. "Father and Dr. Kingston have agreed that the doctor's nephew, Edgar, will be a suitable husband for me. Seems they are both determined I must marry someone, and Edgar does offer certain advantages by association." On these she did not elaborate. How could Mother have imagined Lucinda too eager for her fiancé's embrace?

"I might have argued with Father and gotten my way," the passage continued, "or leastwise a reprieve. Observation has taught me that marriage is the end of all frivolity, regardless of how charming the groom may appear. Still, I cannot refuse Dr. Kingston's advice." Why could she not? Had Lucinda believed herself in some way indebted to him? Or had she been as fascinated with him as were the belles of Magdalene Asylum? "He urges me to make the match for the preservation of my health. My health! When all this time I thought my frailties were what interested men like him, given his specialty. Shall I marry, go slightly mad, and surrender to treatment? He could not neglect me then. Yes, I shall do something, and not die of boredom."

Indeed, experience had taught me that women associated with Dr. Kingston did not die of boredom. Rachel Poncet, Veronique Beaulieu, Lucinda Mallory. Pattern in chaos?

I wondered what Mother and Father had made of their daughter's references to the distinguished friend of the family. Perhaps it was Father who had excised the pages that might have further illuminated for another reader, such as Mother, Lucinda's relationship to Dr. Kingston, her dependence on his advice, her submission to his counsel, her obedience to his wishes. For Father must preserve, even from the grave, his assertion that I, not he, had brought a viper into the house.

I thought back to my first leave. On my arrival, Lucinda's conversation had been full of "Father's friend" Kingston, who came to visit, bringing delicacies the Mallorys could no longer afford, who talked business and medicine with Father, but always had a compliment for her, who called at the house when Father was away, offering his protection to the ladies.

Lucinda wouldn't hear a word against him from me when I had started to grumble about his supercilious manner and reminded me how generous he had been, giving me a recommendation and introductions. But a few days into my leave, Lucinda ceased to talk of Kingston, as he had ceased to visit. I was relieved, not being fond of him myself. But my sister soon fell into despondency. This I had observed, yet saw no mention of it in her diary. No mention, either, of Lucinda's confession to me of her condition, only a gap in the pages where the words should have been. At the time, I had thought of the soldiers coming and going through the town, and assumed my sister and her unnamed lover had succumbed to the desperation of the hour. That I could have understood, and would have sympathized with their desperation, for I had seen it and felt it during my own stint with the army.

The months between my first leave and my second were covered by brief entries that provided me with little insight into Lucinda's state of mind. She made several mentions of feeling downhearted, but who did not feel thus during the fourth year of the war?

Lucinda's diary offered only a spare description of her engagement party, little more than an indifferent recital of fashions and refreshments and gossip, the things I had not remembered. What still lingered in my mind was the expression on her face that night of the party. Posing arm in arm with her fiancé, who had been newly promoted to the rank of major, while Father announced the engagement and Kingston led the toast,

Lucinda had surveyed the crowd of guests. I remember her lips drawn back in a forced smile, her eyes narrowed in defiance of something, someone. For a moment, that look had even been directed at me. My interpretation, perhaps, but I knew her. She was not in love.

After the guests had gone, I had tried to speak to her in private, but she had refused to let me past the doorway of her room. There we exchanged only a few words, the last we ever spoke to one another. I said I didn't want to see her unhappy. She answered that tomorrow I'd return to duty and not see her at all.

In the few remaining pages of the diary, I was struck not so much by the wild discrepancies between Lucinda's story and my memory of events, but by the bizarre accusations she had heaped upon me. If Mother had read these too, and, as it seemed, believed what she had read, it was a testament to her forbearance that she could still stand the sight of me.

At Magdalene Asylum I had been surrounded by those suffering in various degrees and from various forms of madness. But I had not been the victim of anyone's particular delusion. When the patient Hannah had stabbed me, her act had been random violence prompted by her derangement. I would not consider it personal to me. But Lucinda, in her diary, pierced me with words that negated all the affection I wanted to believe she had felt for me.

"He speaks of saving the family's reputation," she had written in sprawling, unsteady script, "of doing my duty, and then, if I'm very good, I might yet find some pleasure in life. When he chooses, how he chooses, at his whim. I will go mad." The "he" of this paragraph was unnamed, and though I could not fit myself into "his" place, my parents must have, for in the next paragraph, Lucinda accused me outright, in a word our father later used against me. "What Robert did to me was unnatural. I understand that now. And I hate him for it." Unnatural. Not what she had said to me at the time. "Darling brother, it's the most natural thing in the world that you should help me, close as we are. Don't be embarrassed."

The sentences in her diary went on contradicting my memory. "I was confused, desperate for his favor. He told me what to do. How humiliated I felt when at last I gave in to his solution to my dilemma." Not my solution, and I would not have guessed she suffered humiliation, not given the look of triumph in her eyes when I agreed to her demand.

"I was so afraid, and Robert hurt me. And then the thing was done, finished and out of my life. No going back." Was this insanity hers or mine? Yes, I believed she had been afraid, that was the only decent excuse I could find for her bizarre behavior. I, too, had been afraid—afraid that my hands would not be steady, that I might injure her, that the bleeding would not stop.

I had seen Lucinda's tears slipping from the outer corners of her eyes as she had lain on the blanket in a clearing in the woods outside of town. We had gone off that morning in the rig for a picnic, she had told Mother. My surgical instruments she had placed in the lunch basket beside the sandwiches, planning our excursion as if it were a lark and lightly assuring me that Mother preferred pleasant lies to painful truth. Lucinda's excuse sounded well practiced, well used. On our return home, she intended to say she was unwell and take to her bed for a day or two.

One last time, there in the woods, I had tried to dissuade her, while she kissed me, then laughed at me. "Oh, Robert, after all the things you must have done in that surgery tent! Think of this as a minnie ball in need of extraction."

Lucinda's brazenness disgusted me. I think that, as much as her earlier begging, her weeping, her cajoling, even her threats to end her own life, had settled the matter in my mind. Some man had not been satisfied to seduce my sister. No, he must make a whore of her. When I destroyed the evidence of her wanton act, I was attempting to hide my own shame as well as hers.

This night I had told my mother that I had taken an action that I believed would save my sister's life. Yet, for a moment in that clearing in the woods, I hadn't believed my sister had any intention of harming herself, but only of getting her own way. I had given her what she wanted, and I had been wrong about her intentions.

The final pages of the diary had been torn out, only ragged edges remaining, the back cover's end paper split from the spine, where the stitching had come loose. There, between end paper and spine, I glimpsed the smooth edge of a folded page and drew it out. That last smudged page contained a last reference to the man who had been Lucinda's seducer. "He will have no more to do with me. His wife is dying, and I would wait, but he won't have me." His wife, under the care of Lila Fentroy. "He knows what was done to me, what I did for him, and now I am finished. I renounced everything else, I worshipped him, and he has tired of me and cast me out of heaven. I am not enough. I am not worthy. I have tried to tear him from these pages, but he comes back. His voice drones on in my head, on and on, telling me what I must do. He has thrown me over, into the valley of the shadow, and he is looking down at me."

I knew the man of whom Lucinda had written far better now than I had in those days. The sting of my sister's condemnation was, in some measure, mitigated by the understanding I had gained of how she was ill-used. I had watched this man set himself above the laws of other men and of God. Easily, he could have walked into my parents' house, long known to Mother and Father, further ingratiating himself to them as he gained influence over Lucinda, a married man, not yet a widower, trusted by my parents, who might well have allowed him to be alone with my sister, to divert her from her melancholia, perhaps to escort her out somewhere. To that clearing in the woods outside of town, for instance. Certainly she had known the way when she directed me there.

I shoved my chair back from the desk and struggled to my feet, the rising sickness clenched in my throat. The presence of her last words convinced me that Lucinda, not Father, had revised the diary. If he had been responsible, surely he would have thrown a few more pages on the grate, destroying all references to the man whom he had introduced to his daughter. For Mother, the idea that Lucinda and her fiancé had anticipated their nuptials was slightly less reprehensible than that Lucinda had carried on an affair with a married man. But Father must have known something closer to the truth, less distorted in sequence, for as far as I knew, he had never condemned Kingston's nephew, never held him responsible for her act of despair. No, Father had condemned me and insisted I name Lucinda's seducer. He was testing my knowledge, already knowing the answer himself, dreading it, I think, for I would not be surprised if the man who ruined Lucinda had also possessed some hold over Father. If I had answered him then as now I was able, would we have struck a bargain? Or would he, whose pride was thicker than blood, still have banished me? Old Dr. Mallory had failed to protect his daughter. I thought of Mr. Rampling, whose heart and mind must have broken on the night Effie was attacked, and felt some pity for him. But it also struck me that turning me out was my father's own way of shooting Lemuel.

Before dawn I woke my mother and took her hand and led her to my room.

"Mother, I haven't touched these crates. You see everything's boxed up and bound just as it was before I arrived. You see that, don't you?"

She nodded, staring at me, bewildered.

"You must have put my medical books and my sickbed journals in here, didn't you?"

Again she nodded.

"I want us to unpack them together, Mother. I want you to see that I have not changed a word nor torn out a page. They are just as they were written."

"Oh, what good will this do?"

"We'll see. I've read Lucinda's diary, and I'm daring to tell you what I know to be the truth, in words I wrote while she was still alive, with no revisions."

Slowly, Mother knelt on the floorboards, the billowy folds of her dressing gown encircling her. She bent over a crate, murmuring, "I recall your journals are in here." Her fingers fumbled with the cord around the crates, and I offered her scissors from my black bag. Then I knelt beside her and extracted one journal after another, opening each for my mother's inspection by the lamplight, until I found the one that included entries written during the month of my first visit home after three years in the war.

Mother's gaze traveled once over the words before she read them aloud. "She has confessed to me what I suspected. She asks that I undo what has been done to her. Though theoretically familiar with the procedure, I am averse to it. But I fear for her wellbeing and her mental balance."

What followed were my notes, gleaned from medical books, on the safest and most effective methods of abortion. Mother scanned these without comment, then read aloud again. "I return to duty tomorrow and am relieved to be going. She seems to be recovering her health, but as to the future, I don't know."

Mother looked up at me. "You don't name her in this."

"I wouldn't. But I name every other patient whose condition and treatment I describe." And I leafed through the journal, showing her example after example.

"Lucinda names you," said Mother.

"Yes, in certain passages she does name me. But in certain other passages she writes of a mysterious 'he' who is not her brother, I swear to you. Look again at her diary. Pages and pages have been torn out, events have been reordered or invented out of nothing. If you'll only look at the dates on which her entries leave off and begin again, look at where the gaps are in her story, surely you'll see that my journal fills those gaps."

But Mother would not, shutting her eyes against her tears.

I continued. "Believe me, I am not the man of whom she writes. That was her seducer who set himself up as the god of a young woman's idolatry. He, not I, was the man who would have no more to do with her. Lucinda was my flesh and blood, and I would have forgiven her anything—anything— if only I had had the time."

Mother opened her eyes and looked not at the diary or the journal I had laid open on the floor before her, but at me, into my eyes. "Do you say that, Robert, as a reproach to me?"

"Oh, no."

"I have prayed for a way to forgive you," she said, her voice unsteady. "Your father told me that he had outlived his children, that he was dying without progeny. I don't want to die that way, too. But I haven't found my way."

"You don't have to," I said. "It's all right. I understand."

"If things happened as you say they did," Mother said, "then Lucinda was wronged by someone other than Dr. Kingston's nephew." To both my parents, Edgar seemed to have had no mark of distinction except his relationship to Kingston. "But even so, you wronged her, too, Robert. And I did when I looked away because I couldn't bear to see the changes in her."

Mother covered her face, weeping into her hands, and this time did not pull away as I reached to hold her. When her sobbing had eased, Mother retreated from my embrace, but gently, patting my arms down to my sides as if she were arranging me in a more seemly attitude.

"I'll be leaving today for Magdalene Asylum," I told her.

Her brow furrowed as she asked me why I planned to return there, after the harsh things I had said about Dr. Kingston, the accusation I had made concerning his business practices. I told her the simple truth. I was still in Kingston's employ, and I was not finished being of service to him. And I told her part of the other truth. Kingston, who had made such a study of the innermost recesses of the female mind, might help me understand how my sister could have been so changed.

"And the girl? What will you do about her?" Mother asked.

"I was hoping you would let Effie stay here for a while. She isn't mad, far from it." When Mother made no response, I added, "Of course, I'll make some other arrangement for her later."

"Well, then I suppose she might…"

"She'll be company for you."

"Yes, she will."

"Thank you."

As Mother left my room, she indicated that this was our parting, that we need not speak again before I left the house.

# Chapter 27

Effie had never spoken to me in daylight. As the sky lightened, panic seized me. I must go to her, wake her, or I would never hear her answers to my questions. I found her in her room, but not sleeping, standing by the window, white shift, bare feet. She was braiding her hair. I drew the curtain against the prospect of morning, faced the curtain, while she stood behind me.

"Tell me who has hurt you," I said. "Those men certainly. And your father in his way. Your sister and her husband. Matron, no doubt. But who else?"

Effie remained silent.

"You said those men wouldn't blur together, not like the way the strokes of a beating blur together. How did you know that's what happens? Did a slave tell you? Or one of your brothers after your father took a strap to him? Has someone beaten you?"

When she answered, Effie's voice sounded almost as thin and distant and unpracticed as it had the first time she spoke to me.

"Straps, whips, unkind hands," she whispered, "devices of tormentors with little or no imagination." Effie drew a long breath, let it go, drew another. "But there is a kind of tormentor whose favorite instrument is the spoken word. With that he destroys affection and hope. He causes a mind to turn in on itself and devise its own suffering for the body."

"Kingston," I said.

"Maybe he understands some of the women in that place. He finds out what they're afraid of, ashamed of, and uses that."

"He did this to you? Tried to?"

"Tried is all. Papa and Jeanetta had given him little enough truth and more than a few lies about me. For a time, Dr. Kingston would guess at one thing and then another, trying to work his spell over me. But in the asylum, Papa protected me as he had not done before and though he was not with me, I never said a word to Dr. Kingston."

"You were never like the others, the ones who admire him and fawn on him. The ones who believe his estimation of them and his distortion of their lives."

"I think that Dr. Kingston needs madness," Effie said softly, "and I have none for him to take."

She was right. She had been an impostor among the madwomen, she and Mrs. Glover and surely others before them. And I felt certain that Kingston's demented following had not always been limited to the bounds of Magdalene Asylum but might well have extended to whomever he found desirably vulnerable, even to the daughter of a colleague.

"Effie, I'm going back to the asylum, leaving this morning." I paused a moment, wondering if she would ask me why. "I must finish my duty to my employer," I gave in unrequested explanation. "I want you to stay here. My mother wants you to stay."

Effie came around and faced me. The sun was well up, and a pale light infiltrated the room despite the drawn the curtain. Standing on tiptoe, she reached up and placed her hands on my shoulders and her smooth cheek against my rough one as I bent toward her. I felt her lips moving close by my ear, her breath soft on my face in proof she spoke to me. And her words were like a kiss. "You are what I have lost."

With one hand I touched Effie's braided hair. The other hand I pressed against the curve of the small of her back, holding her to me, as when I had danced with her in a dream.

After making a few necessary preparations for my journey, I set off on foot, as I had more than a year ago. Mother had shut herself up in her room before I left, and Effie stood on the balcony, very still, her hands resting on the railing.

Again, the Magdalene Asylum was my destination. I walked south and southwest, away from the Mississippi and toward the Atchafalaya. Again, I lugged my satchel and black bag, trudging down farm roads, cutting across fallow fields. Halfway there, a thundershower commenced. And again I was grateful for my cleated boots that gripped at the slick red mud on the tributary tow path.

On my way I had eaten little and slept less, giving myself over to chills no midday sun could thaw, then to fever no spring rain could cool. I gave myself over, as if I were tumbling forward in space and time, careless of myself, but those horseshoe nails in the soles of my boots would not let me fall.

Days had gone by, two or three, I was never sure. Then one evening I drew close to the asylum, of that I was sure. My head began to clear, and stubbornness if not strength drove me on toward the familiar path, the walled garden, the locked gate. But just there, I hesitated then veered off for the piney woods on the outskirts of Lorraine and at nightfall arrived at the Reverend Mr. Jonas's cabin.

The cabin door stood wide open, and lamplight from inside shone out as a glowing band across the narrow porch, where Jonas sat, smoking his pipe, the boy Asa beside him. The Reverend invited me in, and leaving my black bag and satchel outside the door, I followed him. He remarked that I didn't look too well and gave me a slice of cornbread smeared with lard and a cup of chicory coffee. The bread and wine of communion could not have done more to restore my spirits.

I told Jonas I'd been away, seeing to the safe deliverance of a patient who had been released, otherwise I would have gone directly to Captain Purvis about the lynching. "Has anything been done?" I asked, though I had little faith that in my absence Kingston had publicly admitted his patient had taken her own life and not been murdered by Oralia and Wheeler. I had even less faith that the men responsible for the lynching had met with chastisement, let alone justice.

Jonas shook his head. "Nothing, nothing been done." He looked toward the open door, then pushed it nearly shut, and dropped his deep voice lower still. "Asa be taking his sister's passing mighty hard."

"I understand, more than I can say, Reverend. I wish there was something I could do for him."

"Reckon you could take on a lynch mob, Dr. Mallory? Asa been brooding on vengeance, stopping his ears to the word of the Lord."

I shook my head. "For what it's worth, I can take on Dr. Kingston, who started what that mob finished. Without his accusing Oralia, nobody else would have touched her. I intend to hold him accountable for that, and for other things."

"You care to tell me how, sir?"

Choosing to ignore the skepticism in his tone, I said I had been working that out on my way, adding, "I can't promise you or Asa that I can make things any better up at the asylum, but I will make them different."

Swallowing the dregs of my coffee, I rose to go. Jonas saw me out to the porch, where I thanked him for his hospitality and asked the favor of leaving my satchel in his keeping for the night. The Reverend agreed.

Then I transferred my medical journals, with all the information they contained regarding some of Kingston's patients, alive and dead, from my black bag, which I was taking with me, to the satchel, which Jonas said he would stash in his loft. I had no desire to take my journals back into Kingston's territory, not just yet, and didn't wish to be burdened this night with my personal belongings. But I never knew when I might need the instruments of my profession, which were as much a part of me as hand or arm, and did not choose to be parted from them.

Asa stood by, watching me as I rearranged the contents of my luggage. I was intent on separating journals from medical paraphernalia and gave no thought to what was missing from the bag. Then, with no prompting from the Reverend, the boy took up my black bag and offered to walk with me to the asylum gate.

# Chapter 28

Asa knew the way in the dark, knew a shortcut, in fact. The wrought iron gate was locked, I had no key, and the chance of old Gaston hearing my call was less than remote. I contemplated following the wall along to the stockade fence at the river's edge, wading through the water, and climbing up the bank by Hardy's cottage. But again, Asa came to my assistance.

The boy took a cord, from which dangled a key, from around his neck and offered it to me. "This here was in Oralia's pocket," he said.

The key to the gate for her nocturnal comings and goings. "I'm glad you have it, but you shouldn't have it," I said. "Have you ever used it before?"

"No, sir. The women who laid her out give it to me. And I kept it."

I opened the gate, and Asa handed me my bag. "Thank you. You go on back now." I started up the drive, the cleats of my boots cutting into the packed earth. There were lights flickering up ahead at the big house and a faint but sprightly sound of piano music. Kingston must be holding one of his soirees. I heard the gate clang shut behind me and went on.

The downstairs windows were open to the mild night air, the curtains drawn back, and I could see, sure enough, the parlor was awhirl with gaiety, Kingston at its center. Not wishing to disrupt the revels, I made my entrance through a window into Kingston's dark, empty office. There I left my bag, then crossed the hall and mounted the staircase, the cleats of my boots sinking into the thick carpet.

I climbed past the second floor wards, where those inmates not invited to the party stirred and moaned in their drugged repose. On a table on the landing of the third floor, I found a lamp and lit it to brighten my way to the treatment room. And there I set to work.

While some frenetic pair of hands pounded out a dance tune on the piano below, I hauled the crib apparatus to the top of the stairs, dragged it down the three flights, shoved it out the front door and off the veranda into the yard. I followed the same procedure with the restraining chair. Heavier and more cumbersome than the crib, the chair slipped once or twice from my grasp and clattered against the railing, the metal buckles of its unfastened leather straps biting into the varnished banister. An attendant in the wards woke at her post, and shuffled toward me, smelling of whiskey. I assured her that I was simply doing some clearing up for Dr. Kingston, she need not trouble herself. And so she didn't, but shrugged and returned to dozing in her chair.

I pulled the now broken chair and crib away from the house and onto the front lawn, then returned to the third story. From the padded cells, I tore the stained and mildewed mattress ticks from the walls. The nails that had secured them ripped through the striped cloth, and as I dragged the mattresses down the front stairs, their various contents spilled out along the way—corn shucks, Spanish moss, old feathers.

I returned to the house again to retrieve the lamp I had left in one of the cells. That was when I saw that my stripping away of the mattress ticks had exposed a previously hidden door. Forcing it open, I found a narrow spiral staircase. Carrying the lamp, I descended, winding round and round, until I stopped in a space no wider than a single stair. I ran one hand vertically along one corner of the wall in front of me and felt a hinge. I turned the lamplight to the other corner and found a lever. The panel swung open into Kingston's office. How convenient, if he wished to visit a patient in her padded cell, or if he wished to let her out in the night.

I shut the panel. It was papered on the office side and indistinguishable from every other panel of embossed wallpaper, except, of course, to Kingston's eyes. His desk was positioned opposite his secret door, and I recalled how often, when I had sat before him, he had stared over my head at something beyond me.

So absorbed had I been in my undertaking, and after my exertions there was such a ringing in my ears, that I hardly noticed when the piano music ceased and the laughter died away. Out in the yard again, holding the lamp up to survey the wreckage I had created, I heard a rising murmuring behind me. I glanced back over my shoulder. Heads of ringlets peered at me out the parlor windows, and rouged mouths whispered to one another. Turning back to the pile of rubbish, I threw the burning lamp on it, shattered the lamp against the back of the restraining chair. Oil and flames raced over the mattress ticks, and soon the fire crackled in the slats of the crib. Satisfied, I faced the house.

Kingston stepped outside the front door through a cloud of his own cigar smoke, which he waved aside, the better to scrutinize me. Hardy, drink in hand, followed him onto the veranda. Next came the parade of crinolines. And above them all, at the barred windows, appeared a few pale faces of inmates.

For a time, no one moved, no one spoke, as if each of us, myself included, must take in what I had done. I stood close to the blaze, close enough to see the air around it shimmer with heat, and a chill ran through me. Then, over the roar of the fire and the thrumming in my head, I picked out Kingston's voice, raised to be heard by Hardy. "Yes, Joshua, it's him, all right. Robert Mallory has come back to us."

I approached the front steps, empty-handed as I had not been on my first arrival, and presented myself to my employer. In my peripheral vision, I was aware of Hardy sinking back in a wicker chair and of Matron appearing in her dressing gown, shooing the party-goers inside, assisted by a few attendants. But my focus was on Kingston.

"Join me in my office, Robert."

Matron brought a lamp and did her best to cut me with a narrow glance before Kingston sent her off to restore order among the patients.

He took his time, pouring himself a snifter of brandy, holding it to the light, swirling the liquid in the glass. Kingston wanted time, I knew, so that when he spoke, he would be in control.

I sank into a chair, aching with the onset of fever, and yet strangely exhilarated, for it seemed to me that as my body began to fail me, my mind was growing clearer, my resolve stronger.

Kingston spoke in a calculated drawl. "I as much as gave you the girl, Robert. You could have gone anywhere. Done anything."

"No, sir. I could only come here."

"Why? For what?"

"For you. I have come back, sir, to be the part of you that is missing."

He drew in his breath and released it with the twitch of a smile. "And what, pray tell, do you think I am missing?"

My answer came with an explanation, and I was surprised at how quietly and attentively Kingston listened to me. "I have seen with my own eyes your disregard for the lives of others, including Wheeler and Oralia and everyone who cared about them. I have heard you speak of patients and caretakers alike, with contempt. But, of course, what I have seen and heard here is not unique to you. Such behavior is acceptable in a world in which you and those like you set the standard. But there's more.

"While in New Orleans, I called on Mr. Poncet to offer my belated condolences. He didn't know his wife was dead. But you did. And you kept right on charging him your fee. Then, I found the arrangement you made for Effie Rampling was the equivalent of sending her into slavery, and I believe you knew that, too, when you struck your bargain with Mrs. Fabre.

"Tonight, while I was clearing up the treatment room and padded cells—" here his focus shifted from my face to the paneled wall behind me, "I found a door and a staircase leading down here, to your office. How convenient for you to slip upstairs, without even Matron knowing, to treat your special patients—Rachel Poncet, Veronique Beaulieu, and I don't know how many others. Or to let them out when you deemed the time was right to lead them into the valley of the shadow."

Kingston looked back at me.

"You claimed that you came upon Oralia and Wheeler at the riverside. But what if they, in fact, had come upon you?"

He answered me only with an arch of one brow.

"What you are missing, Dr. Kingston, is a conscience. And I have come back to provide it."

"You are out of your head, my boy. You are burning up with fever."

"Oh, not quite, sir. You are missing a conscience as surely as some men are missing an eye or an arm or a leg. Remember how you told me to be sure to call on my mother in Baton Rouge? Well, I did just that. Left Effie with her for company. And while I was there, Mother allowed me to read Lucinda's diary."

Kingston finished the last swallow of his brandy. "So, she wrote of me? Your dear sister…"

"Dear to you?"

"More than you know, Robert. More than someone of ordinary perceptions could ever guess."

I never hated him more than when he spoke of Lucinda, but I made myself ask. "Then since I cannot guess, will you tell me what my sister meant to you?"

Kingston sighed. "We've come so far together, haven't we, my boy? You have unraveled so much. The least I can do is tell you about your sister."

I clenched my jaw and heard him out. "There had been talk among the gentlemen that Lucinda was merely a pretty girl of no particularly striking attainments. Her singing, drawing, needlework and the like hardly distinguished her. But to me, Robert, your sister was remarkable. Oh, my seduction of her was simple enough. A young woman unsure of her charms is an easy mark."

Kingston's face registered amusement, but mine did not.

"Ah, but it was as I grew tired of her that she began to set herself apart from other young ladies. When her body bored me, she surrendered her mind to me and fed my soul—"

"Your arrogance."

"—with the most delicious food. From Lucinda, I acquired an appetite no common whore could satisfy."

My vain and shallow sister. Kingston gave her too much credit, too much blame.

"The more I rejected her, the more she devoted herself to me. The more I ignored her, humiliated her, the more she craved degradation. She would stop at nothing, absolutely nothing, if I ordained it."

She would scorn her father's authority, she would break her mother's heart because Kingston had ordained it.

"My parents were kind to you," I said. "You were a guest in their home."

"And Lucinda would do anything I told her to do. Anything."

"Did you tell her to come to me?"

"She had only to ask you…"

She had only to ask me, "Make me as I was before I met him."

"You told her to marry your nephew," I said. "But she wouldn't go through with it."

"Oh, Robert. I was toying with her. Lucinda would have cuckholded the groom an hour after the wedding, if I had summoned her." Disdain swelled in his voice. "Do you wish to believe that with her suicide she at last defied my power over her? Is that more palatable to you than the alternative?"

"What is the alternative?"

"As I said. She would do anything I commanded her to do."

"You can simply order a woman to hang herself, drown herself, stab herself, and it's done?"

Kingston pursed his lips before he answered. "You refuse to acknowledge that extinguishing a life is as easy for me as blowing out a candle. I am not like you. Unlike yours, Robert, my hands are clean. With a breath, a word, my will is done. I never so much as lick thumb and forefinger to pinch the wick."

I wanted to kill him. Murder was in my heart.

"But death was not easy for Lucinda." I forced my words to come. "Fashioning a noose was among the many things at which my sister was not accomplished. Father told me how she died by slow strangulation."

Kingston eased back in his chair behind his desk. "Are you in need of quinine, Robert?"

"You know I am."

"Everlastingly dosing yourself. You only prolong your suffering. Your case is hopeless, worsened by anemia. You know that, don't you? I have many preparations in my dispensary. You could save yourself a world of pain."

"No, sir. Not yet. I'm not finished with my work. You have restitution to make, and I am here to help you make it."

"Oh, Robert," Kingston exhaled my name with a sigh and shook his head. "Bringing you here, knowing what I know about you, watching you struggle with yourself and yet do my bidding, entertained me for a while. But in the grand scheme of things—"

"Your scheme."

"You are of no real consequence, my boy. You should have stayed gone when you had the chance."

Still, I persisted. "You must repay those you have cheated. You must ask forgiveness from those you have wronged."

Kingston leaned toward me, across his desk, and whispered—or did he imagine he was blowing out a candle? "Robert, you have lost your mind."

The fever seared my eyes, and I could hardly keep them open. But I saw the blur of movement as Kingston rose, moved around his desk and toward me. "What will you have?" he asked. "Opium? Morphine? Belladonna?"

My lips and tongue were too parched to shape an answer. If he had offered me water, I might have exchanged my soul for it.

"Poor boy. You look as if you won't last the night."

Dragging my fingers across my cheeks, I brought my own sweat to my mouth. I was accustomed to Kingston's habit of looking past me, looking through me. It was his staring at me, bearing down on me, that I found disquieting. And then Kingston shifted his attention to something else, quite suddenly, the way he'd often done to show that I was beneath his notice, that he had the upper hand. Except that this time he did not.

Asa was standing in the room with us.

"Who let this boy in here?" Kingston demanded. "You, Robert?"

My voice returned as a rasp. "He came with me to the gate."

"He's been hovering at my gate ever since…"

"Since you took his sister to jail," I said slowly, every word an effort. "He could have entered at any time. He had a gate key, that was in Oralia's pocket at the time of her lynching."

Kingston turned toward Asa. "Why choose tonight, boy?"

Asa lifted his chin and answered. " 'Cause tonight, sir, I got this." He brought his right hand from behind his back, and he was gripping an army revolver, the one to which I had given no thought, had not missed, while taking the medical journals out of my black bag.

Asa pointed the revolver at Kingston, who glowered back at him, and then the boy's hand began to tremble, his whole body to shake. As I pulled myself up from the chair, shaking as well, Kingston strode past me, toward Asa, snatching for the gun. For an instant, the two of them, man and boy, locked themselves together. But in another moment, Asa twisted in Kingston's grasp, still clinging to the revolver, and fired once into the man responsible for his sister's death.

Then the two of them separated, backed away from each other, both of them stunned by the shot. Asa, panting, held the weapon in both his hands, clutched it against his chest, and stared at Kingston, who looked askance at his wounded right arm, dangling at his side. The bullet must have struck at the elbow, for there the fine gray wool of his coat sleeve had been ripped away. The lower part of the sleeve was soaking with blood, blood that poured down over his hand and pooled on the carpet at his feet.

Kingston staggered backward until he leaned against the edge of his vast mahogany desk. I had seen that ashen look of disbelief time and again on other faces. Someone else should take the bullet, someone else should suffer the pain, never oneself.

I went to him. I cleared the top of his desk, swept papers and files and inkstand and blotter onto the floor, and laid him on the desk, with his feet hanging over one end.

Leaving him there, I came to Asa and shoved him toward the open window. "Get out of here," I told him. "Say nothing about this. Go to Jonas and stay with him. You understand me? Don't ever come back here."

Asa nodded, then set the revolver beside my black bag, where I had left it by the window, before he slipped over the sill and was gone.

# Chapter 29

After carrying my black bag near to the desk on which Kingston lay, I fumbled in its depths for what I needed. I had worked time and again in a surgery tent, sicker than I was now, in the hectic flush before delirium overtook me. I would work until I could work no more. Somewhere in the house, beyond the room in which I stood, shouts and pounding footfalls added their clamor to the drumming in my head. If I could keep concentrating on the one task, one procedure at a time, however hurried, then perhaps I could finish what I set out to do.

My hands trembling, I cut away Kingston's coat and shirt sleeves, the scissors chewing through the blood-soaked cloth. I examined the wound. The bullet had shattered the bones of the elbow, severed blood vessels. Kingston's face paled, his eyes grew wild, his breath fitful and interspersed with cries of pain. He must have feared, perhaps understood, the seriousness of his injury, and his desperate expression was as pitiable as any I had ever seen. I tried to stanch the bleeding with a wad of white gauze that was red within a moment. I strapped a tourniquet around his upper arm, above his wound, and as I yanked it taut, Kingston jerked and gasped. The bleeding slowed.

Matron and Hardy were in the room, perhaps with an attendant or two, but it was their voices I heard behind me, Matron wailing that I had murdered Dr. Kingston, Hardy demanding to know what I was up to now. Then they closed in on either side of me, Matron weeping, I suppose with relief to see that her idol still lived.

"I must amputate his arm," I said.

"Oh, my God," Matron cried, "he's going to butcher him."

But Hardy, leaning nearby on his cane, saw my point. "Why, that thing will putrefy in an hour, Lila, if he doesn't cut it off."

"I need more gauze," I said. "And light, I must have more light. Water. Quinine."

Kingston's lips twitched, and Matron bent to hear him gasp out his order to her. "Give it to him. Anything he wants."

"Yes, sir."

I was in no condition to relish Matron's sudden deference to my needs. I was in no condition to do anything until those needs were met for water and quinine. And she must have understood that, for she brought them quickly and all but forced the bitter medicine down my throat herself. It was just as well that I had had little to eat that day. Quinine worked faster on an empty stomach. But the nausea that swept over me sent me reeling, and I dropped into a chair to recover myself.

"You can't fool me with that malingering act of yours," Hardy shouted at me. "Get yourself up and operate." As if blustering were the first step in accomplishing any task.

Kingston was mouthing something to Matron, and she relayed the message to Hardy. "He says to give Dr. Mallory a few minutes. He wants his hands steady."

How strange, in the space of those few minutes, with myself sick and aching, to watch Kingston in far greater distress, to know he waited for my help, depended upon my skill.

Light filled the room as attendants brought a half dozen blazing lamps and a broad mirror to double their illumination. I rose and prepared to go to work. Kingston had lost a great deal of blood, and I could delay no longer. Matron positioned a small table near the desk where my patient lay, and on it I opened my amputation kit, feeling her watching every movement of my hands. I chose the sharpest of the large knives, gripped the handle, and positioned the blade over the flesh between the tourniquet and the wound. Kingston stared up at me. The terror that shone from his eyes coursed as a tremor through his body.

"You can hold him down," I said to Matron and the attendants who gathered behind the lamps, "or Dr. Hardy can give him ether. But do it now."

Kingston jerked his head toward Hardy, who hovered at his left side. His eyes pleaded for the ether.

"Well… I've never used ether," Hardy began sputtering. "Besides, if Robert here is quick enough, it won't matter."

But apparently, it mattered to Kingston, who groaned and bellowed in his agony, and to Matron, who hurried for the ether and thrust bottle and gauze into Hardy's gnarled hands. "You've seen Dr. Kingston use it," she said. "You can't let him suffer."

I was unsure of the meaning of the look Kingston then gave to Hardy, just before the old man sent him off. Was he grateful at the prospect of going beyond pain? Or was he suddenly aghast at the prospect of slipping away, out of control, perhaps never waking?

At the instant Kingston's eyes closed, I brought the blade through his flesh, circumscribing the humeral bone. In the next instant, I exchanged the knife for the handsaw. The bleeding of the wound, slowed earlier by the tourniquet, had begun anew, spewing forth on my trousers and saturating the carpet under my feet. But my cleated boots kept me steady as, with two strokes of the saw's serrated edge, I separated the arm from the body. Patients always appreciated efficiency.

One of the attendants, anticipating my need, had already taken up the discarded knife and had begun heating the blade over a candle flame. When the metal was hot enough to sear flesh, I cauterized the wound. Another attendant, not so adept as a surgical assistant, and Dr. Hardy himself, ever eager to see something lopped off, were both sick to their stomachs.

I dressed the wound with fresh gauze. Then I downed a glass of water, another dose of quinine, another glass of water. The attendant who had heated the knife now brought a blanket to cover Kingston and a pillow for his head. He would not be dragged from the operating table to make room for another patient. Instead he would rest in his ether-induced sleep, watched over by his surgeon. He had a better chance for recovery than many men I had treated, despite his prodigious loss of blood.

I sank into Kingston's red leather desk chair, while Matron reverentially carried the severed arm from the room. Did she intend to bury it, I mused, perhaps between the graves of Rachel Poncet and Veronique Beaulieu?

In the midst of life we are in death. I lost track of how long I observed my patient, watched him capturing each vital breath, holding it, fearing even in sleep to let it go. I surveyed that once forbidding office that looked like home to me now, the home I had known throughout the years of the war, seen through a haze of smoking oil lamps and guttering candles, felt and breathed and heard. It had all become too familiar, blood thickening underfoot, the odor of blood mixing with myriad other odors, someone retching in a corner, someone moaning, someone crying out.

"Robert Mallory." At the harsh sound of Matron's voice, I looked up. She strode through the doorway, pointing her finger at me, for the benefit of those who followed her, Captain Purvis and three soldiers. "There he is. He's the one who shot Dr. Kingston."

Slowly I rose, still unsteady though my fever had abated, and looked toward the captain, whose glance traveled over me and around the room.

The attendants had left some time ago. Hardy, on the corner settee, was quaffing brandy. And I stood alone, in my blood-spattered suit, beside the unconscious Dr. Kingston, both of us encircled by a vast stain of blood. My surgical instruments lay on the table and my revolver on the floor. As I struggled against exhaustion, it seemed to me that Purvis struggled as well to comprehend the scene before him. As he had the first time I met him, the young officer inspired in me an odd sense of kinship, another man doing a job he didn't particularly care to do. The captain's gaze came to rest on Kingston's stump of an arm swathed in gauze. "You did this?" he said to me.

"Yes, sir."

Kingston moaned. A shuddering ran through his shoulders. Then he raised his left arm slightly and moved his hand across his torso, fingers feeling their way toward the other arm that wasn't there, yet ached and throbbed and burned as if it were.

Matron began her discourse on the night's events. I had intruded into the house, she claimed, bent on destruction, had actually burned asylum property. Matron foresaw the danger I represented. Just after Kingston and I had begun our last conversation, she took it upon herself to send Gaston to town, instructing him to fetch Captain Purvis. What had she been thinking of, taking such initiative? Had she lost confidence in her employer? If not for Asa's interference, surely Kingston would have rid himself of any disruption I might have created. By daybreak, he would have seen me dead.

Matron continued, venom wetting her words. "He threatened Dr. Kingston, and he shot him. There it is." She pointed at the revolver, and a soldier lifted it from the rug. "There's the weapon. Oh, when Dr. Hardy and I heard the shot and rushed in, he made a great show of rendering aid to his victim, as if it were some accident. But I know better." She paused for breath.

"Did you shoot Dr. Kingston?" Captain Purvis asked me.

"Of course Robert shot him," Hardy chimed in. "It was just the two of them in here." Douglas didn't shoot himself. Nasty wound, too, close range. Blew that elbow to bits. Ruination of the arm."

"Was there a struggle over the gun, Dr. Mallory?" Was the captain offering me a chance to claim what Matron had already refuted, that the shooting was accidental, or that it was somehow in self-defense? "Did you, in fact, draw on Dr. Kingston? Did you aim to shoot him?"

I hesitated, then answered, "No, sir."

"But you did shoot him?"

I said nothing. Kingston had opened his eyes, and his glance darted from the captain's face to mine.

"Praise be, he's revived," Matron cried, clasping her hands devoutly to her breast, godly being that she was. "Now the doctor can tell us himself how he was nearly murdered." Stepping closer to the desk, she dropped her voice to some approximation of a gentle whisper. "Dr. Kingston, can you speak, sir, and tell Captain Purvis what happened?"

Kingston's eyelids fluttered as if he would slip away again into unconsciousness. But his left hand still moved, seeking the missing arm. Then his eyes flew open, bulged as he arched his neck and looked down at the bandaged remainder beneath his right shoulder. Even when a man knew he must lose a limb, as Kingston had known, acknowledgment was paired with disbelief.

"Dr. Kingston," said the captain, "did Dr. Mallory shoot you?"

I thought of Asa and Oralia. I thought of myself and Lucinda. If Kingston told the truth, I would say he lied. And if he lied, I would leave the truth unsaid.

Matron cradled Kingston's head and gave him a sip of water. There was a grayness in his face, as if he were half ghost already. If he died now, without answering Captain Purvis, what would I do? Hours ago I had wished Kingston dead at least as much as Asa had. Only duty had altered my mind.

Kingston shaped his words, said them aloud, each one distinct and deliberate. "Robert Mallory shot me."

Matron's mouth tightened in an expression of satisfaction. Hardy mumbled something that I doubted was of any importance. Purvis and his men stood silent.

Kingston looked at me—not past me or through me, but at me— triumphantly. If I dared to contradict him, I would feel the power of his word against mine. He could snuff me out with a single breath. I did not need to contradict him, not yet. All I needed to do was wait.

As Kingston and I went on staring at one another, the captain spoke. "Dr. Mallory, have you anything to say?"

Without breaking my gaze at Kingston, I answered, "Not yet, Captain Purvis. Soon."

Did I see a flicker of suspicion in Kingston's eyes, a twitch of apprehension, a question for me there that I would leave unanswered? I knew what was happening to him, for I had seen it happen to other men many times before. A sudden, violent tremor seized and released him. And all of Matron's clinging to him and crying out and cursing me could not reverse his fate. I reached out and put my hand over Kingston's heart, felt it race and pound against my palm as if it would burst from his chest, then the pounding slowed and slowed to nothing.

No heartbeat, no pulse, no breath with which to extinquish other life.

"Dr. Kingston is dead," I announced.

"Murdered!" Matron reminded us all, and commenced sobbing.

Hardy, never one to have much confidence in my opinions, prodded the corpse with his cane just to make sure.

Captain Purvis regarded me with what I could only surmise was an expression of regret. "You understand, Dr. Mallory," he said, "that I must take you into custody."

"Yes, Captain, I understand."

Near daybreak, the captain's men escorted me away from the asylum. The bonfire was burnt out, but the odors of wood smoke and of scorched leather lingered in the air. Attendants, some in uniforms and some in night clothes, and patients, some in ballgowns and some in white shifts, who had gathered to watch the fire, had watched too long and now nodded in sleep. They leaned against the railings or huddled on the steps of the veranda, taking no notice of my departure.

# Chapter 30

I was taken to a private cell in the attic of the building that served as courthouse and jail, for I was something different, the jailer Buford informed me, a gentleman killer, not to be thrown in with the riff-raff in the basement. So, there I found myself locked up across the passage from the cell in which Oralia had been chained.

Shortly after my arrest, the Reverend Mr. Jonas brought my satchel to the jail, and I regretted not being allowed to speak with him and ask after Asa. Captain Purvis took charge of my personal effects. Far better he than the jailer, and he saw to it that I would not only have a change of clothes for the day of the trial, but that I received my journals and writing implements as well to pass the days preceding my day in court.

Naturally, I was not allowed my black bag of medical supplies. What might I have done given my handsaw? But I asked Buford for quinine, begged him for it. I wanted to see clearly, think clearly in whatever time might be left to me. And even as the jailer delayed and scoffed at my request, even before the captain intervened, I set to work.

I leafed through my papers and journals, annotating and arranging. In those pages, I had marked the hours, the days, the years. I had catalogued patients' wounds, symptoms, treatments, cures, and deaths. I had imposed an order, and chaos mocked me. The soldiers and the madwomen and Kingston himself rose up from where they had fallen and walked the earth and crowded into my cell, into my brain. How could I make sense of what had happened to me, what was happening now, when all that had led me to this time and place still existed within me, all at once, without time, without order? And the ringing in my ears, the tolling of bells, the cries of pandemonium shattered the silence and the peace that would not be kept.

On my better days, when quinine brought me a little respite, I occupied myself writing letters to all the families whose names I could remember or had recorded in my journals, who had relatives at Magdalene Asylum. Captain Purvis was generous enough to post the lot of them to Mr. Poncet, whose attorney would know what to do with them.

When I tired and chose to write no more, I looked out the small square window, cut high and barred in the grimy plastered wall. I thought of the little landscape painting that hung in my mother's dining room, that pleasant composition: a swath of high grass flecked with red wildflowers, to the right a spreading live oak, low branches brushing the earth, a higher branch perfect for a swing, upper left blue sky, a smattering of white clouds… And near center stands a young woman in a plain brown dress, near a cauldron of laundry suspended over an open fire. Only the bars in the foreground mar the picture. And of course the laundress never appeared in my mother's painting. Yet I see her as she was that first day, pouring a silver arc of water, her plaited hair draped over her shoulder. Light and shadow and wishful thinking.

A judge and lawyers came from Baton Rouge, and newspaper reporters followed them. As if I had not hurt my mother enough in private, now I must be the source of her public humiliation.

I had not written to Mother, asking her to come, and was startled to see her sitting on a bench near the back of the small, crowded courtroom. I worried that she would be distressed by the proceedings, yet was gratified that she had made the journey, though I could not read the expression of her eyes. Her russet-colored bonnet shadowed her face, and a dark brown shawl covered her shoulders. Was she cold, as I was cold, despite the mild weather and even in such a crowded room? I noticed a space between her and the next occupant of the bench, a portly man in a plaid suit, fanning himself with his hat. Was he offering her a courtesy by keeping some distance, even as other spectators sitting on other benches crushed shoulders? Or was he refraining from coming too close to a relative of the accused?

The man looked familiar. Many of the men in the room looked familiar. I had seen them gathered once before, all of them together, outside the courthouse, along the boardwalk, all of them talking of murder. That was just after I had visited Oralia, the last time I saw her alive.

Some of the men were now seated as jurors, the rest as observers. I, too, was an observer, though set apart from the others, in a small, railed enclosure, under guard. All of us were there, together or apart, to watch the lawyers maneuver and the judge frown and check the time on his gold pocket watch, to hear lies and versions of truth.

Before the day of the trial, I had met once with Mr. Russell, the attorney appointed to represent me—hard to say he was there to defend me. If I'd had the time and means to find better counsel, was there better to be found? Who was most likely to sway in my favor this particular jury? Some of them, the veterans missing limbs, already harbored bitterness toward one of my profession. Some of them had enjoyed special relationships with the deceased: his tailor, his tobacconist, his banker. And some I recognized would as soon lynch a defendant as waste time seeing him tried. Would a nasal-voiced, East-coast educated lawyer or a soft-spoken, newly-educated freedman be more likely to influence the court than the drawling, white-haired learned member of the old order, whom the court had granted me?

The prosecuting attorney was younger and more energetic. While the defense attorney, Mr. Russell, leaned back in his chair, skimming some documents through his spectacles, Mr. Kemble worked the courtroom, greeting spectators, grinning at the jury, nodding at the judge wielding the gavel. Perhaps, in the near future, the fellow planned to run for office.

When proceedings began in earnest, I hardly noticed, except that the din in the room faded to a drone as judge and lawyers took turns holding forth. The shivering, which I had struggled to control lest the jury assume I trembled in fear, abated. Gradually, the ache in my bones became the ache in my muscles as chill became fever. I looked again toward my mother, still wrapped in her shawl, and saw that the space next to her was now occupied. Beside her sat Effie Rampling.

My vision blurred and cleared, eyes straining past the rows of spectators in front of her to catch a better glimpse. Like Mother, Effie sat very straight, chin lifted. They looked well together. Effie wore something soft—an ivory-colored blouse, sprigged with primroses, a bit of lace at the throat. It was something of Mother's, made-over to suit Effie's smaller figure. Somehow, I felt relieved that the blouse had never belonged to my sister. Effie's hair lay unbraided, loosely gathered in a pink ribbon and draped over one shoulder. A cross breeze traveling through the open windows lifted the edges of the ribbon. Effie met my gaze, and for an instant, she smiled. I think she did. Then a man in front of her shifted into my line of vision, and I could no longer see her face.

At the windows, on the lawn outside the courthouse, the Reverend Mr. Jonas and his parishioners had gathered, Asa among them. What had the boy come to hear? Why had he not stayed away?

I was the only witness to the shooting of Dr. Kingston, and there I was on trial for having done the deed. Mr. Russell's best advice to me was to keep my mouth shut and let him raise a reasonable doubt.

Madwomen and black attendants would not be called to describe events on the night of my alleged murderous rampage. That was left to others such as Matron, the first witness for the prosecution, who pronounced her speculations as certainties and labeled me Dr. Kingston's assassin.

"Robert Mallory," she jabbed a finger in my direction, "sneaked through the gates that night and set to destroying asylum property. Built a bonfire in the yard and burnt up everything he could lay his hands on. And then he came after Dr. Kingston with a revolver. That's when I sent the servant galloping into town to fetch help. All for nothing! Captain Purvis and his men arrived too late. That villain had already murdered the doctor."

Mr. Kemble avoided asking Matron anything too specific, such as had she actually seen me holding the revolver? Then, my so-called defense attorney made matters worse, asking her what she supposed my motive could have been in attacking my employer.

"Envy," she asserted. "He had to know he was inferior, even though he was everlastingly putting himself forward. As if the likes of him knew better than Dr. Kingston about treatments and such. Robert Mallory was a troublemaker from the day he arrived. All of you here know what a brilliant man the doctor was, what he did for this community, how you all benefited from his generosity and his fine work. He took this Mallory in as a charity case, as a favor to the boy's father. But he took a viper to his bosom!"

Observing Matron's histrionics in the witness box as she clasped her hands to her heaving breast, I imagined her in future years, Kingston's death the theme of her existence as Lincoln's was for Mrs. Cordelay. Of each new acquaintance, she would demand to know: "Where were you on the night Dr. Kingston was murdered?"

What Lila Fentroy's testimony began, Joshua Hardy's was designed to finish off. According to him, I shot, then butchered Kingston in an attempt to take directorship of the asylum, a position that rightfully belonged to Hardy's grandson, his up-and-coming eminence, Bertram J. Hardy.

"Envy and ambition. Matron hit the nail there."

This time, however, Mr. Russell attempted to do his job, asking, "Dr. Hardy, did you witness the shooting?"

"I didn't have to, sir," he replied in that contemptuous tone he used with patients. "Plain as day, I saw the pair of them go into Dr. Kingston's study. I heard them argue. And I heard the shot." Strange, how Hardy's cloudy eyes and dull ears had been so sharp on that particular night. "When I entered the study, young Mallory pretended to be helping the doctor—as if he didn't know how Kingston had come by that gaping wound! Blood spattered everywhere, flooding over the carpet. Then, under the guise of operating to save the doctor's life, that scoundrel finished off his victim."

"Did you offer to perform the operation yourself, in Dr. Mallory's stead?" Mr. Russell asked.

"Why, I am retired from the medical profession."

"Forgive me if I'm a little confused here, Dr. Hardy. If you suspected my client was trying to finish off Dr. Kingston, wouldn't you come out of retirement on that occasion?"

A glint of amusement shone in the judge's eyes as he prompted Hardy, who had resorted to sputtering, to answer so he and the jury could hear.

"Well, I . . . I hoped Mallory would find his better self and do the job right. Besides, amputations were never my specialty."

"So, rather than risk botching the job yourself, you were willing to trust that Dr. Mallory would make amends, shall we say, for shooting Dr. Kingston," said my lawyer. "Did you not think it possible then that the two men, whom you knew to have disagreed, had struggled over the weapon in the heat of argument, neither one intending to shoot the other? Did you not think, as you watched the defendant make every effort possible to save Dr. Kingston's life, that the shooting was, indeed, accidental?"

Mr. Kemble launched a volley of objections, but seemed satisfied enough with Hardy's answer, given at the judge's insistence.

"The shot was fired from Mallory's own revolver. That's no accident. As for the surgery, I was there to oversee things if Mallory tried something underhanded."

"Which he did, if we are to believe your earlier statement," Mr. Russell countered. "And yet—"

The judge intervened. "Gentlemen, the accused is not on trial for performing surgery. He is on trial for shooting to kill Dr. Kingston. This witness has told us what he knows about the shooting, and he may step down." Then, the judge, whom I had briefly hoped might be a voice of reason, consulted his pocket watch for the third time and murmured to the bailiff, "We should be done with this by dinnertime."

When called on, Captain Purvis stated the facts, as he knew them. No, he had not seen me pull the trigger or perform the surgery. Dr. Kingston had survived his ordeal just long enough to answer the one question the captain posed to him. And then everyone in the courtroom heard him repeat Kingston's answer: "Robert Mallory shot me."

"Were those Dr. Kingston's exact words, Captain?" asked Mr. Kemble.

"Yes, sir."

Had Kingston accused me for his own pride's sake, preferring to blame another white man, however beneath notice he thought I was, than to admit a black boy had gotten the better of him? Or had he despised me so much, after all his looking past me and over me, because I had seen through him?

I swayed under the effect of fever. Had I taken the last of the quinine this morning? Or yesterday, or the day before? I could no longer recall. In my one brief conversation with my attorney, I swore to him that I did not shoot Kingston. Still, Mr. Russell insisted on fashioning some defense about an argument, a struggle, a tragic accident. My head ached as if his convoluted phrases bound my brow.

For a moment, maybe longer, I closed my eyes and let my chin fall to my chest. Then, I felt the rim of a glass pressed to my lips, and I gulped water. One of the guards gripped my shoulders and steadied the glass as I drained it. I whispered my thanks to him.

Above the clanging in my ears, I heard the judge saying something about time, time to be done, time for closing arguments. Panic galvanized me. The trial could not be finished. I had not answered my accusers. I could tell the judge and jury something. Surely, I should be allowed to tell them something. At least let them know that I did not envy Kingston, even if they were determined to believe I killed him.

I searched the crowd for sight of Effie and saw instead the faces of men who blotted her from my sight. I rose, and the guard who had brought me water now gripped my arm.

All the way to taking the stand, I heard Mr. Russell admonishing me, "Stop this nonsense. I'm pleading you guilty to manslaughter. That's the best I can do."

No. Let me tell the truth.

But the lawyer rushed in. "Your Honor, gentlemen of the jury, as you see, my client is not a well man. He was not a well man on the night of the shooting. He is out of his head with fever now, as he was out of his head with fever then, when he and Dr. Kingston had their tussle over the revolver. We know the doctor was shot at very close range, shattering his arm, leaving little chance—"

"Mr. Russell," I called out, putting a stop to his weary sing-song. "Ask me the question. Ask me if I shot him."

Then, with the judge's permission, I was sworn in and, from the stand, I surveyed the room. No need for Kingston's convex mirror here. The distortion was all before me—Matron with her eyes bulging with outrage, Hardy puffing and muttering, waxed side-whiskers aquiver, and row after row of the flushed faces and twisted features of men who believed solely in their rights and their righteousness.

Grudgingly, Mr. Russell asked me, "Did you shoot Dr. Kingston?"

"No, sir. No, I did not shoot him."

"Then who did?" the lawyer asked.

"An intruder. They struggled over the weapon, and Dr. Kingston was wounded."

Mr. Russell looked to the judge. "Your Honor, this is news to me, but with your permission—"

"Get on with it." The judge only patted the pocket in which he kept his watch.

"Dr. Mallory, can you name this intruder?" Mr. Russell's tone was as skeptical as the prosecutor's might have been asking the same question.

Doubt and derision crossed the jurors' faces as they cut their glances, one to another, and whispered among themselves. The onlookers outside drew closer to the windowsills.

"Please, sir, name the intruder," the lawyer prompted me.

"I cannot."

He released his exasperation with an exaggerated sigh. "Well, then describe him to us."

Jonas stood just outside, at the window nearest me, his arm tight around Asa's shoulders. I glanced at the boy, whose mouth trembled, and I wasn't quite sure if Jonas were comforting him, or keeping him from darting away. I turned from the window, not wanting to draw attention to Asa by staring at him.

Mr. Russell spoke again. "Come on now. Do you see the attacker in this courtroom?"

"No, sir."

"Then tell us what he looked like. Was he big or small? Old? Young? A white man? Brown? Black?"

"I can't rightly say, sir."

I wished for another glass of water. I had not thought this far ahead, not thought this through. Half the truth would not suffice for these men, who must punish someone for an attack on one of their own. The judge conferred with the lawyers, something about Mr. Russell getting nowhere and letting Mr. Kemble have at me. Mr. Kemble did.

"An intruder?! You all hear that?" He offered the jury his cordial smile. "An intruder, whom no one else in the house saw or heard." Never mind that only Matron and Hardy were questioned. "Mighty convenient, isn't it, folks? Yet, for some mysterious reason, Dr. Mallory is unable to describe this individual to us. Makes you kind of wonder if the person exists." After pausing to accept the understanding nods of the jurors, Mr. Kemble turned his attention to me, cocking his head and narrowing his eyes. "Are you shielding someone, Dr. Mallory? Maybe one of the inmates? Surely, we could not hold such a creature responsible for her actions. Yet again, I say how convenient that would be. All you have to do is transfer the blame to one who cannot be held accountable."

Or transfer the blame to one who cannot defend himself, not against the machinations of this court of law. I glanced again toward the window. Asa's face was hidden against Jonas's shoulder, and the reverend was saying something to the boy, while keeping his eyes on me. Was Asa hearing the word of the Lord now? What I had said to Jonas regarding the boy came back to me: I wish there were something I could do for him.

I was barely aware of Mr. Kemble, strutting for his audience, speaking gibberish as far as I could understand. Fever seared my eyes. The crowd blurred before me. Then, toward the back of the room, I caught sight of movement and willed my eyes to focus. Effie was no longer sitting beside my mother, but standing, one hand on Mother's shoulder, one at her own breast.

The prosecutor swung back at me, firing questions about the amputation. Wasn't I a surgeon during the Late Unpleasantness? Hadn't I seen wounds like that before? Just how many limbs had I amputated?

"I don't remember."

"Oh, surely, you can provide us with an estimate. Two or three? A dozen? A score?"

"Hundreds."

I must have whispered. Mr. Kemble asked me to repeat the answer.

"Hundreds. I lost count." Maybe I could have filled this room with the limbs I'd severed. Sweat streamed down my neck into my collar. I would not so much as blink, for eyelids could fall like a red curtain. And beyond them lay the mounds of ruined bone and tissue.

Mr. Kemble dabbed at his forehead with a handkerchief before he spoke again. "Dr. Mallory, with all your experience, surely you knew what you were doing when you sawed off Dr. Kingston's arm."

"Yes, sir, I knew."

Suddenly, he changed direction. "We have heard testimony that you envied Dr. Kingston his position and success. Certainly, even if you had thought better of murdering him, maiming him brought you some satisfaction, did it not?"

For a flicker of a second, I wondered if Mr. Russell would intervene, but by then he had washed his hands of me. Manslaughter or nothing for him.

"I did not envy him," I said. "Dr. Kingston was a swindler. He kept the deaths of patients secret from their families and went on collecting his fees for years after the patients died."

If anyone in the courtroom registered shock or disbelief at my statement, I didn't see it. I looked toward Effie, only at her, her blue gaze fixed on me, and remembered the evenings of reading aloud to the ladies of the asylum. Again and again, I would glance from the page to Effie's face and read every emotion in the story written in her eyes, on her lips. If only I could tell her a different story.

"Come now," said Mr. Kemble, "if—I say, if—Dr. Kingston's business practices were suspicious to you, could you not have discussed the matter with the gentleman, who was by all accounts other than yours a generous, gracious, and highly intelligent individual?"

"No, sir. He made it clear that I had no influence to change his ways. He was pleased with himself. With no conscience and no principles, Dr. Kingston enriched himself at anyone's expense and gathered admirers around him, to dazzle with hollow charm and erudition. If any of you here in this room," I looked then at my mother, "if any of you were taken in by him, you were not alone. He could find most anyone's weakness and exploit it. The vanity of colleagues, who were flattered to be linked with his self-styled greatness. The vulnerability of a young lady, who would do anything to please him and could not live with his disdain."

Mother bowed her head. Effie went on looking at me and, as she had in the reading circle, encouraged me with a nod to continue.

"Dr. Kingston used the ignorance and desperation of those who served as his menials. He used the helplessness and shame of families who entrusted him with their loved ones. He used the darkest fears that haunted his patients to control and torment them."

Protestations erupted around me, the guards stepped closer to me, the gavel struck, but I would not be silent.

"Dr. Kingston used the occupants of his asylum as a panderer uses the women in a brothel, turning a profit on their degradation." I heard the rise of other voices but would not stop my own. "And when he tired of someone, or someone got in his way, he blew her out like a candle flame."

"So you blew off his right arm!" Mr. Kemble shouted me down. "Shot him at close range. In cold blood. But even that is not enough for you. No, sir. You go on with your outlandish claims, your vicious rantings. Raving like a madman! Is that what you are, Robert Mallory? A madman? Is that the weakness Dr. Kingston found in you?"

Effie held me in her gaze. Nothing else mattered, least of all the hissing that spun around us through the room and spent itself and dropped to a hush.

"When Kingston found my weakness," I said, "he found my strength."

That was my testimony, all I could give. The guards caught at my shoulders, supported me between them, and took me from the stand.

The lawyers repeated themselves, one claiming manslaughter, the other murder, and the judge got his verdict just after his dinner.

I am not the first to be convicted for something I did not do. Did not do, and yet... Lust in the heart, murder in the heart, a sin in the mind. I was not innocent.

After the trial, Captain Purvis spared the time to speak to me privately in my cell. He stood in the doorway, while I lay on the cot. He seemed troubled by the verdict. I had that in common with him, though I'd come to see it was inevitable, much as I longed for it to be otherwise.

"I wonder about someone who shoots a man," the captain said, "and then does everything he knows how to do to save him. You made a nice job of amputating Dr. Kingston's arm. I've seen worse. I'm surprised he didn't live."

"He'd lost a lot of blood, sir. Maybe I didn't work fast enough." Maybe Kingston needed to die.

"You would treat anyone," said Captain Purvis, softly, almost to himself. "I remember how you came to treat that girl Dr. Kingston had accused of murder." Then he spoke up to me. "That was a bad business. I was away from the courthouse when the lynch mob came, you understand."

"I guess they knew that, sir, and picked their time."

After the trial, I received a letter from Dr. Hardy's grandson, newly qualified as a physician, who had assumed control of the asylum. He had heard from Mr. Poncet's counsel on the subject of the overpayment of fees. Thus, he had written to me, threatening me with legal action if I did not immediately cease my inflammatory correspondence. With what further legal action did Bertram J. Hardy hope to intimidate me? By a court of law, I had been condemned to hang.

The key turned in the lock, and Captain Purvis opened the door. "Dr. Mallory," he said, "you have a visitor. A lady."

Slowly, I turned from the window. The captain stepped back from the doorway, allowing my mother to pass into the cell. My mother. I was grateful that Captain Purvis had escorted her himself, not left the task to the jailer. Then he left us in privacy.

Mother had never been in such a place. Her gloved hands fluttered at her waist like a pair of frightened birds, until I covered them with my own hands and stilled them.

"I can hardly believe what's happened," she said, her voice a little breathless. "To think, Dr. Kingston, your father's old friend…"

"He was no friend to us, Mother, to any of us."

"The lawyer for a Mr. Poncet has corresponded with me," she said, carefully gathering her composure. "He has offered to advise me on how I may proceed to extricate myself from any possible legal or financial entanglement with Dr. Kingston's estate."

"I'm thankful he can help you." I brought her to the cot, where we sat together.

"Now I understand, Robert, that you were quite right in your assessment of your employer, in that regard. He was indeed unscrupulous. But this other…" Her voice broke.

I found Mother's lace-edged handkerchief where it was tucked in her sleeve and drew it out for her to blot her tears before they spotted her skirt.

"Oh, Robert," she whispered, "You had reason to shoot him. You avenged your sister's honor." If that brought her comfort.

"I did everything in my power, Mother, everything within my art, to save him, as God's my witness."

A knock sounded at the door, and Captain Purvis called out, "Mrs. Mallory."

"A moment, sir," she called back.

We rose together, and this time it was she who gripped my hands and steadied them. "You look so ill," Mother said. "Have you taken your quinine?"

"It doesn't matter now."

"But it does matter. Effie explained everything to me. She told me we must come here, we must be with you."

"I know you mean well. But Effie doesn't speak."

"She speaks to me." Determination rose in my mother's voice. "Effie loves you, Robert. She made me promise to say the words to you, to say them out loud for you to hear. I love you."

"And I love you, Mother."

"Son…"

"Please, tell Effie… tell her that I admire her more than I can ever say."

"Mrs. Mallory?" The captain's voice again.

Mother fumbled in her pocket, until she found and extracted a gold coin. Pressing it into my palm, she murmured, "For the hangman."

The executioner's gratuity to insure a sharp ax blade or a well-made noose, a quick death. I tried to give it back to her, but she insisted I take it. "Think of the hangman, Robert. You will be forever on his conscience if you don't pay him for his services."

I dropped the coin in my trouser pocket.

"We'll be with you in the morning," she said. "Effie and I."

"No, you don't have to be."

"Yes, we do." Then Mother repeated a verse I had not heard her say since the morning I'd left home for medical school. "A woman when she is in travail hath sorrow, because her hour is come. But as soon as she is delivered of the child, she rememberth no more the anguish, for joy that a man is born into the world."

We embraced, and her shuddering ran through me. When Captain Purvis opened the door, I guided my mother toward him, for her eyes were hidden behind her lace-trimmed handkerchief.

Again, I was alone, locked in my cell. At nightfall, I lay on the thin mattress suspended over hemp cords, which cut into my shoulder when I shifted onto one side. There was only a sliver of moon at the window, and I turned away from it, into the darkness of the room. The fever, my old companion, was kind and let me drift. It might help me yet to cheat the executioner of his coin.

I heard footsteps approach in the hallway, a muffled voice, the rattle of a key in the lock, the creak of hinges. A band of light crossed the floor, reaching almost to my cot. Through half-closed eyes, I traced the light over the rough boards and upward to its source at the half-open doorway, a man holding a lantern. He and the woman beside him were caught for a moment in silhouette, but this time the man did not lean toward her, presuming intimacy. Instead, I saw the captain step aside, raising the lantern, and allow her to pass by him without touching.

She moved ahead of him, and I could no longer see the light across the wooden planks, yet I saw Effie dancing toward me, barefoot on a marble floor, gliding and turning, fluttering in her white gown like a starlit moth. I sensed her flight, then felt her settling close to me. With one hand, she smoothed the blanket across my chest, and with the other, she caressed my forehead. Her hair fell over my cheek, and I heard her humming and whispering in the hollow of my ear. Her stories were my memories, and they moved like air through gauze netting and iron bars and the intricacies of pain.

When I am gone, may the two women whom I have loved bathe my remains, dress my body in a clean suit of clothes, and lay me to rest. I will ask for nothing more.

# About the author

Rosemary Poole-Carter is a novelist and playwright whose work focuses on the history, the mystery and eccentricity of the American South. Her plays have been produced in the Unitied States and Europe, and include *Mossy Cape*, based on Southern folklore, and *The Little Death*, set in 19th century New Orleans. Her other novels are *What Remains*, an historical mystery, and *Juliette Ascending*, a young adult historical.

Rosemary is a member of Mystery Writers of America and the Historical Novel Society. A graduate of the University of Texas at Austin, she lives in Houston.

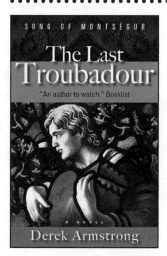

## Women Of Magdalene
### A hauntingly tragic tale of the old South by Rosemary Poole-Carter

An idealistic young doctor in the post-Civil War South exposes the greed and cruelty at the heart of the Magdalene Ladies' Asylum in this elegant, richly detailed and moving story of love and sacrifice.

US$ 24.95 | Pages 288, cloth hardcover
ISBN-13: 978-1-60164-014-7
ISBN-10: 1-60164-014-5
EAN: 9781601640147

• • • • • • • • • • • • • • • • • • • • • • • • • • • • • • • • • • • • • • • • • • •

## On Ice
### A road story like no other, by Red Evans

The sudden death of a sad old fiddle player brings new happiness and hope to those who loved him in this charming, earthy, hilarious coming-of-age tale.

US$ 19.95 | Pages 208, cloth hardcover
ISBN-13: 978-1-60164-015-4
ISBN-10: 1-60164-015-3
EAN: 9781601640154

• • • • • • • • • • • • • • • • • • • • • • • • • • • • • • • • • • • • • • • • • • •

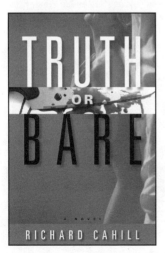

## Truth Or Bare
### Offbeat, stylish crime novel by Richard Cahill

The characters throb with vitality, the prose sizzles in this darkly comic page-turner set in the sleazy world of murderous sex workers, the justice system, and the rich who will stop at nothing to get what they want.

US$ 24.95 | Pages 304, cloth hardcover
ISBN-13: 978-1-60164-016-1
ISBN-10: 1-60164-016-1
EAN: 9781601640161

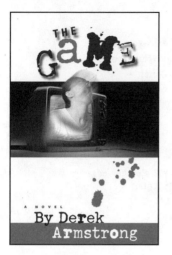

Provocative. Bold. Controversial.

## The Game
### A thriller by Derek Armstrong

Reality television becomes too real when a killer stalks the cast on America's number one live-broadcast reality show.
■ "A series to watch ... Armstrong injects the trope with new vigor." *Booklist*

**US$ 24.95 | Pages 352, cloth hardcover**
**ISBN 978-1-60164-001-7 | EAN: 9781601640017**
**LCCN 2006930183**

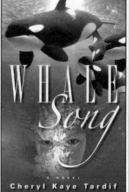

| bang BANG | Whale Song | Shadow of Innocence |
|---|---|---|
| A novel by Lynn Hoffman | A novel by Cheryl Kaye Tardif | A mystery by Ric Wasley |

In Lynn Hoffman's wickedly funny *bang-BANG*, a waitress crime victim takes on America's obsession with guns and transforms herself in the process. Read along as Paula becomes national hero and villain, enforcer and outlaw, lover and leader. Don't miss Paula Sherman's one-woman quest to change America.
■ "Brilliant"
STARRED REVIEW, *Booklist*

**US$ 19.95**
**Pages 176, cloth hardcover**
**ISBN 978-1-60164-000-0**
**EAN 9781601640000**
**LCCN 2006930182**

*Whale Song* is a haunting tale of change and choice. Cheryl Kaye Tardif's beloved novel—a "wonderful novel that will make a wonderful movie" according to *Writer's Digest*—asks the difficult question, which is the higher morality, love or law?
■ "Crowd-pleasing ... a big hit." *Booklist*

**US$ 12.95**
**Pages 208, UNA trade paper**
**ISBN 978-1-60164-007-9**
**EAN 9781601640079**
**LCCN 2006930188**

*The Thin Man* meets *Pulp Fiction* in a unique mystery set amid the drugs-and-music scene of the sixties that touches on all our societal taboos. *Shadow of Innocence* has it all: adventure, sleuthing, drugs, sex, music and a perverse shadowy secret that threatens to tear apart a posh New England town.

**US$ 24.95**
**Pages 304, cloth hardcover**
**ISBN 978-1-60164-006-2**
**EAN 9781601640062**
**LCCN 2006930187**

## The Secret Ever Keeps

A novel by Art Tirrell

An aging Godfather-like billionaire tycoon regrets a decades-long life of "shady dealings" and seeks reconciliation with a granddaughter who doesn't even know he exists. A sweeping adventure across decades—from Prohibition to today—exploring themes of guilt, greed and forgiveness.

■ "Riveting ... Rhapsodic ... Accomplished." *ForeWord*
**US$ 24.95**
**Pages 352, cloth hardcover**
**ISBN 978-1-60164-004-8**
**EAN 9781601640048**
**LCCN 2006930185**

## Toonamint of Champions

A wickedly allegorical comedy by Todd Sentell

Todd Sentell pulls out all the stops in his hilarious spoof of the manners and mores of America's most prestigious golf club. A cast of unforgettable characters, speaking a language only a true son of the South could pull off, reveal that behind the gates of fancy private golf clubs lurk some mighty influential freaks.

■ "Bubbly imagination and wacky humor." *ForeWord*
**US$ 19.95**
**Pages 192, cloth hardcover**
**ISBN 978-1-60164-005-5**
**EAN 9781601640055**
**LCCN 2006930186**

## Mothering Mother

A daughter's humorous and heartbreaking memoir.

Carol D. O'Dell

*Mothering Mother* is an authentic, "in-the-room" view of a daughter's struggle to care for a dying parent. It will touch you and never leave you.

■ "Beautiful, told with humor... and much love." *Booklist*
■ "I not only loved it, I lived it. I laughed, I smiled and shuddered reading this book." Judith H. Wright, author of over 20 books.
**US$ 19.95**
**Pages 208, cloth hardcover**
**ISBN 978-1-60164-003-1**
**EAN 9781601640031**
**LCCN 2006930184**

## Rabid

A novel by T K Kenyon

A sexy, savvy, darkly funny tale of ambition, scandal, forbidden love and murder. Nothing is sacred. The graduate student, her professor, his wife, her priest: four brilliantly realized characters spin out of control in a world where science and religion are in constant conflict.

■ "Kenyon is definitely a keeper." STARRED REVIEW, *Booklist*
**US$ 26.95 | Pages 480, cloth hardcover**
**ISBN 978-1-60164-002-4 | EAN: 9781601640024**
**LCCN 2006930189**